Garden of the Moon

Elizabeth Sinclair

Medallion Press, Inc.
Printed in USA

Garden of the Moon

Elizabeth Sinclair

DEDICATION:

To Sandy Brown, who was there at the beginning, never lost faith, and was willing to spend many sleepless hours helping me bring Harrogate to life

Published 2009 by Medallion Press, Inc.

The MEDALLION PRESS LOGO
is a registered trademark of Medallion Press, Inc.

Typeset in Adobe Garamond Pro
Printed in the United States of America

ISBN: 978-193383698-0

10 9 8 7 6 5 4 3 2 1
First Edition

ACKNOWLEDGEMENTS:

- To my editor, Kerry Estevez, and my friend and critique partner, Dolores Wilson, who are always there when I call for help, advice and general shoring up

- To Helen Rosburg for letting me borrow her incredibly perfect haiku for the opening

- To my husband Bob for his faith, support and timeless love

The Chronicles of Harrogate Plantation

St. Lucius Parish, Louisiana, 1855

My name was Sara Madeline Wade. In my twenty-seventh year, through the benevolent bequest of my beloved paternal grandmother, Alice Wade, I became mistress of Harrogate Plantation. Harrogate is an elegant Greek Revival-style house set among towering, ancient oak trees and a garden so lush and beautiful, it rivaled Eden itself.

To live in my grandmother's house fulfilled a cherished childhood dream. To live there alone was not to be because, when I eagerly moved into my new home, I wasn't fully aware of the extent of my inheritance. I had been bequeathed more than a stately mansion and elegant gardens. I had also inherited Harrogate's darkest secrets.

In the pages to follow, I will attempt to relate my

brief stay at Harrogate as best I can. I don't expect any-one to believe, but I do hope they will try to understand I had to do what I did, because to not have done so would have meant an eternity equivalent to hell.

Little did I realize then that my adventures would actually begin one night before I arrived at Harrogate in the dark, primeval obscurity of St. Claire's Bayou . . .

Sara Madeline Wade
Madeline Grayson

Prologue

A veil of low-lying, white mist hung over the murky, black waters of St. Claire's Bayou. The stink of a mixture of decaying leaves, trees, and the decomposing bodies of dead animals permeated the humid air. A full moon, milky yellow and so big Sara Wade believed she could touch it, hung like a giant ball in the star-studded, black sky. Since she'd been instructed not to bring a lantern because she might be detected, she'd been very relieved when the full moon appeared in the night sky to light her way.

Her grandmother had called the thirteenth moon of a calendar year a seer's moon. Gran said its appearance marked the time of year when the gates between the mortal world and the spirit world opened. Sara would test

Gran's theory later. At the moment, she was just grateful the moon's light served to guide her steps through the treacherous swamp.

The moonlight cast an ominous luminescence over the bayou. The unusually bright light sharply defined the eerie shadows of the moss-draped water oaks, turning them to ghostly specters that, when the breeze blew, seemed to sway and hover silently above her. Here and there Sara could make out cypress knees poking through the misty veil lying low over the black water, as though they were not tree roots, but were instead arms and legs striving for release from the dark waterways flooding this primeval forest.

As she made her way through the thick growth, the low-hanging Spanish moss, damp with the moisture of a late afternoon rain, slithered over Sara's cheek. She shivered and hugged her shawl closer around her body but stayed on the path she'd been instructed to follow.

The soggy ground squished beneath her feet. Cold water seeped into her flimsy shoes. Her new, pink satin slippers would be ruined by the time she returned home, and her mother would be furious, but Sara didn't care. She'd made a promise, and using the concealment of the swamp was necessary for it to be fulfilled. Besides, her mother's disapproval over her ruined slippers would be nothing compared to the rage she'd rain down on Sara if she knew *why* she'd come into the bayou.

The disembodied animal sounds all around her drew her attention back to her surroundings. The slither of something long and slippery through the mud. The crackle of twigs beneath the weight of an unseen creature of the night. The chirp of tree frogs echoing through the darkness. The low growl of a stalking, hungry beast. The plaintive howl of an animal pierced the bayou night and then moments later was answered by another eerie howl from somewhere in the distance.

Holding up the hem of her gown so as not to trip over it, she pushed her unease from her mind and stepped carefully from one bog to another, balancing herself with her outstretched arm. Something slipped through the swamp beside her. She peered down into water as dark as her father's Creole coffee. A very long, very large, scaly tail skimmed over the surface and then disappeared beneath the gloomy depths as if unconcerned by her intrusion into its lair.

Not far ahead of her, a halo of yellow lantern light peeked through the tangle of trees. Here and there, glowing red alligator's eyes glared back at her as if trying to warn her away. But Sara pushed on toward the light.

"Miss Sara?" The quivering female voice was barely audible and was saturated with fear.

"Yes, Lissie. It's me."

Sara stepped into the circle of light. On the ground,

with a lantern at her feet, sat a trembling, wide-eyed black woman. The tracks of recently shed tears glistened on her cheeks. Despite the woman being twice Sara's petite size, her hunched shoulders made her look a lot smaller. Her clothes were soiled and torn, what Sara's father would have called rags and would have thrown away and replaced. The *tignon* covering her hair had once been red, but now, due to the dirt ground into it, the color appeared more like dark burgundy. Her bare feet, though grimy, were caked with dirt and dried blood.

Sara had seen Lissie working in the neighboring plantation's fields and guessed her back carried scars from the whip her owner took delight in applying to his slaves, good and bad, to "keep them in line." Was it any wonder, when the opportunity presented itself, that her husband and son ran? Too bad Lissie had been too sick to go with them.

Thank the good Lord her own father didn't believe in mistreating his people.

Lissie raised her gaze to Sara. The woman's dark eyes reflected stark fear. Sara had no need to guess what generated the fear. If the woman's owner, Sebastian Dubois, caught Lissie, she'd suffer immeasurably under the whip for being here.

Sara smiled in an attempt at reassurance. "I promise that no one will know about this meeting but you and me."

For a while, Lissie stared into Sara's eyes, as if assessing how much she could be trusted. Seemingly satisfied that Sara spoke the truth, the woman's shoulders relaxed, and some of the fear vanished from her expression. Her dark eyes grew big and hopeful. "Dey says you gots the sight."

Sara sat on a tree stump beside Lissie. "Yes, that's true."

Her ability to see ghosts had many names: *the gift, the sight, magic, hoodoo.* Whatever it was called, Sara had accepted it long ago. Deep in her heart, she always felt it was given to her for a special purpose.

"Can you tell me? Is my Moses and Noah alive? Did dey git to freedom?"

Sara laid her hand on Lissie's. The black woman's skin was cold and clammy, and her hand trembled in Sara's. Lissie's intense worry for her loved ones was palpable. Sara had never seen such abject misery in her life. More than anything right now, Sara wanted to ease this woman's pain.

"I'll try."

She smiled weakly. "God bless you, missus."

This was a new realm for Sara. She'd never used what her mother sarcastically referred to as her *affliction* like this before. Normally, the ghosts of the earthbound dead simply showed up. She helped them through whatever was holding them here and then sent them into the light. Never having actually summoned a spirit before,

Sara prayed she could find answers for this troubled woman. The fact that it was the night of a seer's moon might be helpful. Gran always said the spirits were especially communicative on such a night, but until now Sara had never had to test it.

With Lissie's hand clutched tightly in hers, Sara closed her eyes and concentrated. Silently, she called out to Moses and Noah. If they were still living, then neither would appear, and she could put Lissie's mind to rest. If they did appear . . . Sara didn't want to think about what that would mean.

For a very long time, Sara focused on Lissie's men. Slowly, the sounds of the swamp faded, then ceased completely. A profound silence filled the night. A blanket of chilly air enclosed her entire body. She shivered. Sara became weightless, as if she were floating on a cloud. Shadow and light moved in a blur behind her closed eyelids. Then one shadow remained. Its outline was indistinct, so she couldn't tell if it was a man or a woman. Slowly, the image became more defined. Then . . .

"Lissie?"

Sara's eyes snapped open. The tall, semi-transparent figure of a black man stood beside Lissie. His clothes were tattered, his eyes full of tears. He moved to Lissie's side and laid his hand on her shoulder.

Lissie's head snapped up. A brilliant smile transformed the black woman's face. "He's here, isn't he?" Lissie looked around. "My Moses is here. Dear Lord, I can feel him."

"Yes, he's standing beside you," Sara said, trying to keep the sorrow from her voice.

Lissie's joy at her husband's appearance had blotted out what it meant. Moses' spirit materializing could only mean one thing: he was dead.

Moses looked at Sara. His expression had transformed into one of intense sadness, as if he knew what Sara was thinking. "Tell her I didn't make it to Canada, but our Noah did. He's livin' with Lissie's sister."

For a moment Sara, couldn't get her vocal cords to work. Emotion lay in a hard lump in her throat. The chill she'd felt while summoning Moses' spirit now enclosed her heart. She'd never before had to tell anyone their loved one had passed on. Finally, she cleared her throat and pressed Lissie's hand. "Moses says Noah is safe in Canada with your sister."

Tears rolled down Lissie's face. "Oh, thank the Lord dey's safe. Dear Jesus, dey's safe."

Sara swallowed hard and held on tightly to Lissie's hand. "Not both of them. Moses . . . didn't make it."

Lissie stared at Sara for a long moment, the whites of her eyes large and questioning against her dark face. Then as comprehension set in, her expression melted into one of such sorrow, Sara marveled that the woman could tolerate such pain.

"You means my Moses is—"

Sara nodded. "It's the only way he could be here with you now."

Lissie's plaintive wail echoed through the swamp. Sara had never heard such profound agony. It was as though the woman's soul had broken open and was bleeding her sorrow into the night. The agonizing sound shimmered over Sara and slammed into her very soul, weighing her down like a huge invisible rock.

Her gift could not have been meant to bring this kind of agony to anyone.

Moses sent Sara an imploring look. "Tell her I's fine, Miss Sara. Tell her I's goin' to glory. Tell her I be waitin' fo her."

Sara did as he asked. His message seemed to calm Lissie a bit. Now, Lissie simply clutched her middle and rocked back and forth, sobbed quietly, and chanted. "My poor, poor Moses. God rest his soul. God rest his soul."

When Lissie's sobs had quieted to no more than an occasional hiccup, Sara looked to the spirit of the man still standing beside his distraught wife. "She'll be fine now. It's time for you to go into the light."

Moses looked down at his wife and then nodded. To their right, a huge circle of blinding white light appeared. Slowly, he turned and walked into it, disappearing from sight. The light closed in on itself and faded away.

Lissie shivered and rubbed her arms. "He's gone, ain't he?"

Sara patted Lissie's hand. "Yes. It was time for him to move on, Lissie."

The words had barely passed Sara's lips when she caught a movement to her left. Fearing they'd been discovered, she jerked around, her mind already scrambling for an explanation that would preclude punishment for either her or Lissie.

But what she saw was not her father or Lissie's owner, but a stranger. Nor was this man Moses. This man was well-dressed, white, and handsome, and he looked at her as though he knew her. He was also transparent.

Sara's heartbeat picked up. A myriad of unexpected emotions clogged her throat: peace, love—all overshadowed by a profound sadness. She opened her mouth to ask who he was, but no sound would emerge.

Then he smiled. "I'm waiting," he said. Then, like the bayou mist in the light of day, he simply evaporated.

Moongate,
threshold of eternity,
promise forever unbroken.

—Helen Rosburg

Chapter 1

Sara Wade slipped closer to the edge of the carriage seat. Tension gripped her entire body. Excitement flowed through her like warm, mulled cider on a cold October night. She had waited so long for this day and now that it had finally arrived, she had to pinch herself to make sure it wasn't just another of her wild dreams.

Strange dreams had been a part of Sara's life for as long as she could remember. It wouldn't have surprised her if she suddenly woke up in her bed in her family home, Azalea House, in the Garden District of New Orleans, instead of in her papa's carriage driving up the long, oak alley to Harrogate Plantation.

Chills rippled through her to the bone. She closed her eyes tightly. *Please, please, don't let that be the case this time.*

"Laws a mercy!" The whispered expletive came from the young black woman seated beside Sara.

Her eyes popped open, and she turned to her maid. The maid's wide-eyed gaze flittered from tree to bush to flower, then made the same journey again and again, as if she was searching for something. The frantic wringing of her hands in her lap told Sara the maid hoped she wouldn't find whatever she believed lurked somewhere beyond the carriage.

"What is it, Raina?"

Sara's father, Preston Wade, had gifted her with Raina the day of his daughter's birth, and the slave, who had been only four years old at the time, had been her devoted personal maid and friend ever since. To leave Raina in New Orleans would have been unthinkable, like leaving part of herself behind. Not to mention that, even though Sara's mother had virtually pushed her out of the house, Patricia Wade would have never allowed Sara this freedom without Raina to stand guard over her mistress' virtue, even though Patricia was certain that, living in the outback of St. Lucius Parish, her daughter would *wither on the vine* before she ever found a suitable husband. Suitable being defined as non-Creole, rich, well-placed, and tolerably good-looking.

But as much as she loved Raina, right now Sara had

to fight down the urge to shake the woman for scaring the bejesus out of her for no apparent reason. "Raina, what is it?"

Eyes widening, Raina leaned to the side to see around the large body of Samuel, her father, seated atop the driver's bench. "Dis place makes my skin itch, Miss Sara." Frantically, Raina ran her hands up and down her bare arms.

Sara laughed and then looked around. Her laughter died in her throat. Drawing her handkerchief from her reticule, she dabbed at her forehead and top lip, the perspiration not entirely a product of the humid, Louisiana summer weather.

Since she'd been so absorbed in her thoughts, Sara hadn't been paying attention to her surroundings, but now the cause of Raina's alarm became abundantly clear. All along the tunneling oak alley leading to the mansion, the gardens seemed to close in on them. An unexpected spasm of unease coursed through Sara. Had her grandmother's home always been . . . so untamed, so hostile?

Unlike the formality of the grounds outside her father's Garden District home or the Wades' Magnolia Run Plantation just outside New Orleans, the landscaping at Harrogate afforded no sense of order. The careless growth of overgrown foliage seemed to have a mind of its own, as if cloaking the secrets of the old house from the outside world. Without form or design, the branches of the shrubs had interwoven into a tangled, jungle-like setting, giving the impression that they were hiding some long-held mystery within their shadowed recesses, a mystery to which only they were privy and which they would vigorously guard from intruders.

An inexplicable chill ran down Sara's spine.

Suddenly, doubts buffeted her. Was she capable of running this big house? This plantation? Could she care adequately for all who resided there and who would depend on her? Would her gift prove to be an asset or a hindrance?

Had Sara allowed her mother's disdain for something she couldn't and didn't want to understand to cloud her own judgment, to make her take on more than she could reasonably handle just to make a point?

She searched her mind for answers.

She'd always loved this old house. Since the reading of her grandmother's will, five long years ago, she'd dreamed of the day she would be able to live permanently in the only place she had ever felt she really belonged. However, her mother, a socially conscious, cold woman, would hear none of it. It just wasn't seemly for a young, single woman to live alone.

Along with Harrogate, Sara had inherited the ability to see dead people from her beloved deceased paternal grandmother and had long ago accepted it . . . something her mother seemed incapable of doing. Sara's *affliction*, as her mother referred to Sara's ability to see and converse with departed souls, had always embarrassed Patricia.

Then came the *mishap* at Patricia Wade's lawn party, when her mother had caught Sara talking to a dead person. Patricia had changed her mind overnight. Not only would she allow Sara to go to Harrogate; she'd strongly encourage it and couldn't seem to get her daughter out of Azalea House fast enough. Afraid that at any moment her mother might have a change of heart, Sara had Raina packing her trunks before her mother could order tea, all the while trying not to be hurt by her mother's haste to hide her from her society friends.

Affliction. Her mother had no idea, nor did she care, how humiliating and degrading it was to Sara to have her beautiful gift labeled in such a way. Patricia made it sound as though Sara had some horrible, disfiguring disease, when in reality no one could guess by merely looking at her.

Of course, when her mother's smug society friends had quizzed Patricia about why she was sending Sara to Harrogate *alone*, Patricia hadn't mentioned the affliction to them. That would have countered her reason for getting Sara out of the house before anyone discovered her strange behavior. So instead, her mother swept the truth under the rug as effortlessly as Raina swept dirt out the door, and then she lied through her perfect teeth.

"Since poor Sara's passed a respectable age for marriage, I've given up trying to find a suitable man for her. I'm afraid her unmarried state has become somewhat of an . . . embarrassment to her father and me. Allowing her to set up her own home at Harrogate in the seclusion of the country is the wisest choice." She'd paused for effect, and then confided, "Perhaps after living alone for a time, my willful daughter will come to her senses and think twice about her lofty requirements for an acceptable suitor and, hopefully, find a husband. Of course, all the men of her age are already spoken for, so perhaps a widower . . ." The words had faded off into a deep, heartfelt sob and a dramatic dab at her eyes with the corner of a white linen handkerchief.

Her mother's friends had nodded in sympathetic, yet sage agreement and then patted Patricia's shoulder in consolation for having a daughter who would *rain down such embarrassment on her dear mother's head.*

Sara often wondered what they'd think if they knew the real reason her mother was suddenly shipping her only daughter off to St. Lucius Parish. Enraged at her mother's performance, Sara had been seriously tempted to pop out from behind the door where she'd been eavesdropping on their conversation and to tell Mrs. Dubois that her dead husband was smiling at her from right behind her left shoulder or that Mrs. LeFarge's long-deceased father was scowling down at her from his perch on the mantel.

But Sara had controlled her urge for revenge and kept silent. Divulging her gift would have only labeled her as the freak her mother believed her to be, and that would have afforded her mother more of the attention and sympathy she thrived on. Besides, Sara hadn't wanted to do anything that would have enraged her mother enough to change her mind about allowing the move to Harrogate.

Sometimes Sara wished she simply had some physical flaw: a twisted limb or a deformed ear. At least she could hide a crippled leg beneath her billowing gown or a missing ear beneath her chestnut curls. Though she had gotten used to seeing dead people long ago, one aspect of Sara's gift was often hard for her to hide, especially when her mother caught her talking to someone only Sara could see. The dead spirits who sought her out had no discretion about when they'd suddenly appear on the scene.

Unlike her mother, her father had grown up with a mother who had the same *affliction*, so none of it seemed strange to him. He'd even developed a bit of the same talent himself, but he'd never told his wife. It had been something he shared with no one but his only daughter. However, while her father only saw an occasional deceased relative, Sara seemed to find dead people around every corner, or so it seemed sometimes.

Sara shook the doubts away. All this reminiscing was just magnifying her anxiety and taking the edge off her excitement. So what if the gardens were a bit wild? It certainly didn't mean anything sinister lurked out there. It had been, after all, five years since the house had been occupied, and the grounds simply needed grooming.

Papa had promised to send her a dozen of Magnolia Run's best field hands the next day. But the thought of slaves from her father's plantation coming the next day didn't really sweep away Sara's unease. Like Raina, she continued to study their surroundings with a wary eye.

Then suddenly, as if by magic, the carriage rounded a curve in the drive and Harrogate came into view. Her unease did not ebb. Instead, the closer they got to the sprawling mansion, the more intense her anxiety became.

Oaks dripping with amethyst wisteria and ghostly, pearl gray moss surrounded the house. Stirred by the brisk wind, their gnarled limbs seemed to crouch over the roof like protective, disapproving dowagers taking measure of the intruders in their midst. Blazing red azaleas and deep crimson crepe myrtles hemorrhaged their blossoms into the overgrown lawn, spattering the tall grass like droplets of blood. From a tangle of holly shrubs and jasmine vines, marble statuary gowned in sage green lichen peeked at her like naughty children preparing to do mischief. Even the angry puffs of dust nudged into life from the drive by a stiff breeze off the river seemed to voice the very earth's displeasure at their intrusion.

What of the other times she'd visited her grandmother's home? Had it been like this? No. On those occasions, the house and grounds had always been a welcoming presence in her young life. Now they seemed to be warning her away, even angered at her appearance. But in the five years since her grandmother's death, there had been no slaves to keep the place manicured. Naturally, the grounds would be wild and overgrown.

But it wasn't just the overgrown vegetation that made Sara's skin crawl. The heavy atmosphere seemed to suck the air from her lungs, as though something dark and evil lurked in the shadows of the trees and bushes. Something that had been waiting just for Sara.

I'm waiting. The words the ghost had spoken to her in the bayou played through Sara's mind. Was *he* here at Harrogate . . . waiting for her?

She drew her shawl closer around her trembling shoulders. Surely she was being foolish. But the icy fear continued to lie in a tightly coiled ball in the pit of her stomach.

Fighting the inexplicable alarm that had suddenly turned her insides to ice, Sara forced a smile and calmly patted Raina's arm. "It's fine. Just a bit . . . out of hand is all. Samuel will have the men Papa's sending organized in no time, and before you know it, everything will be as beautiful and orderly as when my grandmother was alive."

"Yas, 'um." Raina didn't sound at all convinced. Her wide-eyed gaze continued to dart over the snarled landscaping, and her hands twisted in her lap until Sara thought the woman might remove the skin from them.

Sara shook her morose thoughts loose and peered eagerly ahead of them. Nothing would spoil this day for her. Nothing. Clearing anything that would dampen this moment from her mind, Sara gazed raptly at the house.

Unlike the gardens, the snow-white, antebellum mansion resembled a giant, frosted wedding cake. The identical wings extending from either side of the main house created an image of conformity, order, and balance. Though the grounds had been far from what she'd expected, in her heart, she could feel the welcome the old house extended to its new mistress.

Samuel maneuvered the carriage down the drive and then drew the horses up in front of a wide porch flanked by two sweeping staircases leading to the main level of the home.

Excitement drowned out the anxiety. "Oh, what parties I'll give here." Sara clapped her hands like an excited child. "They'll be just as grand as the ones Gran gave. You'll see."

Raina remained silent, obviously still not finding

anything about the place to feel good about.

"I'll invite all the neighbors to celebrate the reopening of Harrogate, the rebirth of this stately old home."

Raina still didn't reply. She just continued to look around her as if some demon would lunge from the bushes at any moment and devour her.

"Can't you imagine it, Raina?" Sara went on, caught up in her daydream. "Can't you just picture elegant ladies in Worth gowns straight from Paris gliding over the galleries or hurrying down the wrought iron stairs to the veranda?" She giggled. "Maybe some will even sneak into the shadows of the Corinthian columns for a clandestine assignation with their sweethearts, out of the view and hearing of vigilant parents and hovering guardians."

Plans for the future filled her head. Her thoughts bursting with images of her new life, Sara took in the beauty of the house. Closed shutters covered all the windows, save one on the second-floor gallery. She glanced up at the window.

She gasped.

The tall, handsome man from St. Claire's Bayou gazed down at her.

He smiled and nodded as though approving her being there.

She blinked and gasped again.

Like a puff of smoke from one of Papa's cigars, the man had vanished.

Chapter 2

"Oh!" Sara cried, half in surprise and half in disappointment that the man had disappeared.

Raina grabbed her mistress' hand. "What?" Her gaze darted from Sara to the house and back. The woman's eyes widened, nearly popping from their sockets.

Raina had already been spooked enough. No reason to add to her upset. Sara just shook her head and patted the chocolate brown hand clasping one of hers like the jaws of an enraged gator. "It's all right. I was just taken aback by the grandeur of the place. I don't recall it being this immense."

A sigh of relief issued from Raina. "'Peers to me that ain't no reason to scare the bejesus out of a body."

The half lie had slid easily from Sara's lips. Oddly,

the appearance of the unfamiliar man in the upstairs window hadn't caused her any alarm or discomfort. The words he'd spoken in the bayou echoed through her mind again. *I'm waiting.* His slow smile, in some strange way, had been welcoming, as if he knew she belonged here . . . as if he *had* been waiting for her.

Another shiver washed over her. However, rather than apprehension, a wild, rising tide of excitement swelled inside her.

Who was he? He couldn't logically be the same man she'd seen in the bayou. It must have been her imagination that had conjured him. Perhaps he hadn't vanished at all. Perhaps he hadn't been there at all. Or he might have just stepped from her line of vision. But if it wasn't the bayou stranger, then who was he?

Perhaps Papa had sent her an overseer. It wouldn't have surprised her if her father had hired someone to help manage the plantation. He'd been spoiling her without her mother's knowledge for most of Sara's twenty-seven years. Papa's intervention had been the only reason that Sara hadn't found herself walking down the aisle with that pimply-faced Jason Bannister from River Oaks Plantation. Why, the man must have been forty-five if he was a day. When Sara had asked him to leave, her mother had been furious, screaming at her that she'd end up an old maid if she didn't lower her standards.

That night, out of sight of Patricia, Sara had hugged Papa fiercely. Just the thought of sharing her wedding night with that *old* man had made her skin crawl.

As the memories raced through her mind once more, Sara continued to stare at Harrogate's upstairs window . . . waiting . . . inexplicably hoping the man would reappear. When he didn't, she told herself he had merely been a shadow cast by the towering oak trees or perhaps her excitement about finally coming *home*.

Still, the idea that a stranger, captivating or otherwise, could be wandering around in *her* house brought back a small measure of the creepy unease she'd experienced earlier.

"Samuel?" Sara gently poked Raina's father in the side. "Please go inside and make sure everything is . . . in order?"

With a slow nod, the burly black man jumped to the ground, ambled up the stairs, and then entered the house.

To avoid her maid's questioning look, Sara pretended to be absorbed in her surroundings. No need to explain why she'd sent Samuel inside before them. If Raina thought a strange man lay in wait for them inside the house, wild horses wouldn't get the girl in there. As it was, she was already seeing demons in the shrubbery.

A few minutes later, Samuel emerged, descended the stairs, and grinned. "Looks fine to me, Miss Sara."

"Nothing unusual?" Sara stared hard at him.

"No, ma'am."

"You looked upstairs?"

"Yes, ma'am.

"You spectin' somethin' unusual?" Raina blurted, her hands clasping Sara's in a death grip.

Sara pulled her fingers from Raina's grasp. "No, of course not. We're two women all alone with only Samuel for protection. I was just being careful. It's not unusual for vagrants to take refuge in these deserted homes, you know. Do you want to go in there and find some vagrant ready to pounce on us?"

"No ma'am."

"Very well. I suggest you pull yourself together and enjoy the moment. Nothing awaits us inside but a wonderful future."

Her explanation seemed to appease Raina, but apprehension and excitement strained at Sara's insides. The man in the window she thought she'd seen had to have been a trick of the light on the glass panes. But that didn't explain why, when she'd seen that *trick of the light*, her heart had thumped against her chest, nor did it give a reason for the warmth that had rushed over her. *That* had not been her imagination.

Samuel cleared his throat. "You ladies gonna git out da buggy, or ya gonna sit there and chitchat fo the duration?" Chuckling to himself and shaking his head,

Samuel stepped to the side of the carriage. "Fo as much as you gots to say and as long as you been sayin' it, 'peers to me like you woulda said it all by now." The indulgent smile he flashed their way tempered his deep-throated reprimand. Both girls were used to his gentle chiding.

Samuel extended his hand to help Sara to the ground. She rose, cast a last wary look at the upstairs windows, then gathered her skirts in one hand and took Samuel's supporting hand in the other. Carefully, she stepped to the ground, smoothed the travel wrinkles from her voluminous, hunter green traveling gown, and then walked slowly toward the staircase leading up to the first-floor veranda.

Her heart beat out a frantic rhythm against her rib cage. She was about to enter her own home. Sara Madeline Wade's home.

The inside of Harrogate, with the exception of the white dustcovers draped over the furniture, was just as Sara remembered it. The harpsichord, the one at which she and her grandmother Alice had sat and warbled off-key Christmas carols, still filled the large bay windows overlooking the veranda. The settee, where she'd fallen asleep in her grandmother's arms while Alice had related romantic stories of her courtship with Ezra Wade, still dominated the center of the room. Though dusty and in need of laundering, the drapes that puddled on the cypress floor still provided a perfect place for a young girl to hide from a frantic maid at bedtime. Wonderful memories of a happy childhood filled every nook and corner of this magnificent home. All those precious memories, all there, all preserved, all waiting for Sara to come back and relive happier times within these walls.

"Laws a mercy. This won't do. No, sir, won't do a'tall." Suddenly animated, her fears forgotten, Raina bustled around the room, a frown creasing her dark brow, her tongue clucking between sentences. With a newfound energy and dogged determination, she whisked sheets from the furniture and balled them in her arms. "Dey knows you was a comin'. House shudda been ready fo the mistress befo she gits here. Jes pure laziness; dat's what it is all right. Pure laziness."

"Papa said the house servants will arrive tomorrow with the gardeners and the field hands he's sending over from Magnolia Run. The only house servants he sent ahead were your mother to cook and your sister Litisha to help her." Raina's mother, Chloe, would have her hands full in the kitchen cooking meals, and, even very pregnant, Litisha could assume some of the burden. With all the kitchen chores to be done, Sara couldn't ask either of them to do the housework as well. "In the meantime, I can help with this." Sara pulled a sheet from the harpsichord and began folding it, only to have it snatched from her fingers by the irate maid.

"Ain't fo you to do." Raina frowned heavily at her, and then tucked the sheet into the growing pile she hugged against her chest. "Masser Preston should a had dem girls here afore you gots here. Ain't fittin' fo the lady of the house to come home to dis. Ain't fittin a'tall."

A smile tugged at Sara's mouth. Even though the two women had been friends for years, when it came to her duties and Sara's station as her mistress and what tasks she would allow her to do, Raina had always drawn a distinct line. Evidently, folding furniture covers was not one of the duties allowed.

"Dey's jest some things a lady don't do," the diminutive maid declared hotly. "No, suh." She shook her head firmly, making the brightly colored *tignon* covering her hair slip down on her forehead. Impatiently, she pushed the coil of material back in place with her forearm.

Raina hated the *tignon*, but the laws in New Orleans required that a Negro's head be covered at all times because their tight curls offended the white ladies. Now that they were out of the city, perhaps Sara would allow Raina to forgo the hated head-covering. Of course, when neighbors came to call, that might cause some talk. But did she care? Gran wouldn't have. And after all, this was Sara's house now. She could do whatever she wanted, whenever she wanted, and no one could stop her.

She'd have to think about that and add it to the many decisions she would be making as mistress of Harrogate.

"Ain't seemly," the maid continued to mumble. "Jes ain't seemly."

Knowing Raina's outraged, mumbled complaints could go on indefinitely, Sara shut her ears to them and wandered over to the harpsichord. The lovingly cared for rosewood glowed in the afternoon sunlight like the dark honey Gran's cook used to spread over Sara's warm cornbread. With memories of Gran running as thick as cream through her mind and a strange compulsion driving her, Sara ran her fingertips over the keys. A discordant, high-pitched tinkle filled the air. Recalling the beautiful music her grandmother had coaxed from the instrument, Sara continued to run her fingers over the keys. The tinkle filled the silence left behind after Raina's ranting had ceased. Suddenly, several keys reacted with a hollow *thump*, as though something prevented the strings from being struck.

She moved to the side, tipped up the lid, and peered inside. A gold locket and chain lay coiled on the strings. Sara picked it up and examined the exquisite piece of jewelry. Two engraved roses adorned the front, their stems wrapped around each other so completely that it was difficult to tell where one ended and the other began. She opened the catch and flipped the heart open. Inside, an inscription read, *My Love Forever*.

Gran had never worn anything like this. So where had it come from? Perhaps one of her grandmother's many party guests had lost it. Whoever it belonged to, with an inscription like that, it must have been a treasured possession. Absently, she clicked it closed and then tucked it into her dress pocket with the hope of eventually finding its owner.

Hours later, exhausted from an excitement-filled, sleepless night before her departure from New Orleans, the long carriage ride from the city, and the little work Raina had condescended to allowed her to do, Sara climbed into the large, canopied, custom-made bed that had been her grandmother's prized possession.

After harvesting an ancient oak from somewhere on Harrogate land, the wood had been taken to the plantation carpenter who'd constructed a bed to fit Ezra Wade's abnormally tall frame. As a result, Sara's petite, five-foot three-inch body could luxuriate in the vastness of the eiderdown-filled mattress. After her grandfather had died, Sara had spent many nights here with her grandmother, pretending she was floating miles above the earth on a huge, white cloud.

She smiled contentedly and snuggled down into the feather mattress. The full moon spilled through the tall, bedroom windows, coating everything it touched with a silvery-blue cast. Despite her total exhaustion, Sara found it hard to tamp down her excitement and find sleep. Instead, she lay awake taking in the beautifully appointed room, the large windows, and the carved door frames.

Then her gaze locked onto the portrait of the elegant woman over the fireplace. She'd asked her grandmother who the woman was, but Gran had grown impatient and even a bit nervous and said she had no idea. It was just a picture she'd found in the attic and hung above the mantel.

From childhood, Sara had always hated the portrait. She'd gotten the insane idea in her young head that the woman in the picture didn't like her. Whenever she'd entered the room, Sara had often imagined the faint smile on the woman's lips turning down in a frown, her eyes assessing and angry.

"She hates me, Gran. I know it."

"Nonsense, my darling girl. How on earth can a painting hate you?" Gran's smile had held all the indulgence she'd always shown her only granddaughter.

"But just look at the way she keeps staring at me. No matter where I go, she's always watching." Sara had moved about the room to illustrate.

Gran laughed. "Child, her eyes only seem to follow you. Good artists can do that, you know. They can make a portrait's gaze come alive." She'd risen from the end of the bed and taken Sara's hand. "Now, let's you and I go find Matilda and see if her cornbread is out of the oven yet."

With the temptation of Matilda's warm cornbread slathered in honey and the total dismissal of the subject, they'd left the room. But Sara had never forgotten it and made every attempt, when in her Gran's bedroom, not to look at the painting.

Now, once more the object of attention of those frigid, gray eyes, Sara had trouble accepting Gran's explanation. The chill of the unrelenting stare raced through her. Unable to sleep, Sara slipped from the bed and went to the window overlooking the back lawn.

Below, as though lit from within, the full moon painted the entire landscape with an eerie glow. Her gaze came to rest on a large area in the center of the lawn cordoned off by high shrubs on three sides.

On the third side, a moongate afforded an opening to the garden within. Her grandfather had ordered the moongate to be shipped from Japan for her grandmother as a birthday gift after his visit to the Orient. Ten feet tall and almost as wide, the circular gate, fashioned of polished white marble, glowed in the moonlight. On either side, a marble temple dog warded off evil from entering the garden. At the top of the circle, a small plaque read, *Promise forever unbroken.*

A moongate, Gran had explained to Sara, ensured happiness to all who walked through it to enter the garden. And that had certainly been true in Sara's case. No place had provided her with the deep love and unbridled happiness she'd always experienced in what Gran had dubbed "the Garden of the Moon." And, on those rare visits her mother had made to Harrogate, the gazebo in the middle of the garden had been a haven for Sara, a place to escape where she wouldn't be scrutinized and reprimanded for every move she made.

Above the arch, the wide open moonflowers turned their snowy faces to the sky and invited the silvery moths to pollinate them. Their sweet scent filled the night air and drifted to Sara through her open window, bringing with it more cherished memories of the hours she and Gran had spent in the garden. It saddened Sara that by morning the flowers would have closed tightly and died. Though they enjoyed a short lifespan, she loved how they painted the night with color and perfume. When the sun came up again, the moonflowers would be dead, but the garden would be alive with the new beauty of the other flowers: magnolias, azaleas, forget-me-nots, roses, wood violets, morning glories, and camellias—all white.

On many occasions, while peeking out her bedroom window, Sara had caught sight of wisps of smoke floating in the garden. The wisps, unlike the specters she'd been used to seeing, had neither substance nor form. Instead of making her apprehensive, however, they brought with them an overwhelming sensation of warmth, contentment, and a love Sara had never known, not even from Gran. The young Sara had no idea how she'd known, but she'd been sure that love lived in that garden. As she stood here now, that love seemed to rise up from the garden and fill her body, pushing away her restiveness and replacing it with contentment.

Finally at peace, eyelids drooping, Sara made her way back to the bed. She pulled the covers over her, but she was still acutely aware of the steely eyes of the portrait boring into her. Tomorrow, she'd find a suitable replacement, and the hated portrait would be consigned to the attic again, this time forever. Turning her back on the picture, she pulled the covers over her head.

She could almost hear her grandmother laughing at her foolishness.

A soft chuckle escaped Sara. Lord, but she missed her carefree grandmother and the happy times they'd spent together. Sara took a deep breath and surprisingly detected the heady scent of the cologne her grandmother had specially blended in a French Quarter perfumery still clinging to the room. The scent reminded her of the creamy white magnolias that bloomed each year throughout the grounds at Harrogate but most abundantly in the Garden of the Moon. She was glad she'd left the window open to admit their memory-heavy scent.

As drowsiness began to claim her tired body, those cherished memories of Gran lulled Sara toward sleep. Her adored grandmother was seldom far from Sara's thoughts, but tonight those thoughts were more intense, more persistent. It had to be because she was back at Harrogate. Yes, that had to be it. Sara was home.

With a contented sigh, she closed her eyes and allowed the shroud of sleep to envelop her.

"Sara."

Her name being called softly came from a long way off. She stirred in her sleep and settled more comfortably under the down coverlet.

"Sara."

The side of the mattress dipped, as if someone had sat down beside her.

"Raina?" Sara mumbled through the mist of sleep still fogging her brain and snuggled deeper into the warm bedclothes, wanting nothing more than sleep for hours. "It's too early. Let me sleep for a while."

"No, my darling girl, it's not your Raina. It's me, and you must wake up. I can't stay long."

Sara's ears pricked. Only one person ever called her *my darling girl*. Could it be . . .

Unable to believe the possibility and instantly alert, Sara forced her eyes open and pushed the covers off her head. She blinked several times, but the face smiling lovingly down at her remained as solid and as real as the bed in which Sara lay.

Slowly, she sat up, never allowing her gaze to leave the woman at her side lest she vanish. Anyone else would have been frightened half to death. But then, everyone else wasn't like Sara. Hadn't her mother reminded her of that many times over? Sara was used to seeing dead people, and the fact that one had chosen to pay her a nocturnal visit wasn't at all unusual.

What did surprise her was who it was. Sitting beside her, love shining from her blue eyes, her body surrounded by a halo of white light, was Alice Wade, her beloved dead grandmother.

Chapter 3

"Hello, dear," Sara's grandmother said, as though she weren't an apparition sitting on her granddaughter's bed in the middle of the night, but instead a relative who had just dropped by for afternoon tea and some social gossip about what was happening at the neighbor's plantation.

Gran wore the antique white lace dress in which she'd been buried. Pinned on the dress' high neck was the cameo brooch Sara had given Gran for her last birthday. How young, vital, and beautiful her grandmother looked. Gone were the wrinkles of age and the hint of loneliness that had dimmed her eyes and been always present after her beloved Ezra had died. The scent of magnolias surrounded her like a wreath. Instantly, all the love and security Sara had always experienced around her grandmother washed over her.

Suddenly, Sara noticed something in the corner of the bedroom, something almost obscured by the figure of the older woman. A small ball of milky white light pulsated, moving up and down like a child's ball and then back and forth like the pendulum on a clock. She was too excited by her grandmother's presence, though, to delve into what it was.

"Gran, is it really you?"

Her grandmother patted her hand. "Yes, my darling girl, it's me."

"Oh, Gran, I am so happy to see you." Her touch was surprisingly warm, but no less loving than when she lived. "I've missed you so much."

"Oh, my dear, I've missed you, too." She squeezed Sara's hand.

The ball of light in the corner grew bigger and pulsed with a new strength.

Gran glanced at it and then snatched her hand back. "All right, dear. I hear you." She smiled apologetically at Sara. "He warned me not to touch you."

"He?"

Gran dismissed the question with a wave of her hand, something Sara had seen her do many times when she hadn't wanted to be bothered with what she'd considered life's trivialities.

"Life's too short to be giving one jot of time to unimportant things," she'd always say, and then set off on another entirely different subject.

Though excited to be sitting here having a conversation with one of the most important people in her life, Sara was curious as to why, after so many years, her grandmother had chosen now to appear to her.

"Gran, why are you here?"

"My darling girl, I have hung around here for five years waiting for you. I thought your mother would never agree to let you come to Harrogate." She clicked her tongue disapprovingly. "I never saw what your father found so enchanting about that woman. If you ask me, she is stubborn, opinionated, and much too concerned with the dictates of society. Her mother used to say that even as a child, Patricia would dig in her heels and—"

"Gran!" Sara didn't want to talk about her mother. She wanted to hear what had prompted her grandmother's very welcome but unexpected visit.

"Sorry, dear." Gran smiled. Then her expression softened even more. "I came because I needed to tell you there's something very special waiting for you here. *Very* special."

"Special?" Sara blinked. "What is it? What's special?"

Her grandmother shook her head. "I can't say. He'd only let me speak to you if I promised not to say too much."

Sara grew impatient. "Who is this *he* you keep referring to?" She glanced around the room.

"An unimportant detail." The ball of light pulsed frantically, but Gran paid it no heed. "I just don't want you to give up on being the mistress of Harrogate and leave because things get . . . difficult. That would be tragic."

"Leave Harrogate?" Appalled at the thought, Sara shook her head firmly. "I've waited forever to live here. I would never leave."

Gran cast a skeptical sidelong glance at her. "You may change your mind."

"No! Never!" Sara sat straighter. Her chin had firmed into the stubborn pose that, to Sara's everlasting disgust, made her resemble her mother at her most obstinate—but she didn't care. "Why would you even think such a thing?"

An odd expression crossed Gran's face. The same expression she'd always had when Sara talked to her about the portrait of the woman over the fireplace. Back then, Sara had been too young to put a name to it, but now . . . Could it be fear? Shock waves rocked Sara.

The word *fear* and Gran just didn't go together. Gran was the most fearless woman Sara had ever met. One of her favorite pastimes had been to don a pair of her husband's trousers and ride like the wind, legs astride, over Harrogate's lands and *to hell with the neighbors*. When other southern belles were adhering to the strict rules governing female society, Gran was doing as she pleased and laughing in the face of all the frowning matrons while she did it. It was one of the reasons Sara had admired her so much and one of the reasons she had loved coming to stay with her. Sara could be herself here and not have to worry about a flaming reprimand from her strict mother.

Why was Gran afraid now?

But before Sara could ask, Gran hurried on. "As much as I love this old house and want you to live here, I have to warn you that evil lives within these walls."

A cold chill climbed Sara's spine. When they'd come down the drive earlier that day, was that what she'd felt? Did the man in the upstairs window have something to do with it? In the deepest part of her heart, Sara didn't believe he did.

"E—, evil? What kind of evil?"

Gran shook her head. "You have to discover that on your own, my darling girl." When Sara would have protested, Gran held up her hand. "You have the courage. My blood flows through your veins. I know you can do it. I feel it, here." She placed her hand over her heart. "All I can tell you is that the secret to your success, the way to claim victory over the evil, lies hidden in the house and inside you. Find it, and you will find all the answers you seek and happiness beyond your imagination."

"But I'm ever so happy just being here, and I'm not seeking any answers." At least she hadn't been until a few moments ago. "How can you tell me there's evil in this house, then not tell me what it is?"

"Your happiness depends on you learning the answers on your own. They're a part of you, Sara. They always have been." She stood as if to leave. "Search your heart. That's where your destiny lies."

"No!" Sara said loudly. "You can't go. Not yet." She lunged for her grandmother's hand, but Gran stepped out of Sara's reach.

"Now, now, dear. Just remember what I said. Evil may lurk here, but something special also awaits you here." She smiled warmly. "Believe me, no matter how harrowing the journey, it will be worth it."

A million unanswered questions swam though her mind. Would she ever find the answers? Her brain throbbed. She fought to make sense of all her grandmother had said. "But what awaits me? What is so special? How can I find the answers to any of this?"

"Go to Candlewick Plantation and talk to Clarice Degas."

"Clarice Degas? I—"

The older woman sighed. "I must go, my darling Sara." She glanced toward the pulsating light. It had begun to grow brighter and throb more insistently. "Ezra is waiting for me, and if you recall, I've often told you that your grandfather was never a patient man, and bless his heart, he's waited a very long time for me to join him."

"But, Gran, you can't leave me. I need you. I need your help."

Wordlessly, Gran walked toward the vibrating light, and then stopped and turned back toward Sara. "Be careful, my darling girl, and be happy. Above all else, trust in the power of love." Gran smiled and waved, and then she stepped into the light.

In the time it took Sara to open her mouth to protest, the light closed in on itself, and Gran was gone, leaving in her absence only the faint, sweet scent of magnolias and a stifling silence.

Feeling as though she'd lost her grandmother yet again, and fighting back tears, Sara collapsed back on the pillows. Bewildered, she lay in the big, moonlight-dappled bed with her grandmother's warning ringing in her ears, and wondered if she'd dreamed the entire bizarre incident. But in her heart, where the fear had taken root, she knew she hadn't. Levering herself up on one elbow, she glanced toward the portrait above the fireplace.

Had the woman's lips turned up in a sinister smile?

Sara played with the golden pancakes and brown sausages that Chloe, one of the best cooks in New Orleans, had prepared for her. Despite her gloomy mood, Sara smiled. Would her mother ever get over the loss of her cook? Would she ever forgive Sara's father for giving Raina's mother to Sara?

Though her mother had protested hotly at losing both Chloe and Samuel, Sara's father believed strongly in keeping the families of his people together. It never would have occurred to him to separate Raina, her sister Litisha, and their parents. When Sara took Raina from the New Orleans house, it followed that her sister, mother, and father would go with her. Patricia had thrown her usual temper tantrum, but to no avail. Gran would have approved heartily of how her son had stood his ground.

Thoughts of her father's mother nudged Sara's mind back to the night before. She continued to absently push her breakfast around her plate. In her head, she replayed the visit from her ghostly grandmother.

Seeing a ghost wasn't what concerned her. God knows she'd seen here share of them in her lifetime and had gotten quite accustomed to it. What bothered her was the message her grandmother had imparted. Was there really something special waiting for her here? If so, what? And what was the evil at Harrogate? And how was she to fight something when she had no idea what it was?

Then her grandmother's voice played through her mind.

Go to Candlewick Plantation and talk to Clarice Degas.

Unlike Harrogate's austere Greek Revival style, Candlewick's elongated, wooden structure sprawled over the manicured grounds with the lazy grace of a Georgia high-water cottage but on a much grander scale. The house seemed to languish in the shade of the ancient, moss-draped oaks like an elegant lady at her leisure. Shade dappled the expansive veranda, hugging three sides of the house. Each opening between the supporting posts was capped with lacy grillwork. Magnificent double dormers graced the peaked roof. Brilliant white statues of Greek gods and half-naked ladies draped in bits of material with a profusion of flowers at their feet dotted the grounds on either side of the long, curving drive. As was the custom of the homes near the Mississippi, a few of the many lower floor windows were open to allow the cooling river breeze to pass through the house.

Contrary to the first glimpse Sara had gotten of Harrogate upon her arrival yesterday, Candlewick seemed to open its arms to visitors and welcome them with all the charm of its Creole occupants.

Ahead of the carriage conveying Sara and Raina toward

the house, a small black boy raced up the drive, yelling, "Carriage a comin'! Carriage a comin'!"

Sara smoothed her gown self-consciously. She'd chosen one of her best dresses, a lilac gown her father had shipped from Worth's in England. She straightened the lace inset and adjusted the décolletage, then hooked her reticule over her arm. The herd of butterflies that always filled her abdomen just before she saw her mother began to gather in her stomach.

Stop it! She's just an old woman, not a raging beast, and she is certainly not your mother.

Samuel pulled the horse to a stop before the stairs, and Sara stepped onto the stone steps provided to make dismounting from a buggy easier. Her feet had just touched the ground when a slave shuffled onto the porch. The woman wore the drab cream and brown clothes of a house servant, but the *tignon* covering her head was bright yellow, and tight, curly tufts of salt and pepper hair peeked from beneath the edges.

"Good afternoon, Miss," she said in perfect English. Her stern, old eyes thoroughly assessed Sara and Raina.

Smiling, Sara climbed the steps. "I've come to call on Mrs. Degas. I'm Sara Wade, the new mistress of Harrogate Plantation." Though she hadn't meant to, Sara had squared her shoulders, straightened her back, and lifted her chin with intense pride as she said those last words.

The servant's face seemed to pale slightly. "The mistress is resting."

Disappointed, Sara would not be put off. "Then perhaps I'll come back tomorrow at an earlier time." She reached in her reticule and pulled out one of her calling cards, a gift from her father just before she left New Orleans. "Would you please give her my card?"

The servant reached for the card but was stopped by a woman's voice.

"It's all right, Cherry. I'm awake," came a cracked voice from inside the house. "Ask our visitor in." A pause. "You hear me, Cherry?"

Cherry glanced over her shoulder, nodded her head. "Yes, ma'am, I hear you." She stepped to the side. "This way, Miss."

Sara moved past the servant and, with Raina following close behind, entered the cool interior. Cherry guided them through the handsomely appointed foyer with its elegant crystal chandelier and highly polished cypress floors, and then into the sitting room. The room spoke loudly of the Degas' affluence and awed Sara with its luxurious elegance.

Deep burgundy velvet drapes framed windows with hand-painted, stained-glass flowers nestled in the corner of each pane. As was the custom, the drapes puddled generously on the floor as a testimony to the owners' wealth: more fabric than necessary had been purchased to cover the windows. An Aubusson tapestry depicting a unicorn and wood nymphs frolicking through a meadow of wildflowers hung above the Carrera marble mantel. A Baccarat crystal chandelier dripped from the intricate frieze work medallion in the center of the ceiling.

From one of the gold-leafed, French settees, a rail-thin woman in a black bombazine gown and a thick, black shawl gazed at her appraisingly. Her papery skin, drawn tightly over her cheekbones, gave her a fragile look that reminded Sara of a French porcelain doll her father had once given her for Christmas.

For a long moment, Clarice stared at Sara, her open-mouthed expression that of someone who'd seen a ghost. Then, before Sara could inquire if something was wrong, the woman snapped her mouth closed and rearranged her features into a frown. "How long have you been at *that place*?" Though blunt, her strong, brisk voice belied her delicate appearance.

Sara bristled slightly at Mrs. Degas' snide emphases on *that place*. "I just moved into Harrogate yesterday. Are you Mrs. Degas?"

The white head bowed slightly in affirmation. "You may address me as Clarice," she said in a crisp, no-nonsense tone. She looked past Sara, and Raina and motioned for her maid. "Cherry, please bring us some refreshments and some of Bertha's honeyed rice cakes." After Cherry left the room, followed by Raina, Clarice swung her gaze back to Sara. "Please." She waved her blue-veined hand at a gilded chair across from her.

The movement stirred to life the scent of flowers. Not fresh flowers. They rather reminded Sara of flowers that had been dried between the pages of an old book.

Unsure if her welcome would be short-lived, Sara poised herself stiffly on the edge of the chair and waited for Clarice to speak.

"What brings you to Candlewick?" Clarice raised a wizened, wrinkled hand and stopped any reply Sara would have made before it passed her lips. Her ring, earrings, and necklace all contained rubies that sparkled like fresh blood against her pale skin. "Please don't patronize me by telling me it was to pay a social call on a shriveled up old woman you had no desire to meet."

Well, the old lady was frank; Sara would give her that. But what had made Clarice so bitter? Sara swallowed hard, wove her fingers tightly together, and made up her mind to be as frank as her hostess. "I . . . I want to know about Harrogate."

Long ago, her grandmother had told her the house was built by Jonathan Bradford, and completed just before he was to marry Katherine Grayson in 1805. Ezra Wade, Sara's grandfather, had purchased Harrogate Plantation from the Grayson family in 1828, the same year the lone occupant died and Sara was born. Beyond that, she had been told nothing about the house or the people who had lived there. In fact, when she'd asked, her grandmother had often side-stepped Sara's questions by telling her she knew nothing of the former owners, and then skillfully guided their conversation off to another subject. Her reaction to the question was much like what she'd exhibited when Sara had asked about the portrait of the woman.

Clarice raised an eyebrow but said nothing. After studying Sara for several moments, as if deciding if she'd tell her anything, she said, "I lived here when Jonathan built it." She offered nothing more.

"Then you must have known Katherine Grayson and Jonathan Bradford."

Clarice straightened her slim shoulders. The bombazine made a *crinkling* sound, like old, dried paper. "I knew them, but I stopped socializing with my neighbors after—" She broke off abruptly and shifted her gaze to somewhere beyond the windows. A shadow of sadness filled the old woman's eyes. Clarice blinked, then brought her gaze back to Sara. "Until Alice Wade lived there, I never stepped foot in the place after . . . Even when Alice and Ezra owned it, I only went there a few times out of courtesy when she invited me to one of her parties." After taking a long drink of her lemonade, Mrs.

Degas replaced the glass on the table, patted her lips dry with a napkin, and then studied Sara. "What is it you want to know about them?"

Why was Mrs. Degas so bitter about the house and the engaged couple who'd built it? Best not to pry further on that subject. "I'm afraid I know nothing, but I'd appreciate anything you can tell me about them."

Mrs. Degas had started to take another drink, but slowly lowered her glass. Her expression became wary. "Why is it you're so interested in all this, and why come to me to learn about it?"

What was Sara to say? *Because there's evil living in my house, and my grandmother's ghost told me to ask you about it?* All too aware of the reaction she'd get if she mentioned a ghost, she settled for something innocuous. "Curiosity mostly. If I'm going to live there, I thought it would be good if I knew some of the history of the house."

Again, Clarice studied Sara closely before answering. "Like what?" she asked, her tone less severe.

"Why did Jonathan Bradford sell Harrogate?"

"He didn't sell it."

Getting information out of Clarice was akin to getting Patricia Wade to give up the notion of marrying her daughter off to the first pair of trousers who offered. "I don't understand."

A suffocating silence fell over the room. Sara could

hear only the accelerated beat of her own heart and the tick of the tall, rosewood grandfather clock in the hall.

"Then you don't know about the . . . scandal," Clarice said in a whisper so low that Sara had to wonder whether the old woman was talking to herself.

Scandal? At Harrogate? Gran had never mentioned a scandal. Sara shook her head and leaned toward Clarice, eager to hear more.

Clarice stiffened her back, removed the white linen napkin from her lap, placed it on the table, and positioned her glass just so beside it. The woman's already pallid complexion had gone even whiter. Her bloodless lips pursed in a tight line. Finally, she spoke.

"A young man from a neighboring plantation killed Jonathan in a jealous rage on the eve of his and Katherine's wedding."

Rather than being shocked at hearing a murder had taken place at her home and at such a terrible time, Sara felt an inexplicable, all-enveloping sadness descend upon her. The sensation became so overwhelming that she had to fight the sudden urge to sob her heart out. Quickly, before Mrs. Degas noticed, Sara swallowed and cleared her throat, eventually regaining her composure, but the sadness remained hanging over her like a large, black cloud.

Seemingly unaware of Sara's reaction, Mrs. Degas went on with her story, spewing it forth so quickly, it was as though she had to get it out in its entirety or she wouldn't be able to.

"The story goes that this young man had been in love with Katherine for years and had hoped she'd give Jonathan up to her younger sister, Madeline. Maddy, we all called her. When Katherine didn't, the young man decided that if he couldn't have Katherine, neither could Jonathan. So he killed him. Katherine moved away right after the trial and . . . sentencing. Some say Katherine moved to New Orleans, but no one seems to know for sure what happened to her." She lowered her voice. "Now, her twin sister—"

"Maddy was Katherine's twin?"

"Yes. Her fraternal twin. She was a beauty and looked nothing like Katherine. She wasn't unattractive, just not the striking beauty her sister was." Clarice stared openly at Sara, and then went on. "Maddy was . . . exceptional. A beauty not only on the surface, but one whose beauty shone from within as well. Every young man in the parish was in love with her." Unlike the sharp edge it held when she said Katherine's name, Clarice's voice had softened when she spoke of Maddy. "Everyone, except Katherine, loved Maddy, including Jonathan, and we all knew she adored him. If he and Katherine hadn't been betrothed at birth, Jonathan would have asked for Maddy's hand."

"Did Maddy ever live at Harrogate?"

"Yes. Unbeknownst to Katherine, Jonathan had it written into his will that if he died, Maddy was to inherit the plantation. The poor dear lived out the remainder of her life there. Never had visitors. Never wanted visitors. Died a lonely old woman in 1828."

Sara started. The year she was born. Coincidence, no doubt, but very odd.

"Everyone said that over the years, Maddy wasted away from a broken heart. What she felt for Jonathan was one of those everlasting kinds of loves." For the first time, a wisp of a smile tugged at Clarice's mouth. "The kind that a body just never gets past. It just lives on forever."

Forever. My Love Forever. The words in the locket.

Something Mrs. Degas had said earlier suddenly entered Sara's thoughts. If she'd attended parties at Harrogate, perhaps the locket Sara had found in the harpsichord belonged to Mrs. Degas. Digging into her reticule where she'd put it before leaving Harrogate with the intention of asking Clarice if it belonged to her or anyone she knew, Sara extracted the gold locket.

Holding it up by the chain, Sara extended it to Mrs. Degas. "I found this in the harpsichord while we were opening the house. Could you have lost this at one of my grandmother's parties? If you didn't, would you by chance know whom it belongs to? I'd like to return it to its owner."

Mrs. Degas' smile vanished. Her face went sheet white. She recoiled and looked at the locket as though Sara were offering her the hand of Satan.

"No. No. That's not mine."

"Hmm. Then do you know whose it could be? I'm sure whoever it belongs to misses it and would like to have it back."

With her face white and her gaze still centered on the locket, Clarice said, "I'm afraid that would be quite impossible. That's the locket Jonathan gave Maddy for her birthday."

"Maddy? Katherine's twin?"

Mrs. Degas nodded stiffly.

"I know Jonathan loved Maddy, but why would he give Maddy such an expensive gift? Especially one that says *my love forever* inside. Didn't Maddy's husband object to such familiarity?"

"Didn't I mention that Maddy never married?" She pointed a bony finger at the necklace. "And she never took that locket off." Clarice's voice caught. "It . . . it was buried with her." Her complexion had turned absolutely ghostly. "Kather—"

The sound of shattering glass stopped Mrs. Degas mid-sentence. Both women jumped and looked toward the window just as a large, black crow hurtled toward them and landed motionless at their feet. Another shattering of glass followed. Cherry had dropped the pitcher of lemonade she'd just carried into the room.

Mrs. Degas' maid stared in abject horror at the dead bird. "That's a bad omen, a sign from the devil, Miss Clarice." She backed away, oblivious to the broken glass and lemonade puddled at her feet. Her gaze never left the dead bird.

Raina dashed into the room. When she spotted the bird, she stopped cold. Her eyes widened. She stared down at it, just as Cherry continued to do.

The feathers had turned dark crimson with the blood that seeped from its lacerated body. Beneath it, a stain grew ever wider on the Aubusson carpet.

"Call Josiah, and ask him to get this cleaned up." Clarice shuddered, noticeably shaken by the event. She placed her linen napkin over the bird. Almost instantly, crimson seeped through the snow white linen.

"Don't think Josiah'll be touchin' dat bird, Miss Clarice. No, suh." Raina backed up. "It's a powerful bad omen. Crows means somebody gonna die."

Clarice looked from Raina to Sara with something close to hatred flashing from her rheumy eyes. As she hoisted her frail body from the chair, it shook so violently she nearly toppled over. When Sara reached to steady her, she recoiled and glared, her gaze filled with pure venom.

"You brought this here. You and your questions, and your talk of things that should be left alone. Let the past be. You're prying into something that's none of your business." Clarice pointed a bony finger toward the door. "Now, get out of my house, and don't ever come here again."

Chapter 4

When Sara got back to Harrogate, Clarice Degas' stinging words still rang in her ears. The unexpected appearance of the crow seemed to have sparked something in the old woman that made her . . . furious? No, not furious. *Terrified.* But not the same kind of terror the two black women had exhibited. Clarice's terror hadn't just shown in her expression. It had gone much deeper. Perhaps even to her soul. And somehow, she had connected Sara to that fear.

Despite the sun beating through the window in her bedroom, where she sat sipping tea and watching the field hands make order of the grounds, Sara shivered. Did Clarice's reaction have anything to do with the evil Gran had warned her about? No. Gran had said the evil was at

Harrogate, not Candlewick.

Sara shook away the many questions that buffeted her from all sides. She had enough worries right here. No need to add Clarice Degas to the mix. Still, Sara couldn't entirely erase the incident from her mind. What had taken place at Candlewick had some connection to Harrogate and her; otherwise, her grandmother wouldn't have sent her there. But what was it? And, if Clarice refused to share everything she knew, how was Sara supposed to find out?

Inexplicably, Sara's gaze was drawn to the portrait of the woman hanging over the mantel. A sinister smile curved her lips, and a strange light filled her eyes. That had to be stopped, now. Her imagination or not, the portrait gave Sara the creeps. It had to go. She set down her teacup and saucer, and gave the embroidered bell roped beside the bed a yank.

Moments later, Raina stepped into the room. "Yes, Missus?"

Sara pointed at the portrait. "Take that down, and come with me."

Raina frowned, but did as she'd been told. Painting in hand, she followed Sara down the hall. At the end of the hall, Sara hoisted the hem of her gown in one hand, threw open the attic door with the other, and then climbed the stairs.

The attic was dirty, hot, and lit dimly by a shaft of light coming through the one tiny, dusty window. Stacked everywhere were discarded or forgotten possessions ranging from furniture to clothing and filling every available bit of floor space. Travel-scarred trunks, moth-eaten carpetbags, shattered lamps, broken furniture, and more—all of which had occupied a place in the rooms below at one time, but now lay forgotten and forlorn in the dark recesses of the attic. A narrow pathway wound through the clutter.

Cobwebs hanging in wispy veils from the rafters tangled in Sara's hair like phantom fingers trying to prevent her from doing what she'd come here to do.

Impatiently brushing away a cobweb that had attached itself to her cheek, Sara glanced over her shoulder at her maid. Raina was obviously not at all comfortable about being here. The maid's large brown eyes shifted frantically in their sockets, attempting to take in all corners of the attic at once. Sara didn't blame her. Truth be told, her skin had begun to crawl the moment she'd mounted the first step.

"Put that portrait anywhere, and then help me look for a painting to replace it."

"Yes, Missus." Raina propped the woman's portrait against the closest trunk, making certain the painting faced away from them, then scanned the semi-dark room.

"I don't see no more pichurs, Miss Sara." Raina remained at the top of the stairs, no more than a foot from a quick getaway should something pop out of the darkness.

"You're not looking, Raina. Check behind some of the furniture. There has to be more here. Lord knows, there's enough other junk." Sara shoved aside a chair on which the seat's material had been nearly obliterated by layers of black mildew. Dust moats floated up and danced in the weak shaft of sunlight. Sara sneezed.

Raina still hadn't moved much farther than a few steps.

"Just *look*, Raina!" Sara's eagerness to leave this place filtered into her voice as a harsh command, and she immediately felt bad for taking out her impatience on Raina. It wasn't her fault the painting gave Sara the creeps. She cast a guilty look toward Raina.

Raina went immediately to the closest pile of discarded junk and began pawing through it. Moments later, she was engrossed in digging through a group of paintings she'd found leaning against the wall and nearly concealed by an old, dilapidated sideboard. Suddenly, she stopped and stared down at one of the paintings.

"Laws, Miss Sara, you never told me Miss Alice had your pichur painted."

Sara ceased her search through a stack of oil paintings and turned to her maid and frowned. "She didn't." The only portrait she'd ever sat for was by a New Orleans artist, and it hung over the mantel in the Wade's Garden District home.

Raina shook her head. "No, ma'am. She sho nuff did. I gots it right here."

She held up a painting, but Sara couldn't see it through the dust moats and gloom. Using her foot, she pushed aside a chair with its legs missing, and then made her way across the attic to the maid. Raina tilted the painting to allow the filtered light from the window to fall on it.

Sara stopped abruptly. Her mouth fell open. She could feel the color draining from her face. Icy shock waves danced over her hot skin. She had to fight to keep her knees from buckling.

"Miss Sara, you okay?"

Sara nodded dumbly, barely aware of moving. Her gaze remained glued to the painting.

Though her chestnut hair was piled on the top of her head and tiny ringlets of curls framed her face and neck, a style that hadn't been in vogue for a very long time, and her empire-waist dress was totally out of date as well, the woman's face . . . her eyes . . . could have been . . . Sara's looking back at her from the canvas.

"Look here. Dey's a gentleman, too." Raina held up another canvas, the same size and with the same frame style. It appeared as though they'd been painted as a matching set.

Dragging her gaze from the unknown woman's portrait, Sara glanced at the second painting. Disbelief, then surprise, vibrated through her from head to toe. It couldn't be, but there was no mistaking who the man in the portrait was. He was the unknown man who had appeared to Sara in the swamp and in the upstairs window.

Speechless, she sank weakly into a Queen Anne chair, oblivious to the way the chair tilted to the side, and to the dust that would cling to her dress.

This couldn't be. It just couldn't be. Who were these people, and why were their paintings in Harrogate? Propping them against her legs, Raina stood them side-by-side for Sara to look at.

It was then that Sara noticed it. The locket hanging around the woman's neck. The same one that was on her dressing table downstairs. The locket Clarice had said Maddy never took off, the one that had been buried with Madeline Grayson. There was no doubt in Sara's mind that this portrait was of Madeline Grayson.

Her gaze shifted back to the man's face in the other portrait. Was he Jonathan Bradford? Something that stirred next to her frantically beating heart told her it was.

But what of the other painting, the one she'd removed from her bedroom? Could that be Katherine? After what Clarice had implied about Katherine's dislike of her sister, if Maddy and Sara looked that much alike, then Sara finally understood why the woman in the portrait hated her. She also understood Clarice's initial reaction to her: the wide eyes and the paling of her complexion. She probably thought Maddy had come back from the dead.

"What's dis?" Raina rummaged around at the back of the painting.

The sound of the backing being ripped away brought Sara back to the moment. "Don't damage the painting."

"I's not hurtin' the pichur none. I's tryin' to—" Whatever Raina had been working at freeing from the back of the painting let loose, almost throwing the maid backward. Catching her balance, she stood erect and raised something in the air. "Look here! Dey's a book, too."

In somewhat of a daze, Sara took the small, leather-bound book. A light layer of dust nearly obscured the writing on the cover. Using the hem of her gown, she wiped the cover clean. Written across the black leather in gold leaf were five words: *The Diary of Madeline Grayson*.

Sara's head grew light. Her temples began to throb. She swayed.

Raina's steadying hand on her shoulder roused her from her stupor. "You's lookin' poorly, Miss Sara. We needs to git you out a dis dust fo you takes sick. No tellin' what kind of sickness is hangin' 'round up here." Taking Sara's elbow, Raina lifted her from the chair. "Jest lean on me."

Sara tucked the book in her pocket, took two steps, and

then stopped. "Get the paintings, Raina . . . both of them."

Raina looked back and forth between the paintings and her wobbly mistress. "But—"

She smiled weakly at the maid. "I'll be fine. Just get the paintings."

Reluctantly, Raina did as she was told, but kept a sharp eye on Sara. Juggling one portrait under each arm, Raina followed Sara down the steep attic stairs.

After supervising Samuel, whom Sara had summoned to hang the replacement paintings above the mantel, she sat at the foot of the bed and stared at them. Her resemblance to the woman in the portrait was uncanny. Her chestnut hair, the exact same shade as Sara's, outlined her heart-shaped face with tight ringlets. They shared the same upturned nose, stubborn chin, and high cheekbones. Even the tiny mole Sara had on her neck just below her ear had been added to the painting. She and Madeline Grayson looked more like twins than Katherine and Maddy did.

Her eyes, the same shade of emerald green as Sara's, glittered with some inner secret happiness, a happiness Sara had seen in her mirrored reflection of late. If what Clarice had said about Jonathan and Maddy being in love was true, Sara didn't have to try hard to figure out what secret Maddy's happy smile hid, but it didn't explain her own smile.

With that thought, her gaze slid to the painting of the man. He had to be Jonathan. His hair was black as night, his eyes the color of Spanish moss. Sara had no trouble understanding why Maddy had fallen in love with him. Just staring at his picture made Sara's heartbeat race. How she longed to touch him . . . really touch him.

Impulsively, she went to the mantel and ran her fingertip over his cheek, then down to his lips. The skin on her fingers seemed to warm, as though she were actually touching human flesh. She pulled her hand back, but the sensation remained.

The words he'd spoken in the swamp echoed through her mind. *I'm waiting.* Had he, for some reason, referred to her arrival at Harrogate?

Sara took a step back, needing to distance herself from this mesmerizing, yet unsettling, man. Something hit the side of her leg. She touched her pocket. Maddy's diary. Carefully, she withdrew it. Hugging the book against her heart, she glanced once more at Jonathan's captivating smile and then walked to the chair next to the window overlooking the Garden of the Moon. She sank into the chair, eager to learn what Maddy Grayson's deepest thoughts were. She opened the cover. The faint odor of old roses drifted up to her.

Then the door opened, and Raina poked her head in.

Sara frowned, impatient to be rid of her maid and get back to the diary. "Can this wait, Raina?"

"No, ma'am, Miss Sara. Dey's a lady downstairs what says she knows you. Says Massah Preston sent her here."

Reluctantly, Sara placed the diary on the small table beside her. "Did she give you her card?"

"No, ma'am." Raina looked at the floor and shuffled her feet. "She'd don't appear like the kind what would have a card. Dress looks worn, hair hangin' all loose 'round her shoulders. No, ma'am, not the kind to have a callin' card."

Growing increasingly impatient, Sara stood. "Well, did she at least give you her name?"

"Yes, ma'am, she sho nuff did. Says she's Miss Juliana Weston."

"Julie!"

With unbridled delight propelling her, diary forgotten, Sara bolted from the chair and nearly knocked Raina off her feet in her haste to get downstairs to see her dearest friend from boarding school.

Julie stood in the middle of the sitting room. Her

raven-black hair, tied up with a blue ribbon, hung loosely down her back. Her faded, travel-worn, navy blue gown was wrinkled and soiled. But all Sara really saw clearly was her dearest friend. A friend she sorely needed right now. Julie understood her. Julie knew about Sara's gift and never doubted her or laughed at her or belittled her because of it.

Sara squealed, rushed forward, and then hugged Julie so tightly, she gasped for air. "I can't believe it!" She stepped back to feast her eyes on the friend she hadn't seen for almost four years. "You must tell me everything that's happened to you since I last saw you." She grabbed Julie's hand and ushered her to the settee, calling orders over her shoulder to Raina to bring them refreshments.

Once they were seated, the questions poured from Sara. "I thought you were still in Richmond. Why are you in Louisiana? How long can you stay? Are you married? Did you bring him with you? Who is he? Where is he?"

Julie laughed out loud, the sound musical and light, but, to Sara's ears, a bit forced. "My word, Sara, which one of those questions do you want me to answer first?"

The hollow smile Julie flashed at Sara lacked sincerity. This was not the Julie Sara had known at boarding school. That Julie had bubbled with life. Nothing dampened her spirit. When Sara had confided her problems to her, she'd always found the bright side of everything.

But now, the inner light that had always made Julie shine was gone. Something was terribly wrong.

Taking Julie's cold hand, Sara looked her in the eye. "Tell me."

Julie's beautiful gray eyes filled instantly with tears. The forced smile vanished from her lips. Her shoulders slumped. "Papa's dead." She grimaced, as though the words slashed a wound in her heart.

"Oh my goodness, Julie." Sara pulled her friend into her arms and cradled her like a small child while Julie sobbed quietly. "I am so very sorry."

Sara knew how much Julie had loved her father. Their love for their fathers had been what initially brought Sara and Julie together as friends. Julie's mother had died in childbirth, and her father had transferred all the love he'd had for his wife to his infant daughter. He'd raised and adored Julie and, from what she'd told Sara, they'd been inseparable. Her father had been the center of Julie's life, and now he was gone. Sara couldn't begin to imagine the pain of her friend's loss.

After a few moments, Julie's sobs ceased. She sat up and dried her tears on a handkerchief she'd pulled from her reticule. "I'm sorry. I just can't speak of it without crying." She laughed weakly. "Seems that all I do these days is weep." She glanced at Sara, then lowered her gaze to her clasped hands.

"There is nothing to apologize for." She took Julie's cold hands in hers. It struck her that the skin was callused and rough and totally unlike those of the well-groomed lady that Sara had befriended at school. "When did it happen?"

"Three months ago. His heart failed."

"Three months ago? And you waited all this time to come to me?"

"I couldn't come any sooner." Julie rose and went to stare out the window. "There's more, Sara."

Silence followed Julie's statement. She continued to study the scene beyond the window, as though deeply engrossed in what the field hands were doing. Unwilling to hurry her friend, Sara waited patiently for her to go on.

"Two years ago, the crops failed. I won't bore you with the details. I'll just say that poor Papa did everything he could to save them, but it was too late." Her voice caught again. She swallowed hard, straightened her shoulders, dabbed at her tears, and went on. "He tried to get a loan to get us through the year and buy seed for the spring, but the bank wouldn't take a chance and everyone we knew had suffered the same setbacks, so no one was willing to part with money they'd need to recover their own losses." She glanced at Sara and then came to sit beside her. "He never got back on his feet, either financially or emotionally. Oh, we tried. I even worked the fields beside

72

him and our slaves."

Julie's worn, faded gown and the calluses on her hands now made sense to Sara.

"But it was too little too late. That final failure took the heart right out of him." Julie shook her head as if to clear away unwanted memories. "When the bank took the plantation after he died to pay off Papa's debts, I had to find somewhere to go. What with us not having any living relatives, the only place I could think of to go for help was you. So I went to New Orleans to find you, and your father sent me here."

"I'm so sorry, Julie." The words sounded hollow and so . . . useless.

Sara knew how precarious the financial well-being of a plantation could be. A couple of years of bad weather or insect infestation could mean disaster. Often, a neighbor who had not suffered the same hardships could share his seed or provide the financial help for a planter to make it to the next year, but not if the neighbor had suffered the same losses.

Lifting her chin and looking more like the proud girl Sara had met at school, Julie forced a smile. "I didn't come here for either your pity or your charity. I need a place to stay until I can find a position as a nanny or something and support myself. It'll only be for a month or so." She shrugged. "If you don't want me here, I'll understand."

"Don't want you here?" Sara sprang to her feet. "That's just foolish talk! I won't hear of you leaving. You'll live here for as long as you want to stay with me. I'm all alone in a big house with more rooms than I'd fill in a lifetime. Truth be told, my mother would probably be very pleased if I wasn't living here alone." She pulled Julie to her feet and hugged her. "Now, Raina will take you to your room. You get some rest, and we'll talk more at dinner."

As Julie started from the room, Sara stopped her. "Julie, if it helps make this any easier, I need you now as much as you need me."

Chloe outdid herself with dinner that night. Julie hadn't seen that much food in over a year. The table should have collapsed under the weight of a platter of crispy, brown roast pork with raisin sauce, candied sweet potatoes, yellow cornbread with honey butter, stuffed, plump tomatoes, and chocolate cake so rich and sweet that every bite made Julie want to swoon.

Her months of hunger finally satiated, Julie sighed contentedly, wiped her mouth on her napkin, and sat back in her chair. "If you just moved in here, where on earth did you get all this food?"

Sara shrugged. "My cook, Chloe, said Papa sent it with the house slaves. As usual, he's thought of everything."

"Well, my stomach thanks him. But a few more meals like this and I'll have to let out all my gowns . . . not that I have that many to let out," she added, and her smile vanished. She looked down at the gown she'd chosen to wear for dinner. While it was clean and by far the best of the gowns she owned, the many washings it had gone through had made the material almost threadbare and had faded what was once bright pink to almost white.

A little over a year ago, her closet had bulged with her fashionable gowns. But that was before they'd had to sell them to buy food. She glanced at Sara and could almost see what she was thinking. Sara had always been a problem solver. If someone was in need, she'd be the first to offer help. This time, Julie was the one in need, but she couldn't allow it.

"I didn't say that to suggest anything, so don't even think about buying me clothes, Sara. I can make do with what I have."

"Nonsense." A grin spread across Sara's face. "I won't take no for an answer. Besides, I wasn't thinking of buying you new dresses. We're the same size, and Papa has always spoiled me by buying me more gowns than I can ever hope to wear. I'll sort through them and see what will suit you."

"Thank you for not saying you'll give me what you don't want."

Sara frowned. "I would never give you my castoffs."

"Well, whatever you choose to call them, I can't accept them." Pride was about all Julie had left.

Sara's frown deepened. "This is not a question of you accepting them or not. I simply refuse to take no for an answer. If it makes you feel better, then consider them on loan until you can get your own. I'll have Raina bring them to your room as soon as I can sort through them. And if it makes you feel any better, since I don't have a head for figures and you seem to have experience with it, you can help me balance the plantation's account books."

The stubborn set of Sara's mouth, a gesture that oddly enough made her resemble the one person in the world Sara had no desire to emulate—her mother—said it all. There was no use fighting her on the issue.

"Thank you." The thanks came as much for the offer of a place to live as it did for Sara's sparing Julie the humiliation of taking charity.

"It's the least I can do after all you've done for me." She grinned. "Why, if it hadn't been for you offering to go with him, I would have had to attend the Spring Cotillion with Jordan Longstreet." Sara wrinkled her nose in disgust.

For the first time in ages, Julie laughed, really laughed, with happiness. "Come to think of it, you do owe me. I had to suffer through the entire night with that dolt walking on the toes of my new blue slippers. He made such a mess of them I had to throw them out, and my toes took weeks to recover from the abuse."

Sara giggled, sounding much like she had back at school when they'd shared secrets after the lights went out.

"As I also recall," Julie continued, "the reason you didn't want to go with him was because you'd seen his grandmother's spirit hovering over him, and you refused to accompany a man who took his dead grandmother to a dance with him." Julie knew all about Sara's gift and, rather than being repelled by it, had found it fascinating. Another reason the two of them had become inseparable friends. Julie simply accepted Sara for who she was.

Julie's expression had sobered. "Speaking of grand-mothers . . . I never said how sorry I was to hear you lost your grandmother. I know how close you were to her."

Sara's laughter, along with the light in her eyes, died. She became very solemn, then stood and laid her napkin on the table. "Let's go into the garden. I need some fresh air."

Julie followed her without a word. From the look on her face, Sara needed more than fresh air.

The garden was like none other Julie had ever seen. Everything, from the unusual circular gate with the two white marble dogs stationed on either side, to the profusion of snowy flowers, went far beyond anything she could have imagined. In the distance, she could see the outline of a gazebo. She and Sara wound their way silently toward it through the maze of gravel pathways that zigzagged through the garden.

Julie waited for Sara to speak. When she didn't, Julie consigned her friend's silence to grief she was still felling about losing her grandmother. She could have kicked herself for mentioning Sara's grandmother. "I'm sorry I brought up your grandmother. I just thought that after five years—"

Sara raised her hand to stop Julie's apology. "Please, don't apologize. That's not why I asked you to come out here." She glanced at Julie. "I have something to tell you, and I didn't want anyone else to hear us talking about it."

Julie understood. Servants were well-known for *hearing* everything that went on in the big house and then spreading the gossip like cottonseed throughout the slave community.

"Does this have anything to do with what you said earlier about needing me now as much as I need you?" She hesitated before going on. "Does it have anything to do with that . . . that . . . thing you do?"

Julie was well aware, after having heard Sara's complaints on her return to school from every vacation, how much her mother's attitude toward her gift upset Sara. Being treated like a pariah by her own mother had to have been hard for her. Maybe it wasn't wise to bring up the subject when Sara was in such an agitated state, but the words were out, and it was too late for second-guessing.

Sara stopped walking and swung around to face her friend. As Julie had feared, anger tinted Sara's cheeks a bright pink. "You're my friend, and I've never hid my gift from you, so there's no need for you to tiptoe around it. Just say it. I see dead people."

Julie took a step back and held up her hands, palms out to ward off more of Sara's anger. "Okay. You see dead people. What does that have to do with what's bothering you? Talk to me, please."

Instantly, Sara appeared contrite for her outburst. "I'm sorry."

She dropped her gaze to her feet. Evidently, the wound her mother's disapproval had inflicted on Sara's heart hadn't healed. And evidently something had happened to aggravate the situation.

Julie placed her hand on Sara's forearm. She tilted her head to better see her friend's face in the moonlight. "Sara?"

Without a word, Sara took Julie's hand and led her

to Gran's favorite white, wrought iron bench nestled among a grouping of budding rosebushes and sheltered beneath the spreading branches of a towering magnolia tree. The tree's deep green, leathery leaves glistened in the moonlight, and the heady mixture of the perfume from its saucer-sized, creamy blossoms vied with the moonflower's intoxicating fragrance for dominance of the night air. The mixture made Sara lightheaded.

Once seated, Sara searched for the words to explain what had happened to her in the last few days. She raised her gaze to her friend's. A strange light over Julie's shoulder snagged Sara's attention. The words froze on the tip of her tongue.

"Sara, what is it?"

Sara bolted to her feet. She could hear Julie, but she only stared mutely at the apparition taking shape in the corner of the garden.

After few moments, the image was complete. A few feet from them stood the figure of a man. Not just any man. It was the man from the window, the man in the portrait hanging in her bedroom. This time, her frantically beating heart told her he was Jonathan Bradford.

Chapter 5

Sara opened her mouth to explain her strange behavior to Julie, but before the words had passed her lips, the man's image shimmered like heat waves and then vanished, but not before he smiled at Sara. Once more, the two women were alone in the garden.

"Sara? What is it?" Julie glanced over her shoulder, then back to Sara. "You're white as a sheet." She stood and laid her hand on Sara's brow. "Are you feeling all right?"

The concern in her friend's voice roused Sara from the stupor brought on by the apparition of Jonathan appearing so suddenly out of nowhere. She forced a smile to her cold lips.

"I'm . . . fine." The words rang with insincerity.

"You don't look fine. You look like you're going to

faint at any moment." Julie moved to her side and then guided Sara back to the garden bench. "Sit down."

Not until Julie said it did Sara become aware of the pain in her chest from her air-deprived lungs and the watery weakness invading her legs.

"You rest there, and I'll go get Raina."

Sara grabbed Julie's hand. "No. I don't need Raina, and what I have to tell you will just frighten her."

This time, it was Julie's face that was drained of color. She sank onto the bench beside Sara. "Very well. I'm listening."

Even though Julie was aware that she saw dead people, Sara still had trouble finding the right words to tell her friend about what had happened at Harrogate in the past two days. This went far beyond just seeing specters and sending them into the light. In fact, it went beyond logical explanation, but if she was to get Julie's help, she had to try to explain it.

"When we came down the drive to Harrogate, I was convinced my life was perfect. I was finally free of my mother, and I was coming home to the one place I'd always felt secure and at peace," she said, pushing the words out before she could change her mind. "But when we stopped in front of the house, things began to happen that I couldn't explain. At first I thought it was fatigue from the journey, or the shadows of the trees playing tricks on me, but I soon learned that it wasn't." Words continued to tumble from her in quick succession.

Once she started, she talked nonstop for the next hour, leaving almost nothing out, while Julie listened. By the time she'd finished, Julie knew everything: the man in the swamp and the upstairs window, the locket, her grandmother's nocturnal visit, the visit to Clarice's, the dead crow, the portraits, the diary, her uncanny resemblance to the dead Madeline Grayson, and the overwhelming sadness she'd felt when Clarice told her of Jonathan's murder.

The one thing Sara did omit was the unprecedented physical reaction she had to Jonathan Bradford's ghost. Until she understood it herself, she couldn't very well explain why she longed for the touch of a dead man.

"Are you sure you didn't just dream about your grandmother visiting you? You'd just made a very long journey from New Orleans and worked most of the day opening the house. You were probably sleeping very deeply. It could have been that you thought you were awake, but you weren't." The lack of conviction in Julie's voice told Sara her friend was grabbing at straws. "As for the sadness . . ." Julie went on, "well . . . it's probably no more than the same fatigue or grief you'd naturally feel for someone who died so violently."

Sara shook her head. "If that were the case, then

how do you explain that the locket I found was buried with a dead woman and that the ghost of Jonathon Bradford appeared just now." She inclined her head in the direction where the ghost had been.

"Just now?" Julie glanced over her shoulder. "Is that what you saw? Is he still here?"

"No. He's gone, but he was right over there." This time Sara pointed at the exact spot beside a flowering azalea bush where she'd just seen him.

Relief evident in her expression, Julie sat back. For a few moments, she remained deep in thought. "You're sure the man in the swamp, and the window, and the portrait, and the one who just showed up here are all this Jonathan person?"

"Bradford. His name is Jonathan Bradford." Sara swallowed hard. "I saw his portrait. There is no doubt in my mind."

"Could he be the evil your grandmother warned you about?"

Sara thought about it. The man's eyes were the kindest she'd ever seen. His smile warmed her through and through. Somewhere deep inside, she knew he didn't want to hurt her. "No. I don't sense any evil about him at all."

"None?"

"No. None. I just wish I knew what he wanted."

"If you don't sense evil around him, then I'd say

84

what he wants is pretty clear." Smiling, Julie laid her hand on Sara's. "If you look as much like Maddy as you say, then I think he believes his Maddy has come back, and that's why he's here." She paused. "And he did say he was waiting."

Sara stood. "That's absurd." She walked to where the specter of Jonathan Bradford had been. The shrub rustled with the evening breeze off the river. But there was no sign that anyone had been standing there moments earlier. "Why would he be waiting for me? I'm not Maddy." She turned to Julie. "Am I?"

That night, after the house was silent, Sara made a trip to the attic on her own, determined to find anything else that would help her unravel the mysteries plaguing her and Harrogate. Armed with the pitiful light from a single candle and with no idea exactly what it was she was searching for, she began to dig through the myriad of stored family objects. She dug into drawers in half-rotted dressers, pawed through trunks of dusty, yellowed clothing, opened books, and fanned through pages that fell apart at her touch. She looked behind, over, and under anything she thought could be concealing something, and even ran her fingers along the overhead beams.

After almost an hour of fighting clinging cobwebs and choking dust, she'd found nothing that would shed light on any of her questions about anyone with a role in Harrogate's past and the short, tragic life of Jonathan Bradford or Maddy Grayson or the evil that lurked here.

Discouraged and about to give up, she noticed a large trunk pushed under the slanting rafters, behind a pile of boxes. Placing her candle on a nearby hatbox, she shoved the boxes aside, kneeled beside the trunk, and then pried open the lid. Since the hinges had rusted, it took several tries before it finally budged enough for her to lever the top up. Inside were items obviously belonging to a man: shirts, trousers, coats, several accounts ledgers with the name *Harrogate* written in gold leaf on their covers, and a box that had contained a set of engraved dueling pistols. One was missing. But there was nothing to answer any of the questions plaguing her.

About to close the lid, she spotted a white porcelain shaving mug with the gold initials *JB* on it. She picked it up and traced the initials with her fingertip. This had been *his*. She knew it as well as she knew her own name. As when she'd touched the painting, her fingertips grew warm. The awareness rushed throughout her body, making her tremble. Suddenly, the sensation of millions of butterflies taking wing in her stomach made her weak all over.

What did all this mean?

Movement near the head of the stairs caught her attention. Thinking Raina had followed her, she turned to tell the maid she would be down directly. But the words never passed her lips.

Standing at the head of the stairs was the transparent image of Jonathan Bradford. Clutching the shaving mug to her breast, she froze, waiting for whatever would come next. None of the ghosts she'd ever seen had attacked her, but with Gran's warning of evil in the house ringing in her memory, this could well be a first. Perhaps, contrary to Julie's belief that he'd come back because he had Sara confused with Maddy, this man chose to appear because he had something malicious in mind for her. If that were the case, why didn't she feel it? Why did she feel nothing more than a magnetic tug drawing her toward him and a warmth that went so deep inside her, it became a part of her?

For a very long moment he just studied her, as though drinking in the sight of her. Then he smiled and beckoned her to follow him. When he started down the stairs, Sara roused herself and quickly closed the trunk, grabbed the candle and, clutching the shaving mug, hurried after him. In the downstairs hallway, he stopped from time to time and looked back, as though to make certain she was still there. At her bedroom he paused, looked back again, and then disappeared through the closed door.

"Wait!" With her heart beating heavily against her bodice, she raced after him. An intense eagerness to speak to him, find out what he wanted, pushed her past any fear of danger.

But when she entered the room . . . it was empty.

With a sigh of defeat, Sara set the mug on her bedside table. Needing time to digest what had just happened and not wanting to explain her disheveled state, she refrained from summoning Raina. Instead, she stripped out of her soiled gown and then washed away the attic's dust and grime from her face and arms in the bowl on the washstand. Once clean, she slipped on a pale green nightdress, picked up the mug, then settled into a chair and peered into the darkness beyond the window overlooking the Garden of the Moon.

Below her, the full moon illuminated the white flowers, making them appear as tiny ghosts against the dark foliage. While she stared into the night, she caressed the mug. That warmth that now was familiar filled her.

Why was Jonathan taunting her, teasing her with words and actions she didn't understand? Why didn't he let her know what he wanted from her? Frustration and confusion besieged her from all sides.

Maddy can tell you.

Her grandmother's disembodied voice echoed inside her head. The words undulated through her mind like ripples in a pond and consumed any other thoughts.

Sara came instantly alert. "Gran?"

She glanced around for the ball of white light into which Gran had disappeared, but the room remained dark except for the flicker of the candle's flame on the table beside her. Defeat again weighed heavily on her shoulders.

What could Maddy tell her? Maddy was dead. How was Sara to get those answers if Maddy's ghost would not appear to her? But if Gran was right and Maddy had the answers . . .

She *must* speak to Maddy.

Closing her eyes, Sara concentrated. She'd only summoned a spirit once before in the bayou, so she had no idea if it would work again or if she'd just been lucky that one night. But at this point, she had to try. Several minutes of deep concentration passed without results. It was no use. For some reason, she couldn't communicate with Maddy.

Fatigue suddenly overcame her. Tomorrow was another day. Perhaps when she was refreshed from a good night's sleep, she would be more successful. Standing, she set the mug on the side table.

Thunk!

Something hit the floor.

Sara looked down. At her feet lay Maddy's diary.

Suddenly, her grandmother's words made sense.

Maddy can tell you.

The answers Sara sought must have lain hidden in Maddy's diary.

All sleepiness vanished from her body. Sara picked up the book and then returned to her chair in front of the window. She drew the candle closer to illuminate the pages, and her gaze was drawn to Jonathan's portrait. His expression had changed to a smile of satisfaction. In her heart, she knew he'd lead her to the source that would satisfy all her unanswered questions. Feeling just a bit foolish, she smiled back at him and nodded, and then opened the diary and began to read.

In the first few pages, much of Maddy's elegant handwriting documented her day-to-day activities: tea with her mother and their neighbor's wife and daughter, a shopping trip to New Orleans, and her excitement about her upcoming birthday and the barbeque at Candlewick Plantation. The mention of Clarice's home piqued Sara's interest. Perhaps now she would learn why Clarice had reacted so strangely.

She turned the page.

June 17, 1805

Momma, Katherine, and I went to town for the final fittings of our gowns for tomorrow's barbeque at

Candlewick.   Momma and Katherine argued again over the color of Katherine's gown.   Momma said crimson is not what a demure lady wears.   However, Katherine, being Katherine, refused to change her mind.   I sometimes think my sister takes delight in being obstinate and seeing how deeply she can shock poor Momma's sensibilities.

I chose a lovely, sky blue silk.   Momma fawned over me and showered compliments on me.   She said it would go well with my hair, and all the gentlemen would swoon at the sight of me.   Oddly, I found myself feeling bad for Katherine.   Momma consistently criticized Katherine's choices, and warned her that the ladies would all snub her, and she would become a social outcast.   I wish Momma would be nicer to her.   Katherine can be trying on one's nerves, but I think if she were treated differently, she would react differently. I think Momma's constant, caustic criticism is the reason Katherine's disposition seems to get worse every day.

I really chose the color of my gown because it's Jonathan's favorite.   He said the dining room in Harrogate, the house he's building, will be sky blue.   Harrogate is almost complete, and we're going to stop by to see it on our way home from the Degas' barbeque tomorrow evening.   I can't wait.   I just know it will be breathtaking, because Papa's seen it and says it's truly magnificent, and I believe him.   After all, Jonathan designed it.   How could it be anything less than grand?

It does, however, break my heart that it's Katherine who will be its mistress and not me. But I'm trying not to think dismal thoughts. I'm too excited about tomorrow.

Jonathan will be at the barbeque. He says he'll have a special gift for me, but seeing him will be the best birthday present I could ask for. My heart pounds at the mere thought of seeing him again. Because Jonathan is Katherine's unofficial fiancé, I know I shouldn't, but I do love him so. I have ever since we were children. He's so kind and so gentle. I just know, deep down, that he's my soul mate, and if I can't have him, I would rather spend my life alone.

Warmth invaded Sara. She knew what that special gift was—the locket. She picked it up and clutched it in her hand, then glanced at the portrait of Maddy's love. Clarice had been right. Maddy had truly loved Jonathan. For a moment, Sara gazed dreamily off into the dark night beyond the window and wondered what it would be like to love someone so passionately and to have them love you likewise in return. It certainly wouldn't be like the distant, often tolerant, friendliness her parents shared. It would have to be more like the forever kind of love that Gran had felt for Ezra Wade.

Perhaps someday, Sara would be lucky enough to find the man who would make her heart sing at the mere thought of him. An image of Jonathan Bradford drifted into her mind's eye. That now familiar longing to touch him accompanied it.

Shaking herself free of her impossible yearnings, she rubbed her thumb over the engraved roses on the locket and turned to the following day's diary entry.

June 18, 1805

The day of the barbeque has finally arrived. I primped for hours getting ready. I want to look perfect for Jonathan. I'm so excited I can hardly hold the pen to write this. It's also my birthday, and I feel as though my heart will burst from my chest at the prospect of celebrating and seeing Jonathan, my love, my soulmate. Katherine, who's more concerned with how she looks than seeing the man she's supposed to love, doesn't seem to care one way or the other, and I fear my suspicions are right. She doesn't love Jonathan. She never has. Perhaps she will break off their relationship. I can only pray it will be so.

A blank section separated the first entry from the next.

We're home, and the day was one I will cherish in my heart forever. It's very late, and I should be exhausted, but I'm not. I'm much too excited to sleep. I just have to tell someone what happened and since I can't tell my family, writing it down here will have to suffice. My heart is singing. On our way home from Candlewick, we stopped to see Jonathan's house. It's just as I pictured it—magnificent. I can feel his love for the place in every room, in every piece of furniture, and in every drape.

While everyone was taking a tour of the rooms, Jonathan and I slipped away to the garden. He told them it was to show me the roses, which he knows I love, but it was really to give me my birthday gift.

It was all so very romantic. I remember every second of our time together. The balmy night was enchanting, and Jonathan looked especially handsome in his burgundy coat, white shirt, and tan breeches. The moonlight tinted his ebony hair silver. He smiled, and I swear I saw love glowing in his eyes. My heart began to beat triple time. He held a small box out to me. My head grew light and . . .

Suddenly, a wave of dizziness overcame Sara. She clutched the locket close. The cold metal became hot against her skin, but she felt no pain.

Her vision blurred. Weightlessness, more intense than she'd experienced in the bayou, lifted her body from the chair. Just as suddenly, she was thrown into a long tunnel that ended in a swirling vortex.

Multicolored, bright lights flashed all around her.

The air grew thick and heavy, becoming difficult to breathe.

She tried to grab something to stop the spinning, but her arms wouldn't obey.

Round and round she spun.

Intense dizziness made her stomach churn. Nausea rose in her throat from the constant circular motion.

Then as suddenly as it had started, the spinning stopped. To her utter shock, Sara was no longer in her bedroom. Instead, she found herself sitting on the bench in the Garden of the Moon.

But the garden was different. The plants were noticeably much younger. The magnolia tree that had towered over her and Julie earlier now barely reached above the back of the bench. Ezra's moongate was gone, as were the temple dogs that guarded the garden against evil.

However, though shocking, the changes in the garden did not surprise her half as much as her clothes did. The pale green nightdress she'd put on that evening had been replaced by a sky blue silk dress with an empire waist.

"What's happening?" she asked the silent night.

"You've come back to me."

Chapter 6

The deep, male voice coming from the garden's lengthening shadows startled Sara, yet it also brought with it an overwhelming sense of eager excitement and love. She strained to see the speaker's face, but a cloud covered the full moon. All around her, everything—the garden, the night, the unseen creatures—seemed to be poised . . . waiting, expectant, as though preparing for . . . something. Even though there was no moonlight, the white flowers glowed brighter, as if straining to illuminate the dark corners of the night. Their inexplicably intensified fragrance permeated the night.

An owl hooted.

A dog barked.

Some small, nocturnal animal scurried through

the bushes.

A soft breeze whispered through the treetops.

And then a twig snapped.

Sara spun in the direction of the sound.

Nothing.

Then that voice came again.

"I've waited a long time for you." The velvety tones slid over her skin like warm bathwater.

Suddenly, she knew she'd been waiting all her life for this moment. All the frustration and confusion that had filled her for days vanished on the gentle breeze.

The bushes rustled. Then very slowly, the source of the voice stepped from the shadows. As if summoned, the moon slipped from behind the cloud cover, revealing the man's face, a face as familiar to her as her own.

Jonathan Bradford held out a small, black velvet box to her. "Happy birthday, my Maddy."

Oddly, she felt no need to correct him. In fact, she wasn't sure if he *should* be corrected. As she stared at his handsome face, Sara Wade faded from her being, and Maddy's spirit took over. In that soft, quiet moment she unmistakably became Madeline Grayson. Without conscious thought, she held out her hand and took the box.

"Thank you, Jonathan." Maddy lifted the lid and stared openmouthed at what she found. Nestled against a white silk background was a heart-shaped, gold locket engraved with two roses, their stems tightly entwined, their unity engraved in gold for all eternity.

"Oh, Jonathan, it's lovely."

"Open the heart." He took a seat beside her on the bench.

His nearness, the scent of his cologne, the warmth emanating from his body made her head swim. She took a moment to regain her balance. Then, using her fingernail, she freed the catch. The front of the locket sprang open. Inside an inscription read *My Love Forever*. Tears burned her eyes.

Jonathan took her free hand. "It's true, Maddy. No matter what happens, I will love you until time ceases to be."

Her pounding heart threatened to burst from her chest. She believed him because she felt the same love for him. Yet, despite her joy, a wave of utter sadness washed over her. "Nothing can happen. Nothing will change. You're betrothed to my sister."

He shook his head. "I'm going to ask Katherine to release me from the betrothal. Then you and I can get married. That's how it always should have been, how it was meant to be."

Maddy gazed into his dear face. For one fleeting moment, hope blossomed in her. But it quickly died. She bowed her head. "Katherine will never agree to that."

Placing his forefinger under her chin, he raised her face so their gazes locked. He smiled and then wiped away the lone tear on her cheek with the pad of his thumb. His gentle touch sent shivers of longing through her.

"We won't know if we don't try. Why would she want to marry someone who doesn't love her?"

Memories of all the times Katherine had taken her toys, pushed her aside for attention, and generally tried to outshine Maddy at every turn rushed through her mind. "Because Katherine never gives up anything, especially to me."

Jonathan sighed and pulled her into his arms. She snuggled against his shirtfront, wishing she could stay enclosed in this warm cocoon forever.

He kissed her hair and whispered, "We can't lose hope. I refuse to let you go."

"You may not have a choice."

"There has to be a choice."

He lowered his head and placed his lips gently on hers. Warmth spread through her every nerve ending. A need rose up in her so strong she felt like she would cry out for wanting . . . wanting. What was it she wanted so very badly?

The bushes rustled near the garden's entrance. "Jonathan? Are you there?"

Katherine!

They sprang apart like naughty children. Jonathan quickly moved to the far side of the path. Maddy nervously smoothed the wrinkles from her gown. She glanced at Jonathan and saw him open his mouth to answer Katherine.

But she never heard the words.

Maddy stared at Jonathan, but was unable to speak. Then she began to feel very strange . . . lightheaded, unable to focus her muddled thoughts. She could feel the spirit of Maddy weakening while Sara Wade got stronger. Though she fought to retain her existence as Madeline Grayson, the connection grew more and more tenuous with each passing moment.

Panic filled her. This couldn't be happening. She must remain here with Jonathan, where she was safe and loved. As she reached for Jonathan, his image blurred, the edges grew fuzzy, and he began to fade.

Before she could call out, she was once more sucked up in the vortex of swirling colors.

Sara awoke to find herself sitting in the chair by the window, the locket still clutched in her hand and the diary lying open in her lap. Once more, she was Sara Wade. The spirit of Maddy Grayson had remained in the past with Jonathan. Sara's heart ached with an inexplicable emptiness.

What had happened? Had Katherine discovered them? Seen them embracing? Kissing? Had she, after seeing them and realizing they loved each other, given Jonathan up? No. Clarice had said someone . . . the jealous man . . . had killed Jonathan, and Maddy had never married.

The intense despondency that overcame her was like a knife being plunged into her heart. Her very soul cried out for Jonathan. Trying to make sense of this intense sorrow she felt for the loss of a man she'd never known, Sara turned to his portrait.

She gasped. Both Jonathan's and Maddy's paintings were gone. Katherine Grayson's portrait leered down at Sara. The satisfaction in Maddy's sister's triumphant, painted smile was unmistakable. She'd won again.

With tears burning her eyes and too exhausted both mentally and physically to care that the paintings had been switched, Sara collapsed onto her bed. Not even when her beloved Gran died had she felt so wretched, so lost, and so very, very alone.

Faced with the smirking painting the next morning, Sara called Raina to her bedroom. She had no idea how the painting had been returned to its spot over the mantel, but it had to go. It might be just the dream she'd had the night before of Maddy meeting Jonathan in the garden or the childhood memories of her dislike of the portrait, but whatever it was, she could not stand another moment of that woman's likeness hanging on her bedroom wall.

"You wants me, Miss Sara?"

"Who changed the paintings over the mantel?" She pointed at the portrait of Katherine Grayson.

Raina stared at it, looking as puzzled as Sara had been the night before. "Don't know. Far's I know, ain't nobody touched it."

This was just insane. Someone had to have changed those paintings. But that mattered little. What did matter was that the portrait had to be taken down . . . now. "Please have Samuel change them back. I don't want my—" She stopped herself. Had she almost said *my sister's picture*? "I don't want that woman's picture in here."

"Yes, ma'am, right away." Raina threw her a quizzical glance, and then backed out of the room.

Sara frowned. *My sister.* What had made her want to say that?

Not really understanding why, she felt an even stronger, deep-seated dislike for Katherine than she'd felt yesterday. It had to be connected somehow to Jonathan and Maddy. Had Maddy hated Katherine so much that the feeling had been transferred to her? She laughed.

Now, that was really insane. How could a dead person transfer anything to the living? She'd had enough inter-action with the dead that if someone was going to make her feel things she wouldn't ordinarily feel, it would have happened long ago.

But hadn't Jonathan made her feel things she'd never felt for a man in her life? If his spirit could do it, why couldn't Maddy's spirit do it as well?

Her head swimming with unanswered questions and the remnants of a very real dream torturing her thoughts, Sara waited until Samuel switched the paintings.

"What you want me to do with dis?" Samuel held up the painting of Katherine.

"Burn it," Sara said. Her crisp order surprised Sara almost as much as it did Samuel and Raina.

Moments later, Sara watched out the window as Samuel laid the portrait atop a pile of burning brush. Not until the flames had consumed the entire thing— canvas, frame, and all—did she move away from the window. At last, Katherine Grayson's likeness was gone for good.

"Did you sleep well?" Julie motioned for Raina to add another sausage patty to her already overburdened breakfast plate. She wondered absently if the hunger of the last few months, when she was living hand-to-mouth, would ever be assuaged. When Sara didn't answer, her attention was pulled away from the delicious-looking breakfast awaiting her. She looked at her friend. "Sara?"

Sara started, as if roused from deep thought. "Oh, I'm sorry. Yes . . . yes, I slept very well. And you?" She picked up her fork and began moving the food randomly around her plate.

Julie frowned. Sara didn't look as though she'd slept well. Faint bluish circles ringed her eyes. Her complexion had all the color of a northern winter, and as she reached for her coffee cup, her hand trembled slightly.

Covering Sara's hand with her own, Julie squeezed it lightly. "Have you forgotten? I'm your best friend. I know when you're lying."

Sara dropped her hand to the table and curled her fingers into a fist. Her nails dug scars in the linen table-cloth. She gave a small nervous laugh. "I guess I'm no better at deceiving you now than I was at school." She glanced at Julie through a fringe of chestnut lashes. "No, I didn't sleep well. As a matter of fact, I had a most disturbing dream. The strange thing is, I'm not at all sure it was a dream."

After pushing back her plate, Julie leaned her forearms on the table, ready to listen. Sara glanced at her, then quickly averted her gaze again, the gesture telling Julie of her friend's reluctance to talk about this dream.

"Well, tell me about the dream."

"You'll think I'm crazy," Sara finally said.

Julie laughed and patted Sara's arm. "You talk to dead people. If I were going to think you're crazy, wouldn't I have done it long ago?"

To Julie's relief, Sara actually laughed. Swallowing hard, she related the dream she'd had the night before. "When I woke up last night, the paintings of Maddy and Jonathan were gone, and Katherine's was back over the mantel."

"It was just a dream, Sara. Nothing more. We all have them. At the time, they seem real, very real, but when we're awake and can think logically about them, we realize they were nothing but images that came to us during sleep."

"No, I don't think it was *just* a dream. I think there was a message for me in it and that it had something to do with what Gran told me."

"Sara," Julie said, leaning back in her chair and repositioning her plate, "I think you're so desperate to solve this mystery that you're forcing yourself to see things when there's a perfectly logical explanation for it. Your grandmother's warning and what took place last night were just dreams brought on by the worry you've been expending to figure all this out."

Sara shrugged, but she didn't look convinced. "Perhaps you're right. I'm probably making a lot out of nothing." For a few moments, she went back to rearranging her breakfast plate. Then she frowned. "But how do you explain the switched paintings?"

Julie swallowed a mouthful of pancake. "Paintings don't just hang themselves. One of the servants did it. That's the only logical answer."

"But I asked Raina, and she said no one had touched them. And if what you say is true, why would they do it?"

Julie laughed again and added another generous dollop of butter and a splash of maple syrup to her pancakes. "As to the why, I'm afraid I have no explanation for that. As to Raina swearing no one touched them . . . it wouldn't be the first time a servant lied to stay out of trouble."

Sara huffed with obvious indignation. Straightening her shoulders, she glared at Julie. "Raina has never lied to me."

Julie cocked an eyebrow. "That you're aware of."

After breakfast, Julie hustled Sara back to her room to rest. Even though Sara protested that she had plantation business to see to, Julie would hear none of it. "I ran my father's plantation for a long time. I think I can be trusted for one day to see to your duties without your supervision. Now, get into bed and sleep and forget about Harrogate for a while."

For once, Harrogate was the furthest thing from Sara's mind. Allowing Julie to take over her duties was easy because it gave Sara the opportunity to work on solving the puzzle of the dream without interruption.

As she settled herself in the chair beneath her bedroom window, her dream of the night before claimed her attention to the exclusion of everything else.

But was it a dream? Everything—Jonathan's arms, his kiss, the balmy evening breeze, the scent of the flowers— had all seemed so very real at the time. Now she had her doubts.

"Be sensible, Sara," she chided out loud, "you can't go back into the past. What else could it have been but a very vivid, very realistic dream?"

What else indeed?

She picked up Maddy's diary and, for a moment, ran her fingertips over the gold embossed letters of the woman's name. When, as Maddy, she'd been sheltered in Jonathan's arms, she'd felt so safe, so cherished. It had been unlike anything she'd ever experienced before. How lucky Maddy had been to know the kind of love Jonathan had given her. If only—

Stop it, Sara! You're letting your fanciful imagination

get away from you.

Opening the book, she began to read from where she'd stopped the night before. To her amazement, Maddy's recounting of what had taken place in the garden matched Sara's dream exactly, right down to the words of love that Jonathan had spoken, the description of the locket, and the promise to ask Katherine to release him from their betrothal.

How could that be? There was only one explanation. Sara must have read it before she fell asleep, and then she'd dreamed it exactly. But when she'd awakened, the diary had been open to the same spot where she had left off before she'd gotten so dizzy and drifted into . . . What had she drifted into? But she hadn't just drifted off. There had been that terrible spinning, the nausea, the colors.

Her head began to throb. Covering her eyes with her hand to shut out the blazing sunlight streaming through the window, she laid her head back and sighed. Would she ever find the peace at Harrogate that she'd so longed for and expected when she'd come here?

"Miss Sara?"

Turning toward the voice, she found Raina standing in the doorway holding a small silver tray. On the tray was a glass of milk.

"Yes?"

Raina came to her side. "Miss Julie told me you was

feelin' poorly. She said to bring you dis glass a warm milk, and to stay right here 'til you drinks it." She extended the tray toward Sara.

Sara stared at the glass, but made no move to take it. She hated warm milk and had never quite figured out what medicinal benefits a cow could put into it that would endow heated milk with a cure-all for everything from gout to hysterics.

"No, thank you, Raina. I'm just fine. I don't need any milk."

Raina's mouth set in a stubborn line. "Miss Julie says she'll have my hide if you don't drinks dis here milk."

Sara had to laugh. Julie didn't have a mean bone in her body. The threat, undoubtedly, was as empty as a used-up tub of lard. Nevertheless, Sara decided it might help to ease the throbbing in her temples. Shrugging, she took the glass and drank until the milk was gone. Setting the glass back on the tray with a loud *thunk*, she made a face and then smiled up at Raina.

"There. Are you both happy now?"

Raina grinned, her white teeth glowing against her chocolate skin. "Yas, 'um." She made no move to leave.

"Is there something else, Raina?"

Raina nodded. Her *tignon* wobbled and slipped over her forehead. With her free hand, she pushed the bright green turban back in place. "Miss Julie says I's to tuck you in for a nap."

Being treated like a child raised Sara's hackles. It reminded her vividly of her mother. She made a mental note to talk to Julie about it at lunch.

Sara stood, placed her fists on her hips, and glowered at her maid. "You know better than anyone that I haven't been tucked in for a good many years, Raina. I'm sure I can manage a nap without your help." She made her way to the bed and stretched out on it. "See?"

"Yas, 'um." Raina, failing miserably at hiding her satisfied grin, left the room.

To Sara's surprise, her eyelids quickly grew heavy and she began to drift off. Just before her eyes closed, she heard the echo of a woman's mocking laughter.

Chapter 7

Sara bolted upright in bed. All sleepiness vanished from her body. Immediately, Sara's gaze shot to the mantel. Expecting to see Katherine's portrait there again, she sighed in relief when she saw that Jonathan and Maddy's portraits hung exactly where Samuel had placed them. How foolish of her. She'd watched Samuel burn the painting. How could it possibly be there now?

The woman's laughter again drifted over the still air.

"Raina? Is that you?"

No reply.

"Julie?"

Still no reply.

Was this someone's idea of a tasteless joke because she'd ordered Katherine's portrait burned? That was impossible. The only ones who knew about her hatred of the portrait were Julie and Raina, and neither of them would be cruel enough to do something like this.

Then a thought occurred to her. Maybe—and her blood turned icy cold at the thought . . . Could it be Katherine's spirit laughing at Sara's fanciful daydreams of Jonathan? Could Maddy's sister be expressing her delight at winning again by seeing to it that Jonathan could never be Sara's . . . Maddy's? This was becoming ridiculous. She'd begun to confuse herself with Maddy.

A ray of sunlight shafted through the window, its beam coming to rest on the mantel just below the portraits. Though the sunbeam had caught her attention, not until Sara left the bed and approached the mantel did she notice something else. At the foot of one of the porcelain candlesticks, haloed by the ray of sunlight, was a small, black velvet box . . . the same one that had contained Maddy's birthday locket. Sara blinked, testing the veracity of what she was seeing. The box was still there.

This just could not be.

It simply *was not* possible. Though she fought to deny it, the proof lay right before her eyes. The box couldn't be here . . . unless what had happened in the garden had *not* been a dream and she'd actually lived through a period of time in the past and brought the box back with her.

Her knees gave way. She collapsed onto the end of

112

the bed. Confused, she stared at the mantel while she tried to make sense of the nonsense.

Could she have actually gone back in time? Could she, for those few moments, have entered Maddy's body and relived an event that had taken place over fifty years ago? Was that possible? She pressed her shaking hand to her chest and felt the quickened rhythm of her heart, knowing it beat with the same magic it had in her dream. The dream had felt more real than any she'd ever known. No matter how she tried, she could not come up with an alternative, plausible explanation for any of this.

Sara's own lifelong experiences of seeing things that no one else could see had taught her that phenomena most people believed impossible were, indeed, very possible. After all, she talked to dead people, saw dead people. The dead occupied a parallel plane, so why not past events? So why was the notion of time travel so hard for her to accept? Deep inside, she knew why she continued to fight the probability—fear she would never be able to repeat the experience, never be held by Jonathan again and, as a result, have to suffer a disappointment so heart-breaking she would be unable to live with it.

Her heart began to pound faster. The idea throbbed through her head. Was she losing her mind? Still she continued to allow the possibility entrance into her thoughts. Could she go back to Jonathan? If the 1805 box had ended up here in 1855, hadn't she'd already done it once? But how?

Something must have triggered it. Frantically, she looked around her.

Overwhelmed and entranced by the prospect of being with Jonathan again, she retraced mentally the steps she'd taken the night before.

She'd come downstairs from the attic, washed, changed into her nightclothes, and then sat in the chair with the diary. No, she hadn't picked up the diary then. The mug. She'd been holding Jonathan's shaving mug. Sara sat in the chair and grabbed the mug from the table and clutched it to her chest.

Nothing.

What had happened then? The diary had fallen to the floor, and she'd picked it up and held it securely alongside the mug. Carefully, she repeated her movements exactly. The diary felt warm against her skin.

Nothing.

Then she recalled having looked at Jonathan's portrait and his smiling at her in satisfaction. She dropped the mug and the diary to her lap and spun in the chair. She stared hard at the picture of the man who had claimed Maddy's love. Last night, his expression had changed from the wooden one which the artist had captured in oils to one that reflected love. Today, it remained unmoved.

Jonathan, help me. Show me how to come back to you, she implored the painted face.

Still nothing. No dizziness; no spinning; no lightheaded weightlessness. Nothing.

Tears welled in her eyes. Setting the diary and the mug aside, she leaned forward; her chin came to rest against her upper chest. Something resting against the bodice of her dress glimmered in the sunlight.

The locket.

Of course. She'd been holding onto the locket when the room had begun to spin.

Quickly, she grabbed the gold heart, closed her eyes, and summoned Jonathan's spirit. For a long time, she just sat there holding onto the necklace with a death grip and . . . waiting . . . and waiting . . . and waiting. Finally, when nothing happened, she opened her eyes. She was still sitting in her bedroom at Harrogate.

That she'd never see Jonathan again was more than she could stand. Unreasonable despair unlike anything she'd ever experienced in her whole life overcame her. She buried her face in her hands. Heartbreaking sobs tore from her very soul and violently shook her entire body. Agonizing pain, like a knife being buried in her heart and slicing through her, caused her to double over with the physical and mental anguish.

Sara had no idea how long she'd cried. All she knew was that her heart was so broken it would likely never mend again. Then a gentle hand touched her cheek.

"Sara?" Finding her friend in such a desolate state, Julie tried to keep the panic from her voice and failed miserably. "What is it? Why are you crying?"

Sara didn't answer. She continued to cry as though her heart were broken in a million pieces. Never, in all her life, had Julie heard such terrible, wrenching sorrow issuing from another human being. Whatever had caused this weeping had to be something that was tearing Sara apart because nothing consoled her.

Finally, while she waited for the sobbing to cease, Julie sat on the arm of the chair and held Sara's head against her chest. Her friend's agony burned through her own body. When she could stand it no longer, Julie squeezed Sara's shoulder and said, "Sara, you're going to make yourself ill. Please stop crying, and tell me what has happened."

Sara raised her face. Her swollen, red eyes, drained of all emotion, reflected only an awful hopelessness. Tears glistened on her ghostly white cheeks. As she tried to bring her weeping under control, her bottom lip quivered.

"I'll never . . . see him . . . again, Julie." Tears welled

in her eyes again. Several spilled over and ran down her cheeks. "Never."

Julie frowned. To her knowledge, there was no *him* in Sara's life. "See who? Who is it you'll never see again?"

"Jonathan." Sara wrung her hands.

Again Julie frowned. Then it struck her. No. She had to be wrong. Sara couldn't possibly be talking about Jonathan Bradford. Forcing her voice to be as calm as possible, she asked, "Jonathan who, dear?"

With a new flush of tears cascading down her face, Sara pointed to the picture over the mantel.

Julie's heart dropped. Obviously, she'd underestimated the degree of Sara's obsession with her dream and her grandmother's warnings. Frantic for a way to help her friend, Julie led Sara to the bed. Though she fought to find them, no words came to mind to ease Sara's pain or to convince her that Jonathan was nothing more than another ghost who had sought her out, that seeing him had been nothing more than a dream, and that she had to give up this . . . *notion* of seeing him again.

She eased Sara back against the pillows. "Close your eyes and take a rest. When you wake up, we'll talk, and then things won't look so bad."

For the next few minutes, Julie sat beside her distraught friend, stroked her forehead, and murmured reassurances.

Despite Julie's cautions and vigilance, in the following days Sara didn't improve. All she could think about was the dream, and how she could get back to Jonathan. It possessed her every waking moment. She could think of nothing else. It was as if she'd lost her ability to control her thoughts and actions . . . as if some unseen force were driving her.

She no longer recognized the woman who looked back at her from her mirror. Dark purple circles ringed her sleepless eyes. Her lackluster hair hung limply around her face. She barely slept or ate, and her already fragile-looking body became more so. Her clothes hung loosely on her, so she stopped getting dressed and spent the days in her nightclothes. She jumped at the slightest noise, and her temper seemed to be on edge all the time.

Frustrated, she spent every day and half of every night going over again and again in her mind her actions of the night she was convinced she'd gone back in time. But nothing she tried produced the desired reunion with Jonathan. Then she'd collapse in a torrent of sobs until she cried herself to sleep, only to wake the next day and start the ritual all over again.

When her efforts came up empty, she would spend

hours just staring at Jonathan's picture, begging him silently to come for her. But even his ghostly appearances had ceased. Since the night in the attic, aside from what she adamantly believed was her journey back to 1805, Sara had not seen Jonathan again.

Sara could tell from the look in Julie's and Raina's tight expressions and how they put their heads together and whispered when they thought she wasn't looking, that they were worried about her well-being, but she couldn't seem to stop herself. Finding the answer had become an addiction that gnawed at her heart, her soul, and her common sense with every waking moment of every day. The only peace she found from her quandary was when she slept, and even that was fitful.

Harrogate had ceased to matter and, had it not been for Julie, would have suffered from lack of supervision and attention. Thanks to Sara's friend, the sick slaves had been tended, the fields plowed for planting, meals planned and served, and the house kept clean. But Sara barely noticed. Her life as she'd known it before she'd been held in Jonathan's arms had almost ceased to exist.

Over two weeks had passed since Julie had found Sara convulsing and in tears. Now, Julie lay in her bed listening to the sound of Sara's footsteps as she paced her bedroom floor, and knew that nothing she had said to her had eased Sara's mind. Frustration at how to save her friend swamped her, robbing her of sleep. Sara was becoming weaker every day, and if Julie didn't find something to deter her, she had no doubts that Sara would die of a broken heart.

But how did Julie stop her and make Sara see the absurdity of what she believed to be true? If she could, Julie would conjure up a way to send Sara back to Jonathan. But to do that, she'd have to believe it was possible, and she didn't. To her thinking, time travel was a fool's dream. Julie truly believed that Sara could see dead people. But traveling back in time? It had to have been a figment of her imagination, a dream and nothing more, and the sooner Sara accepted that, the sooner they could get her on the road to recovery.

In the meantime, Julie had to put the dilemma out of her mind and get some sleep. Otherwise, she'd be no better off than Sara and no help to her at all. Julie rolled to her side, pulled the covers over her shoulder, and closed her eyes.

A heavy *thud* came from Sara's room.

Without hesitation, Julie shot up in her bed, threw back the bedclothes, and then raced down the hall to Sara's room. For a fraction of a second, she stared at the door. Icy fear danced up and down her spine. Terrified of what lay beyond, she grabbed the knob, turned it, and then pushed the door open.

Next to the bed lay the crumpled form of Sara. Julie rushed to her side. Her motionless body and pale face reflected Julie's worse fear. The lack of sleep and food had finally taken its toll. She leaned over her and listened for her breathing. A faint wisp of air touched her cheek. Relieved, she gathered Sara's limp body in her arms and held her.

"Raina!" Julie's shrill voice echoed around the room. "Raina!"

Scant moments later, Raina raced into the room, her nightclothes flapping wildly around her feet, her hair in disarray, her eyes wide, and her lightened complexion relaying her fear. "Yes, Miss—" When she caught sight of her mistress' prone body, she stopped dead. "Oh, Lawd a mercy!" She began wringing her hands.

"Raina, help me get her into bed." Julie's fear for her friend imbued her voice with an unrecognizable tone of command. "Now, Raina!"

Roused from her state of shock, Raina hurried to Julie's side and helped lift Sara into the bed. Once Sara was on the bed, Raina stepped back and gawked at her mistress, tears shimmering in her wide eyes. "Lawd, Miss Julie, is she dead?"

Julie shook her head. "No, but I'm afraid she will

be if we don't get a doctor. Send Samuel for Dr. Norris."

Raina made no move to do as Julie asked. She just kept staring wide-eyed at Sara's motionless body, her shaking hands pleating and unpleating the skirt of her nightgown.

"Do as I say, Raina! Now!"

The maid ran from the room hoisting her muslin nightgown up to her knees. Julie clasped Sara's cold hands in hers, trying to warm them. With concentrated intensity, she watched her friend's chest rise and fall and silently begged her to keep breathing.

Choking back tears, she fought down the clawing fear that had claimed her body. This couldn't be happening. Why hadn't she seen how bad it had gotten, how truly sick Sara was?

Leaning down, she whispered in Sara's ear. "Don't you dare die on me, Sara Wade. You hear me? You can't die."

Then she heard laughter, delighted laughter. But when she looked around, no one was there.

Chapter 8

Dr. Norris, a portly, older man dressed all in black and sporting a snowy beard to mid-chest, entered the sitting room where Julie and Raina had been silently awaiting word of Sara's condition. His expression looked grim. Julie's heart sank.

Please let her be all right, she prayed.

Julie stood on shaky legs and faced the doctor. "How is she?"

He set his small, black satchel on the table and shook his head. "She's a very sick young woman. I've given her a dose of laudanum, and she should sleep for a good while."

Relief that her friend was at least still alive weakened Julie's knees. She sank into the closest chair and motioned for him to take a seat. He took the offered chair, set his satchel beside his feet, and looked from Raina to Julie.

"When was the last time she ate?"

Julie looked to Raina. The black woman shrugged. Had it been so long that neither of them could recall? Julie knew Sara had been picking at her food for the last week, but she had assumed she'd consumed some of it.

"I'm not sure. Perhaps it's been a couple of days ago since she actually ate a whole meal. Her appetite hasn't been what it should be lately. She's been . . . upset and hasn't been terribly hungry. But neither of us thought . . ." She turned to Raina for confirmation. Raina nodded in agreement.

For a moment, he seemed absorbed in his thoughts. Stroking his beard, he stared out the window. Finally, he looked at Julie. "I'd say she's showing very early signs of malnutrition." Julie gasped. He held up his hand. "No need to panic. We caught it in time. It can be reversed with sleep and food. When she wakes up, give her a light broth. No solid food for a while. For now she's to have just liquids: broths, tea, fruit juice. Her system has to be acclimated to accepting solid food again."

He opened his satchel and withdrew a small bottle labeled *laudanum*. "Give her a little of this in the afternoon and evening. It'll help her get some much needed healing rest. It's been mixed with sweet cider to kill the bitterness. You should decrease the dosage each day; otherwise, there's a risk of addiction."

He stood and retrieved his satchel. "It's going to take a few days, but she should be good as new very soon. Call me if you need me. I'll check back with her in a couple of days." He started to leave, and then turned back to Julie. "Any idea what brought this on?"

Taken aback by his question, Julie searched for a reasonable explanation. She couldn't very well tell him Sara was pining away for a ghost. "I think opening the house was a bit too much for her."

His arched eyebrow told her he had doubts that simply opening a house could cause this degree of illness, but he gave her no argument.

While Raina showed the doctor to the door, Julie tucked the medicine bottle in her pocket and then collapsed on the settee. Relief surged through her. Sara would be all right. Slowly, her nerves unwound from the tight ball they'd formed when she'd found Sara on the bedroom floor.

Just as quickly, they coiled up again. Never in all the time she'd known Sara had Julie seen her so driven, so obsessed with anything as she was with this idea that she could go back in time. Was this just a short reprieve? When Sara awoke, would she go back to living as she had before she'd collapsed? Would she once more start searching for an answer to a puzzle that had no answers?

The side of Sara's bed dipped. Through the haze of sleep, she felt a strong hand cover hers and then squeeze it reassuringly. For a moment she thought it might be Raina or Julie or even the doctor, but the touch of that hand changed that. Vaguely familiar peace, the first she'd felt in days, ebbed through her.

Warm breath caressed her cheek, and then a deep, gentle voice whispered in her ear. "You must sleep and get well, my love. I need you to come back to me."

She tried to open her eyes, but it felt as though lead weights rested on them. Her voice wouldn't work. Frustrated tears gathered behind her eyelids. Warm moisture trickled from beneath them and down her cheek.

"Please, don't cry. It breaks my heart." The voice quivered as though the speaker was trying to hold back painful emotions. A kiss fluttered across her skin, and the moisture was gone. "I know you tried, but don't give up. You'll find a way to come back to me. I know you will. But first, you must get well and stay well. You must eat and rest and stay strong." A hand smoothed her forehead. "Now, sleep. Sleep, my love."

Sara sighed and allowed herself to be lulled back into a deep sleep by the hand caressing her cheek.

In the next days, Sara often felt the touch of that hand and heard that loving voice urging her to get well. With each visit from the disembodied voice, she found new strength. Then another voice, a woman's, had penetrated the fog in which Sara was enclosed and pressed her to swallow something that was sometimes bittersweet, sometimes salty. Whenever she thought about refusing it, that tender voice would fill her head . . . *You must get well, my love.*

In her cloudy state, she didn't know why, but she knew she had to obey the voice. *She had to.* There was something she needed to do, something very important, and she had to get well to do it. What that something was, she couldn't focus in on; she just knew it was urgent.

Gradually, as the days passed, the man's voice came less often than the woman with the funny tasting liquids did. And slowly, Sara became more lucid, more aware of her surroundings.

She had no idea how long she'd been ill, but one morning, she woke up to sunshine pouring through her windows and bathing her face in warmth. Birds sang in the trees outside and, although weak, she found herself feeling much better than she had in days. As she lay there, she shifted her gaze from the beautiful day outside the window to the painting above the mantel.

In her heart, she knew it had been his voice that had come to her and given her the strength to fight her way back. And she knew why. Now that she was well again, she had to renew her search for the key to going back to Jonathan's time. But this time, she'd do it sensibly and not let it possess her every waking moment. She had to be well to go back to him.

Jonathan's hand had stroked her brow and whispered loving words to her. He had encouraged her to get well, and she would not let him down.

She smiled at Jonathan's portrait. "Thank you."

"Who you talkin' to, Miss Sara?" Raina stood in the doorway, her brow furrowed, her hands clutching Sara's breakfast tray. The woman's sharp gaze scanned the empty room.

For a moment, Sara had no answer. Then she grinned weakly. "You, Raina. I was thanking you for taking care of me. You did nurse me back to health, didn't you?"

On the bedside table, Raina set down a tray containing a cup of steaming tea and a small bowl of Chloe's special oatmeal slathered in sweet cream and warm honey. "Course I did. Me and Miss Julie. Course, I did the biggest share. Miss Julie was just too upset to be any help a'tall." Raina avoided eye contact with Sara, and she knew the maid was embellishing her part in nursing her back to health. "That girl fretted over you somethin' fierce. I thought she'd be takin' to her bed, too, and I was gonna be nursin' both of you." She clicked her tongue in typical Raina fashion.

Sara struggled to sit up, but Raina stopped her.

"I want to sit up to eat," Sara protested.

"Don't you be doing too much right off. Here, let me help." Raina leaned Sara forward, fluffed both her pillows and piled them behind her back, and then tucked the eiderdown quilt close around her body. "Now, you just leans back, and I'll put dis tray on your lap."

Finding that even if she wanted to, she wasn't strong enough to protest, Sara did as she was told. She picked up the spoon.

"Now, you eats slow. Hear? You ain't had solid food in you for a time. Gobblin' down that food ain't gonna do you no good. Doc Norris says you's to eat slow."

Sara nodded and took a half spoonful of oatmeal. As she slid it into her mouth, she glanced at Raina, who was standing over her like a guard over a convict.

"When you's done, Miss Julie is gonna have you carried down to the veranda so's you can get some air and put some color in dem cheeks."

The thought of being able to feel the sun's warmth on her skin again made Sara want to wolf down her food, but with Raina's stern gaze taking in her every movement, she didn't dare. Instead, she forced herself to eat at a measured pace.

Samuel carried Sara through the front door and onto the veranda. The warm sun caressed her face. She took a deep breath. Coming into the sunshine and being able to breathe fresh air again was like being reborn. Samuel deposited her gently onto the chaise that he'd brought out earlier under Raina's watchful eye. Julie arranged the folds of Sara's nightdress around her legs and then covered them with a light quilt.

"You're looking better already." Julie sat in the rocker beside Sara. "You gave us quite a scare."

Sara took Julie's hand. "I'm sorry. I was being so foolish. All I could think of was—" She looked at their clasped hands. "Well, no need to tell you what I was thinking." She raised her gaze to her friend. "Raina told me that you've been taking very good care of Harrogate while I was ill. Thank you."

Julie smiled. "You've allowed me to think of this as my home. I could do no less."

"It is your home, Julie. It will be your home as long as you want it to be." Julie began to fidget, and it wasn't embarrassment because of Sara's praise or her promise of a home. Something else was bothering her. "What's wrong? What's got you worried?"

"You." Julie looked away, then back at Sara. "You were very ill, Sara. You almost— You have to promise me that you won't do what you did before and make yourself ill again."

Shaking her head firmly, Sara took Julie's hand. "You have my promise that I won't be so foolish again." Despite her promise, though, Sara had to make Julie understand she would not be giving up on her quest to return to Jonathan. "But I will continue to try and find the secret to going back to him."

Like the petals of a flower wilting under a scorching sun, Julie's shoulders sagged. "This is crazy. Going back in time is not possible, anymore than going forward is. Today is today, and nothing can change that. You have to give this up, Sara, before it consumes you again."

It was hard to ignore the pain in Julie's eyes, but Sara couldn't do as her friend asked. The love she felt for Jonathan was far stronger than her love for her friend. "All I can promise is that I will not allow myself to be obsessed with it again." She squeezed Julie's fingers in an attempt to show her the importance of what she was about to say. "While I was ill, he came to me and begged me to get well. I know that it was because of him and his love that I fought my way out of that fog. He asked me to return to him. I fully intend to do just that, no matter what it takes."

As the days passed, Sara became stronger and stronger, and little by little, she improved physically until she was once more herself. At the same time, she was constantly aware of either Raina's or Julie's watchful gaze following her around the house. Since the day on the veranda, she and Julie hadn't spoken of Jonathan or her search for the key to going back to him, but Sara knew it was not far from her friend's mind. And when she couldn't be around, Julie had enlisted Raina in what she came to think of as the *Sara watch*.

Without a word, and making a very bad attempt at trying to look innocuous, either Raina or Julie hovered about making sure Sara didn't do anything that would make her ill again. They encouraged second helpings at dinner, suggested early bedtimes, and, by using some foolish excuse for the visits, checked in on her before either of them retired for the night. While Sara found their concern endearing, she also found it annoying. It reminded her of being back in New Orleans with her overprotective mother standing guard over her virtue. But Julie and Raina's watchfulness could not dampen

Sara's determination to be with Jonathan again.

Knowing her room proved to be the one place relatively free of Raina's and Julie's anxiety, she took refuge there. Settled on the chaise lounge Raina had directed Samuel to bring back up from the veranda and put in Sara's room for the afternoon naps the maid and Julie insisted upon, Sara settled back and closed her eyes. She hadn't yet regained all of her stamina, and it took only moments for her to feel the shroud of sleep enclose her.

The face of a woman with brown curls framing her not-so-handsome face gazed down at Sara. The woman's wide, brown eyes reflected rage unlike any Sara had ever seen.

Katherine Grayson.

Aware that this was nothing more than a dream, Sara struggled to rouse herself from sleep and from this nightmare, but she couldn't.

"What do you want?" Sara's voice trembled with the terror that had claimed her entire body.

Katherine threw back her head and laughed. The sound echoed around the room, chilling Sara to the bone. Continuing to glower down at Sara, Katherine pointed toward the bedroom wall.

Despite the paralyzing dread gripping her, Sara

turned her gaze in that direction. What she saw made her heart cease beating for a moment. Knots of fear coiled tightly in her stomach. Numbing terror covered her like an icy mourning shroud.

On the wall, in letters that appeared to be written in blood, had appeared a bone-chilling message.

Return to him and die!

Chapter 9

Sara bolted upright, eyes wide, heart racing. Quickly, she swung her gaze to the wall where the blood writing had been. It was, as it had always been, covered in flowered wallpaper. The only marks on it were the kiss of the rays of the afternoon sun. Nothing else.

Gradually, her heartbeat slowed, and the fear that had invaded every nerve in her body ebbed. It had been a bad dream. Nothing more. She swung her legs over the edge of the chaise lounge and felt the reassuring firmness of the floor beneath her feet.

A light tapping sounded on the door. "Yes?"

The door opened slowly, and Julie peeked around it. "You're awake." She stepped inside and then stopped abruptly. "Are you okay?"

Sara frowned. "I really wish you and Raina would stop worrying over me like a dog with a bone. I'm fine."

Julie didn't look convinced. "You don't look fine. You look peaked."

"I just woke up. I doubt I look like the belle of the ball." Though she tried, she couldn't keep the knots of irritation tying up her nerves from coloring her tone. "In fact, I feel so fine, I'm going for a walk by the river." She stood, slid Maddy's diary off the night table, and stuffed it in her pocket for later reading, then swept past Julie and out the door.

Julie followed close behind. "But do you—"

Sara stopped and turned on her friend. "Alone."

Looking abashed, Julie hung back and let Sara proceed down the stairs and out the front door.

The day couldn't have been more beautiful. The sun glittered like a bright gem in a clear blue sky, not a cloud in sight. Sara luxuriated in the caress of a gentle breeze blowing on her sun-warmed skin. Beside the road, the lazy Mississippi slipped by on its way to the Gulf of Mexico, its muddy waters lapping the shoreline as it flowed slowly south to the Delta.

Despite the beauty and serenity of the day, Sara felt

very guilty about snapping at Julie. She was mindful that, had it not been for her friend, Harrogate would have been ignored during her illness. She knew Julie had her best interests at heart, but if she was ever to figure out how to get back to Jonathan, she had to have time alone to think. With Raina and Julie hovering over her every minute of the day, that had become a near impossibility. Sara made a mental note to apologize when she returned to the house.

As she walked along the riverbank, her thoughts monopolized by her quest, Sara suddenly got the unmistakable feeling someone was following her. She stopped and turned to find . . . no one. Squinting against the bright sunlight, she scanned the trees and bushes, but still saw nothing except bees busily pollinating wildflowers and the gentle sway of the roadside foliage in the breeze.

She shook her head and chuckled. "Your imagination is getting out of control, Sara Wade."

But after all that had happened lately, she couldn't be too hard on herself. It wasn't every day that paintings replaced themselves, that messages written in blood appeared and disappeared on one's bedroom wall, or that one was catapulted fifty years into the past.

Dismissing her misgivings, she patted her skirt pocket to make sure Maddy's diary still resided safely within its folds, and continued on along the riverbank. Up ahead, a fallen tree extended out over the water and was shaded by the widespread limbs of a majestic water oak. Enough of the trunk still rested on land to ensure stability, and two of the limbs provided a perfect place for someone to sit and read in the shade without being disturbed. Since it was close to high noon and the heat of the day was at its most intense, River Road saw little traffic, so her chances of finally finding some peace and quiet were very good.

Sara gathered her skirts and settled herself within the embrace of the two Y-shaped vertical limbs. Her feet dangled over the muddy waters. Allowing the child in her to emerge, she swung her feet to and fro. The tree swayed gracefully in response. A bird sitting in the far reaches of the branches that extended over the water squawked and took flight. Evidently he too was looking for privacy. She smiled and leaned back against the branch that served as a backrest.

From her pocket, she withdrew Maddy's diary and let it fall open to the last pages she'd read. Just holding in her hands the book that contained stories of Jonathan and Maddy's relationship brought with it that warm blanket of love. Sara ran her fingers lovingly over the yellowed paper covered in Maddy's elegant handwriting. As the contentment that always accompanied thoughts of Jonathan washed over her like a warm spring rain, she began to read.

June 19, 1805

Every time I feel the warm metal of the locket against my skin, I think of Jonathan and wish it were his hands instead. I know that's shameless, but I so want our love to be complete. Our time in the garden last night was too short, and I'm so weary of stealing a moment here and there. I want to be with Jonathan forever, every minute of every day until the end of time. But unless Katherine releases him from their betrothal, I'm afraid that's impossible, and I will have to settle for the few moments we can steal.

In my darkest hours, I try to imagine a life without Jonathan, but I can't. The very idea of spending my remaining lifetime alone and without his love sends such pain through my heart that I can hardly breathe. Jonathan is my life, and without him I will just shrivel up and die.

One thing I'm certain of . . . for whatever selfish reason, Katherine is determined to wed Jonathan. She cannot make him happy. I can.

Tomorrow, Jonathan and his parents will come to Brentwood for dinner with our family. I won't even allow myself to think about the reason for this gathering of the two families. But in my heart I know it's to set the wedding date. However, I must guard my reaction carefully, and so must Jonathan. I don't know what terrible thing will happen if we are discovered.

Katherine has been watching me today. I fear she may

have guessed of my love for Jonathan. We'll have to be even more circumspect. I'm afraid what she'll do if—

A twig snapped behind Sara, but before she could turn to find the source, something shoved her shoulder. The diary flew out of her hands. She was catapulted forward into the river. As she slipped beneath the muddy water, she could hear that horrible, familiar sound of a woman's maniacal laughter.

She had just enough time to suck in a breath before the water closed over her head. Her voluminous skirts and multiple petticoats swirled about her, imprisoning her legs. Struggling to free herself of their cloying manacles, she kicked her legs and flayed her arms to pull herself back to the surface, but the water and the saturated material impeded her movements, dragging her down.

Silt and muddy water filled her mouth. Her lungs screamed for air. Could she hold her breath long enough to get above the water?

Panic quickened her movements. The current tugged relentlessly at her body. Even with her eyes open, she could see nothing through the opaque water. Totally disoriented, she continued to fight against the water and the material holding her prisoner. Turning this way and that, she searched blindly for land, but the water was too dense and dirty for her to see more than inches beyond her nose. Her skirts tangled more firmly around her legs. Her arms churned frantically in the water attempting to push her upward, but they quickly grew tired of their battle.

I'm going to drown. I'll never see Jonathan again.

The thought renewed her strength. Her muscles burning with the effort and lungs about to burst for want of air, she again tried to propel herself up. But the current, along with the weight of her wet clothing, fought just as hard to pull her down into its watery confinement. It was no use. She could never win by pitting her feeble efforts against the strength of the mighty Mississippi. All strength drained from her.

I'm going to die.

Her tired arms gave up the fight. Her body went limp. The current carried her along with little effort. Water burned her nose and throat as she gave in to her natural reaction to suck air into her lungs.

Her head grew light. The muddy water seemed to glisten like diamonds in the sunlight. She felt detached from herself. The body that had been fighting so hard to survive gave in to the will of the river. Her drive to keep up the battle to live evaporated. Sara allowed the gentle rhythm of the water to envelop her.

Then strong hands grabbed her under her arms and dragged her to the surface. As her head broke free of the river, she gasped at the life-giving air. Slowly, the hands pulled her to the shore and deposited her on the warm, heavenly solidity of the riverbank. For a long time, she just lay there, coughing and choking out silt-laden water. When she could breathe again, she looked around for her savior. No one was there. Not even wet footprints that should have been left behind by whoever came into the river to pull her to safety.

It took only a scant moment for her to realize who had saved her from a watery grave . . . Jonathan. But, at the same time, she also became aware of whose hands had likely pushed her in . . . Katherine's.

Then she remembered the diary. Frantically, she ran the few yards back up the road to where the fallen tree trunk was. She looked around for the book, but it was nowhere to be found. Desperation propelling her, she parted the tall grass and ran her hands over the earth. Nothing. Springing to her feet, she walked in circles, foraging in the bushes and weeds. Still nothing. Falling to her knees, she crawled through the tall grass. Her legs became tangled once more in the confines of her muddy, wet skirt, inhibiting her in what proved to be a fruitless endeavor. Eventually, she gave up.

Had Katherine taken it after she'd pushed her in? Had it fallen into the Mississippi? Either scenario meant she would never see it again.

Filled with despair at having lost her only connection

to Jonathan, perhaps forever, and dripping with muddy river water, she ambled back to the tree. Tears streaked her cheeks. What if the secret to returning to Jonathan was hidden within the pages of the diary? What if, with its loss, all chances of her ever seeing him again vanished?

Hours later, muddy, wet, and despondent, Sara walked into the front hall of Harrogate.

"Laws a mercy, child." Raina rushed toward her, eyes wide, mouth hanging open in astonishment. "Whatever did you do to yourself?" She cradled Sara close to her side and guided her toward the staircase. "We needs to git you out of dem wet clothes." Turning, she called over her shoulder, "Miss Julie! Miss Julie, come quick."

"Raina, there's no reason to alert the entire household. I fell into the river. That's all." She had no intention of sharing the full details of what had occurred on the riverbank. "I just need to get washed up and changed. I'm fine otherwise."

Raina clucked her tongue. "You call fine bein' all muddy and wet? And you jest gettin' out of the sick bed 'n all?" She shook her head so hard her *tignon* slipped to the side. She ignored it and continued to reprimand Sara. "Now you is gonna get washed and into your nightclothes. Den

I'm gonna have my momma make you some nice hot broth."

Sara gave up. She had neither the strength nor the inclination to fight Raina.

Below them the rustle of material and the sound of running footsteps told Sara that Julie had entered the hall. "Raina, what is it?"

"Dis one's done fallen into the river. She comes traipsin' in here like dis and says she's fine." Raina kept propelling Sara up the stairs. "Anybody with an eye in dey head can see she ain't fine." Raina began clucking her tongue again. "She coulda drowned. Thanks be to the Lawd she didn't."

Hurried steps behind them told Sara that Julie was hot on their heels. "How did you fall in the river?"

Sara opened her mouth to speak, but Raina got there first. "Didn't say. Jest said she fell in. If she don't take to her sick bed again after this, it'll be a miracle. Yep, a miracle." Raina continued her tirade, but Sara blocked her out.

They were doing it again—treating her like a child without a brain in her head.

When she could ignore Raina's ravings no longer, Sara stopped short and turned to her maid. "If you don't mind, I can speak for myself. I still have a tongue in my mouth. The water didn't wash it away. Now, let go of me and go get me hot water for a bath."

Raina opened her mouth as if to protest, but then,

when Sara stared her down, just as quickly, as if thinking better of it, she snapped it closed and turned to go downstairs. Sara swung toward Julie. "Now, if you come with me, I'll explain what happened."

Without waiting for a reply from her friend, Sara tromped up the remaining stairs. She could hear Raina's retreating footsteps. Julie followed close behind her. Once in her room, Sara slumped onto the bench at the foot of her bed.

Julie sat next to her. "Well?"

Without leaving anything out, Sara related the happenings at the river. "I have no idea what happened to the diary. I searched everywhere, but I couldn't find it." She clutched Julie's hand. "What am I going to do? I'm sure that finding the way back to Jonathan is somehow connected to the diary. If Katherine took it or if it fell into the river, I'll never see it or Jonathan again—" Suppressed tears choked off the rest of her words.

"Perhaps you overlooked it," Julie said, hope imbuing her voice. "If you promise to bathe, change your clothes, and then take a nap, I'll send Samuel to the river to look for the book."

Although Sara knew in her heart that Samuel would come back empty-handed, a faint spark of hope ignited within her. "Thank you. You're a good friend, Julie."

Samuel slipped into the room and deposited a large copper tub in the center of the room. He was quickly followed by several maids carrying buckets of steaming water.

"Samuel, Miss Sara lost a book down by the river. Take several of the men and go see if you can find it."

"Yes, 'um." When the tub had been filled, Samuel hurried the women from the room.

Julie stood and pulled Sara to her feet, spun her around, and began to unbutton the long row of tiny buttons down Sara's back. "Humph! Good friend. If I was truly a good friend, I'd make you see sense and stop all this foolishness," she mumbled, barely loud enough for Sara to hear.

Too despondent and too tired to argue, Sara simply sighed and acquiesced to being undressed and then helped into the tub of water. Leaning back, she closed her eyes and allowed the warmth of the bath to ease the problems from her mind.

But the respite didn't last long.

Before too many minutes passed, her thoughts went once more to what had happened at the river. Someone had pushed her in, and Sara no longer had to wonder what was the evil at Harrogate that Gran had referred to.

She had recognized that laughter, and even if she hadn't, only one person who wished Sara harm came to mind —Katherine Grayson.

That admission gave rise to another question: how far would Katherine go to keep Sara from Jonathan?

Chapter 10

Sara ate little at dinner that evening. As long as Maddy's diary was still missing, she could concentrate on little else. Samuel and some of the field hands had searched the riverbank until the sun had set, and found nothing. It just didn't make sense. The book couldn't have just vanished into thin air. Could it?

Sara had to smile ruefully at that thought. With all that had been going on around here in the last weeks, anything was possible.

"Want to share what you find so amusing?" Julie's voice roused Sara from her thoughts.

"I wasn't really smiling because I find anything humorous. It just hit me that the idea of a vanishing book shouldn't surprise me. After all, life around here hasn't been exactly *normal* of late, has it?"

Julie laughed. "No, not exactly."

"I'm sure it will turn up eventually." The forced lightness in her voice nicely covered her intense worry as to its whereabouts. Laying down her fork, Sara covered Julie's hand with hers. "About this afternoon in my room . . . I know I don't always seem so at times, but I'm truly grateful for everything you've done for me and Harrogate, and I know you only have my best interest at heart. It's just that sometimes—"

"You get frustrated with Raina and me hovering over you." Julie turned her palm up, linked her fingers in Sara's, and squeezed. "Maybe we did get a bit over-zealous, but we love you."

"I know, and I love both of you for caring so much."

Julie let go of Sara's hand, straightened her back, and picked up her fork. "Nevertheless, I promise that from now on, I'll be more of a friend and less of a mother hen." Then she frowned. "But you have to promise to take better care of yourself."

Jonathan's words rang through her mind. *You'll find a way to come back to me. I know you will. But first, you must get well and stay well. You must eat and sleep and stay strong.*

She smiled at Julie, and the words came easy. "I

promise."

The rest of the house had been asleep for hours. All except Sara, who sat staring out the window that overlooked the Garden of the Moon. After promising Julie she'd take care of herself, Sara felt a bit guilty for not being asleep, too. But her mind just wouldn't slow down.

Over and over, she relived the events of the day, looking for something she'd missed that would lead her to the location of Maddy's diary. But try as she might, she could think of nothing that would lead her to the diary.

She'd tried everything else to return to Jonathan. The diary was the only thing she hadn't eliminated as a possible way to reach him. Something about the diary held the key. But she'd never know for sure if she didn't find it.

Suddenly, movement in the garden caught her attention. A veil of soft white light seemed to glide amongst the flowers and shrubs. She sat forward and studied it for a long time, trying to make out what it was.

Indistinct and formless, it flowed like liquid silver through the garden, never disturbing anything it touched. Then it paused, and she felt as though it saw her, too, and beckoned to her.

Jonathan?

Her heart began to race. Excitement filled her entire being.

He's come back. He's waiting for me.

She jumped to her feet and, forgetting that she wore nothing more than her nightdress, dressing gown, and slippers, she bolted from the room and fled down the stairs, through the house, and out the French doors toward the garden. She stopped between the temple dogs, just outside the moongate, to catch her breath.

Not until she got there did she consider it might be Katherine laying a new trap for her. With measured steps, she moved slowly through the moongate and down the path leading to the area where she'd seen the white mist.

Light from a half moon shed pitiful illumination on the path. Then it disappeared behind a cloud. Several times, when she'd lost her way momentarily in the resulting darkness, Sara stumbled over a bush, its branches snatching at her clothes and skin, but she pushed on. Her heart beat triple time in her chest, and despite the coolness of the evening, sweat beads dotted her forehead. Her flimsy nightgown clung to her damp body, and the cool night air penetrated the thin material, chilling her skin. Her head pivoted from side to side, eyes ever watchful for Katherine and whatever she may have in mind this time.

When Sara had finally reached the spot where she'd seen the mist and stopped at a safe distance away, she slipped behind the broad trunk of an old magnolia tree and peered around it. Able to make out nothing but Gran's favorite bench, the place Sara had thought she'd seen the floating mist stop, she sighed in frustration. There was no sign of the mist or anything else—at least nothing she could see in the darkness.

Then the moon came out of hiding, and Sara could see a dark patch on the bench. She squinted to make out what it was, but from this distance, it remained a mystery. Carefully, she looked around her to make certain Katherine wasn't lurking somewhere nearby, ready to pounce. Satisfied that she was alone, Sara crept out of her hiding place and approached the bench.

Not until she was nearly on top of it did she realize the small dark patch was . . .

Maddy's diary!

She had no idea how it had gotten here from the riverbank, nor did she care. All that mattered was that it was here. She snatched it up and cradled it against her breast. The second her hands touched it, that now familiar sensation of peace and love washed over her. Holding it tightly, she turned to flee back to the safety of her bedroom. Out of the corner of her eye, she caught a glimpse of that misty apparition she'd seen from her window.

"Who's there? Show yourself." Though her words sounded brave, her insides curdled with fear. "Who are you?"

"It's me, my darling girl."

"Gran?" The fear melted away like butter on a hot day.

The transparent mist slowly took the familiar form of Sara's grandmother.

Sara breathed a sigh of relief. "I was afraid you were—"

"Katherine?"

"Yes. I think she tried to drown me today, Gran."

"That she did. Had it not been for Jonathan, she would have succeeded."

Jonathan, her savior. She knew in her heart it had been he who had snatched her from the jaws of a watery death, so she didn't need Gran's affirmation, but it was nice to have her supposition verified.

Gran drifted toward her, skimming over the ground like a soap bubble blown by the wind. She stopped just beyond Sara's reach. "Katherine can't come into this garden, child. You're safe here. The temple dogs guard it from any evil entering here."

Sara recalled what Clarice Degas had told her. "But the night Jonathan was killed, Katherine was here, wasn't she? She just stood by and watched Jonathan die. Anyone who could do that had to be evil."

"Yes, but there were no dogs back then."

"Of course. Grandpa Ezra put the dogs outside

the moongate."

Gran nodded. "You're not the first person who's been the object of Katherine's wrath. Do you think I wanted her face staring at me from that picture day after day? I tried to remove her portrait from my bedroom many times, but the next day it would always be back there, and I'd always hear her laughter when I discovered it had been replaced."

So Gran had also come face to face with the evil that lived at Harrogate. For the first time, it made sense why her grandmother would not talk about the portrait Sara hated so much.

"She's a malevolent presence in the house, and you don't have the protection of the temple dogs outside the garden. Be careful, darling girl."

Sara nodded. "I will. Thank you for returning the diary to me. How did you get—"

Gran stopped her words with that wave of the hand that dismissed things she found trivial and then smiled that beautiful smile Sara knew so well. "You're very welcome, darling girl. Guard it closely."

"Don't worry. I'll guard it with my life."

"Let's hope it never comes to that. Now, I suggest you return to your room before you catch your death."

The figure of a man took shape behind Gran. For a moment, Sara thought it was Jonathan, but when he moved closer, she realized it was her grandfather. Gran glanced over her shoulder and smiled.

"I must go now. Be safe, darling girl. And be happy."

Gran turned and drifted back to where Sara's grandfather waited with a loving smile curling up the full mouth nearly hidden behind his profuse black moustache. A moment later, hand in hand, they vanished. For a long time, Sara clutched the diary to her and stared at the spot where they'd been. As she'd done many times, Sara wished she'd known Ezra Wade. Unfortunately, he'd died before she was old enough to remember him.

How much in love her grandparents were. A love that had spanned time and space. A love like Maddy and Jonathan had shared. A love that Sara longed for with every ounce of her being.

The next morning, she awoke refreshed and happy. Instead of reading the diary as she'd so wanted to, Sara had gone to bed, the diary tucked safely under her pillow. She'd promised Julie and Jonathan she would take care of herself, and sitting up half the night reading would not have been the way to do that. However, this morning she was already planning to retire early this evening— which should please Julie and Raina—and read. Perhaps she would find the way back to Jonathan. Excitement bubbled up in her.

She tamped it down. First, she had to get through the long hours of the day. So when Julie suggested Sara help supervise the slaves while they butchered a pig Sara's father had sent to Harrogate, she readily agreed. It was a dirty job, but one the plantation mistress was expected to supervise. It was also tiring. By the time it was finished, Sara was ready to go back to the house and relax with a cold drink. But that was not to be.

After the last of the butchering had been done and the meat had been moved to the smokehouse for curing, she and Julie were called to one of the slave cabins to help deliver a baby for Litisha, Samuel and Chloe's youngest daughter.

As it turned out, their services weren't needed. Floree, an old, freewoman midwife, who lived in a shack a couple miles down River Road, had beaten them to it. Samuel had fetched her, and by the time Sara and Julie had arrived, Litisha had given birth to a beautiful little girl. The baby was bathed, wrapped in a length of white flannel, and nursing at her momma's breast. Rather than go inside, they stood just outside the door to the crowded cabin, marveling at the arrival of the tiny new life.

Before long, Floree began shooing everyone out of the cabin so the mother and baby could sleep.

Sara stopped one of the girls as she slipped through

the doorway. "Tell Floree we thank her for helping Litisha. Tell her to go into the kitchen in the big house, and she'll find a basket of vegetables waiting for her."

The girl's eyes grew large. "Oh, Missus, Floree won't step foot in da big house. Never has fo years." She hurried on, leaving Sara to stare after her in puzzlement.

"Strange." Then she shrugged. It wasn't all that uncommon for a slave who didn't work in the main house to refuse entry. The poor things were imbued with a fear of anything that wasn't a part of their everyday world. "Well, I'll have Samuel take the basket to her house." Then she looped her arm through Julie's. "Right now, I'm too tired to think about it. I need a bath and some food."

Julie agreed.

Tired, but still elated with the sight of the mother and her new baby, Julie and Sara made their way along the dirt path that led back up to the main house from the slave quarters.

"Who was the midwife?" Julie stepped around a puddle in the road.

"Raina said she used to a be a slave on one of the neighboring plantations, but she helped nurse her mistress through yellow fever years ago and her master was so grateful, he freed her and gave her that tiny house she lives in."

"I'm sorry we missed the birth of Litisha's baby," Julie mused. "Delivering babies is one of the chores of the plantation mistress that I always loved. Seeing that tiny new life come into the world is like watching a miracle happen."

As Sara recalled the many births she'd witnessed at her father's plantation, her throat choked with emotions, and she could only nod.

"Do you ever think about having children?" Julie shifted the small black bag that held their medical supplies to her other hand.

Sara considered the question for a moment before answering. "I always thought I'd fall in love with some dashing man, marry him, and have a boy and a girl."

"Why both?"

Sara grinned at her companion. "A girl for me to dress in ribbons and lace, and a boy for his father to teach how to ride and hunt."

Julie nudged her with her elbow. "Well, if you don't settle down and find that man, you may as well forget about those children."

Sara's footsteps faltered. She sort of had a man. But how could one produce children with a ghost?

Back at the house, their conversation about children was soon forgotten. The house was filled with the aromas of baked ham, creamed peas, fresh baked bread, and peach cobbler. Famished after their arduous day, both women hurried through washing and dressing and were back in the dining room before Chloe could serve up the food.

When Raina delivered the meal to the dining room, she was grinning ear to ear with the news that she had a beautiful little niece.

"I saw her, and she's jest the prettiest thing the good Lawd ever put on this here earth. Yes, she sho is." She fairly sang out the words.

Julie and Sara laughed. "She is that," they agreed in unison.

"Has Litisha named her yet?" Julie helped herself to a large slice of pink ham and added it to her plate.

Sara noted absently that Julie's appetite had diminished a little since her arrival. She hoped she'd finally gotten over the idea that each meal would be her last.

"She's namin' her Rose, jes like the flower."

As though some unseen force had shoved it into her mind, Sara immediately had a vision of the white roses growing around the gazebo in the Garden of the Moon. Suddenly, the siren's call of Maddy's diary became almost overwhelming. Fighting it down, she dug into her dinner with a gusto that elicited satisfied nods from Julie and Raina.

Sated and eager to get to her room, Sara forced herself to sit in the parlor with Julie and exchange banalities until she could go to bed without giving rise to questions from her friend. The mantel clock ticked away the endless minutes. Each minute was like a pin prick. Outside, twilight descended on the plantation grounds. Sara glanced at the clock. Eight thirty. Still too early to retire for the night. Barely aware of what her companion was saying, she nodded and inserted appropriate replies, their vagueness escaping Julie's notice. Or so Sara thought.

Julie laid aside the embroidery she'd been working on. "You're very quiet tonight, Sara." Pulling a length of crimson floss from the basket at her side, Julie threaded her needle, knotted the ends, and went back to work on the sampler.

Sara sighed and closed the book she'd been pretending to read. "I guess I'm just tired. We had a very busy day."

Immediately, Julie lowered her embroidery, and that all-too-familiar look of concern came over her expression. For once, Sara didn't mind.

"Then perhaps you should make an early night of it, and go to bed. It hasn't been all that long since you were ill."

Relieved, Sara had to fight to keep the smile from her lips. "Perhaps you're right. I think I'll take your advice," she said, rising from the chair with a lethargic movement to underline her exhaustion. "See you in the morning."

"Good night. Sleep well."

As she left the room, Sara nodded, but she knew there would be little sleep for her that night.

Settled in her chair, Sara lifted Maddy's diary into her lap. She ruffled the pages and began to wonder about Maddy's last entry in the book. Taking it firmly in her hands, she attempted to open the book toward the back but couldn't. It was as if the pages were glued together. Over and over she tried, but always with the same result. Then she went to where she'd left off reading and tried, and the pages fell opened with little effort on her part.

She smiled. Evidently she was not supposed to peek at the ending.

With overwhelming excitement at the prospect of seeing Jonathan again, even if just through Maddy's musings, she started to read.

June 20, 1805

My heart is shattered. The reason for the family gathering was as I feared. Tonight, my father announced Katherine's betrothal to Jonathan. Sadly, now it's official. Though I waited and prayed for my sister to say she didn't want to marry the man I love, as Jonathan had predicted she would, Katherine didn't object. Instead, she just smiled at me, her expression filled with satisfaction. She doesn't love Jonathan, but she's taking great delight in knowing I do and in making me suffer.

Our father spared no expense on the elaborate celebration dinner of roast capons and French champagne. The guests were as ostentatious as the food and drink: Clarice Degas and her son, Phillip, of Candlewick Plantation, the Watsons of Riverdown Plantation, the Madisons of Magnolia Rest Plantation, and even the governor of Orleans Territory, William Claiborne.

I had little to eat. The food stuck in my throat. It's hard to eat when your heart lies in a million pieces in your breast.

Sara paused in her reading and ran her fingertips over the dried tearstains on the page. Maddy's heartache mirrored the pain stabbing into her own chest. She had no idea what was going to happen after this, but she knew it was as though it were happening to her and not this woman who had walked the earth fifty years before her. This connection she shared with Maddy Grayson was uncanny. Oddly, Sara felt as if she, and not Madeline Grayson, had been the one living the distraught woman's life.

Sara hadn't even realized she'd been shedding tears of her own until one dropped to the yellow pages to join Maddy's. Drying her tears, she read on.

How am I going to live the rest of my life without him, watching him father children with a woman who is incapable of love, never feeling the touch of his lips on mine again? The agony of merely thinking about it is almost unbearable.

Tonight, I hid in the background of the celebration going on in the sitting room, hugging my sorrow close to my heart. No one noticed me. They were all too busy fawning over Katherine . . . everyone but Mother. Oddly, she sat to the side looking almost as unhappy as I felt. Occasionally she'd cast a glance in my direction, her expression filled with pity. Pity? For me?

My morose mood had just about paralyzed me when Jonathan whispered in my ear to meet him in my mother's garden . . .

The room began to spin out of control. Sara swirled helplessly through a long, bright tunnel. Colors swam before her eyes. Her stomach heaved. Panic seized her. But this all seemed familiar, as if it had happened to her once before. And it had. The night she'd found herself in the Garden of the Moon with Jonathan on her birth-day . . . Maddy's birthday.

Elation filled her twisting and turning body. She'd finally found the secret to going back to Jonathan. All she'd ever had to do all along was read Maddy's diary.

She ceased fighting the whirling vortex and waited,

knowing that at the end of this dizzying journey, she would once more find the man she loved.

Maddy escaped the parlor filled with people cele-brating the betrothal and slipped out to meet Jonathan. Easing down the long hall to the back of the house, she heard voices coming from her father's study. Careful, and not wanting to risk being discovered, she stopped outside the door. It was slightly ajar, and Clarice Degas' familiar, French-accented voice came to her through the crack.

"You must forget her. She's betrothed to another man now. Pining over her will serve no purpose except to make you ill, *chère*." A slight pause followed. "Please, *bien-aimé*, you must move on with your life."

"I can't, Mother." Maddy recognized the anguished voice of Philip Degas, Clarice's only child. "I've loved Katherine for too long to just sweep her from my thoughts and my heart. This *Américain* does not deserve her."

Maddy's mouth fell open.

Phillip was in love with Katherine?

That answered many questions she'd had over the years: Phillip's continual and everlasting patience with a woman who had a tongue like a viper; his animated face whenever Katherine entered a room; the lavish pearl necklace he'd given her for her birthday, despite the impropriety of such a gift to a woman on the verge of betrothal to another man; how he sought her out at every social gathering.

The fact that she wasn't the only one with a bleeding heart made Maddy feel a tiny bit less alone, even if she couldn't share her feelings with Phillip.

"He can't have her, Mother. I'll stop him. I'm not sure how, but I *will* stop him." The gritty, threatening tone of Phillip's voice sent chills down Maddy's back.

Before Clarice could reply, Maddy slipped past the door and hurried toward the front door. Slipping outside, she skirted the pool of light pouring from the drawing room window and hurried around to the back of the house. The garden was dark, but the moon shed enough light for her to see Jonathan waiting for her at the far end, partially hidden by a large azalea bush.

"My love." He enfolded her in his arms. "I'm so very sorry. I really thought she'd back out of the engagement."

Maddy said nothing. She couldn't. Her throat was so full of emotion, the words would never have come through. She buried her face against the soft linen of Jonathan's shirt front.

Jonathan set her at arm's length. "All hope is not lost. The wedding date hasn't been set, and perhaps she'll call it off before then."

Maddy pulled from his embrace and moved a few feet away. Thinking about anything while enclosed in Jonathan's arms, except how very much she loved him, was nearly impossible.

"She won't, you know. We're only fooling ourselves if we believe that." She smiled weakly. "I will always love you, but I think it's our destiny never to be together."

"No!" Jonathan strode angrily toward her. "I won't listen to such talk. We *will* be together. I'll find a way." He took her shoulders in his big hands, his voice gentler. "I'll find a way. I promise you I will, and I have never broken any promise I ever made to you. Have I?"

She shook her head. He was right. He'd never broken a promise, but she was very much afraid that this, through no fault of his, was one promise he would not be able to keep.

Maddy looked into his dear face. There was no way they would ever be together. She knew it in the depths of her heart, and if Jonathan wanted to be honest with himself, he knew it as well.

"Jonathan, I just heard Phillip tell his mother he loves Katherine, and he plans on stopping you from having her." Maddy took a step toward him, but stopped before she got close enough to touch him. "He sounded desperate. If he loves her half as much as I love you, that desperation could lead him to do things he wouldn't normally even consider. Please be careful."

Jonathan laughed, the sound strained and bitter. "My God, I'd give her to him gladly, if she'd just release me from this charade of a relationship." He ran his hand through his thick black hair. "I must find a way to get out of this. I can't live my life estranged from the woman I love." He closed the gap between them and hauled Maddy back into his arms. "I refuse to wake up every morning and not find you beside me."

Maddy knew there was no way that was ever going to happen. Talking about it further would only hurt both of them. Filled with despair, she pulled from his embrace and kissed him briefly. "We'll be missed. We have to go back inside."

She turned and ran from the garden, unable to be near him with such a deep chasm separating them.

Outside the parlor door, she stopped long enough to dab at the moisture on her cheeks. Her eagle-eyed mother would see it immediately and want to know why she'd been crying.

"Ah, Jonathan, my boy, there you are," her father bellowed.

Maddy assumed Jonathan had reentered the parlor by the dining room door. Satisfied that no trace of her tears remained on her skin, she slipped into the parlor in time to hear her father's announcement.

"Good news," her father went on. "We've settled

on a date. You and Katherine will be married in two weeks right here at Brentwood. The weather will still be favorable, so we'll have the wedding in the garden." He raised a glass of champagne and toasted the couple. "To Katherine and Jonathan. May their lives be long, happy, and fruitful."

Maddy's head began to spin. Catching hold of a chair back, she waited for the dizzy spell to pass, but it didn't. The sensation increased. The lightness invading her head grew worse. Soon a swirling mass of light swept her up and away from the mass of people. All sound around her ceased. Her feet seemed to have been lifted from the floor. Just at that moment, she was thrown into a long, endless tunnel of light.

Chapter 11

With a start, Sara became conscious of her surroundings. The intense pain slicing through her heart was almost physical. She . . . no, Maddy had lost Jonathan to Katherine, a woman who wanted him only as a means to hurt her sister. And what of Phillip? The poor man, although she couldn't imagine why anyone would love Maddy's sister that much, would be crushed. Like Maddy, he'd suffered a heartbreaking loss.

With a heavy heart, Sara laid the diary aside and gazed blankly out the window. How could she live with this pain? How did Maddy live with it? Why did Katherine hate Maddy so much?

Then she recalled the conversation she'd overheard between Clarice and Phillip in the Graysons' library.

Clarice would know why Katherine was so bent on hurting her sister and destroying four lives in the process. And what of Phillip's threat to have Katherine for himself? Was Phillip the young neighbor man Clarice Degas said had killed Jonathan?

The last time she spoke to Clarice, the old lady said Katherine hated Maddy for her beauty—but it must have been more than that. And Sara knew in her heart Clarice could tell her the real reason and whether Phillip had made good on his threat. Despite Clarice's warning not to return to Candlewick, tomorrow Sara would go see her and get some answers. Right now, she had to give in to the sudden exhaustion that claimed her body.

Putting the diary safely away, she crawled into her bed and pulled the eiderdown quilt under her chin. Almost before she had time to think about it, her eyes drifted closed, and she sank into the oblivion of sleep.

"Wake up, my love."

The gentle voice whispered in Sara's ear. Warm breath wafted over her skin and sent shivers down her spine. She pulled the down quilt closer to her body.

"Wake up, Maddy."

Maddy?

Sara's eyes flew open. Instantly, she was vividly aware of another presence in the room. Straining against the enveloping darkness, she pushed herself up and gazed around. Sitting beside her on the bed was Jonathan. At first, elation filled her. But it was followed quickly by intense fear. If Katherine knew he was here, what new madness would she visit on them?

"You have to leave, Jonathan."

He smiled, looked deep into her eyes, and stroked the side of her face with his fingertips. "Why? Don't you want me here?"

Not want him here? She wanted him here more than she wanted her next breath. But Katherine's wrath was beginning to frighten her more than a little. "Katherine—"

He stopped her words with his fingertips. "Forget Katherine."

"But—"

"Shh. Trust me."

Oh, God, she did trust him. She trusted him with her life, but what if Katherine found out? What would she do?

"Why are you here?"

"I've missed you." He picked up a lock of her hair and wrapped it around his hand. "Your hair." He rubbed a strand of it over his cheek. "Your eyes." He kissed each eye. "Your creamy skin." He bent and placed a kiss on the hollow of her throat. She gasped at the strength of the thrill that raced through her body. "Your sweet, sweet smell." He buried his face in her neck. "Your lips." He brushed them with a butterfly kiss. "I had to taste the sweetness that is my Maddy."

Sara's head was swimming. It cost her every ounce of willpower to push him away. "Jonathan, I'm not Maddy. I'm Sara Wade."

He shook his head. "You *are* Maddy. You have *always* been and will *always* be my Maddy."

"But Maddy's—"

Again he stopped her words, but this time with a feathery soft kiss, and then he drew back and looked deep into her eyes. "Maddy is not dead. Haven't you figured that out yet? She lives in you."

Sara recalled how easily it had been for her to slip into Maddy's body when she'd gone back in time. Vaguely, she remembered Gran talking about a Hindu belief that a human soul had the ability to live on beyond the death of one body and then be transferred into another body, but carry the soul of the first. She'd even had a name for it—reincarnation.

Was that what had happened? Had Maddy's soul taken possession of hers? Had she truly been Maddy in another lifetime?

Before she could make sense of her thoughts, Jonathan was kissing her again. This time it wasn't just a light brushing of their lips. His kiss had become intense, demanding, hungry, devouring her with its passion. The dizzy sensation that had taken possession of Sara at this moment and imprisoned her willpower mirrored the one she'd experienced every time she'd spun though the swirling vortex, and just before she'd slipped into Maddy's identity. But this time she retained her identity as Sara and remained in her room and in her body.

Helpless to resist, she allowed Jonathan to hold her, to kiss her, to devour her. Exhaustion forgotten, her entire body came alive with a new energy, a need far beyond anything she'd ever experienced before. Even when he slipped her nightdress over her shoulders and trailed kisses down her neck and into her exposed cleavage, she couldn't find the strength to resist.

Need sprang to life inside her and swelled to overwhelming proportions. She wanted this man more than she'd ever wanted anything before in her life. More than the return of her beloved Gran. More than her freedom from her mother. More than Harrogate. More than her next breath. She shivered.

Jonathon pulled back. "Are you cold?"

Cold? Heaven help her. Her body felt like it could rival the fire burning in the hearth for heat. "No, I'm not cold."

"What then?" When she didn't answer, he grinned knowingly. "I excite you."

Suddenly hit by a wash of shyness, she averted her gaze. Her cheeks felt as though they were burning up. "Yes."

Hooking his finger under her chin, he raised it until their gazes met. "Good. I want to excite you. I want you to want me so much you can think of nothing else."

"I do want you, but—"

His lips stopped her protest. This time she gave in to the arousal rushing through her every nerve ending. Sara wrapped her arms around his shoulders and pulled him down to lie beside her on the bed. Impatient with the blanket and sheet that prevented her from being as close to him as she needed to be, she kicked them aside. They slithered to the floor, unnoticed. The cool night air washed over her burning skin, but it did nothing to alleviate the fire inside her.

Jonathan continued to kiss her mouth, her neck, and her breasts until Sara felt the only way to release her emotions was to call out, but she knew that would only bring Julie and Raina, and the last thing she wanted right now was anyone to interrupt this exquisite torture.

Suddenly a high-pitched woman's scream rent the air. It seemed to echo off the walls like a crazed ball bouncing madly from place to place.

Sara stiffened, her own scream building in her throat. She clung to Jonathan's broad shoulders, seeking protection within his arms. Her ears began to hurt. But the scream continued on and on until Sara opened her mouth to beg it to stop.

But the words never emerged from her throat. A loud crack drowned out the scream for a fraction of a second. Sara's head jerked toward the side of the room. A shaft of moonlight illuminated the mirror over the dressing table. A jagged fissure ran diagonally across the surface.

Then Jonathan vanished.

The scream ceased.

Sara lay staring at the ceiling, wondering if she'd dreamt the entire thing. Had Jonathan really been there at all, or had it been a product of her fevered imagination, her overwhelming need to have him beside her? And the scream . . . Had it been Katherine objecting to what was happening between Jonathan and Sara? Or had that, too, been her imagination? And the mirror? Had it really broken?

She rose from the bed, lit the candle on her nightstand, and carried it hesitantly to the dressing table. Holding it aloft so she could better see, she gasped. Running from one corner of the mirror to the other was a zigzag crack.

The next morning, haunted by both fear and the ecstasy from the night before, and armed with the determination to get answers to the myriad of questions racing through her mind, Sara ordered a carriage to take her to Candlewick Plantation.

When Cherry, Clarice Degas' maid, opened the front door, Sara, foregoing the good manners her mother had instilled in her, swept past the surprised maid without waiting for an invitation. After her last visit to Candlewick Plantation, Sara wasn't sure of her welcome, or whether there would be any welcome at all, and she couldn't risk taking any chances that she'd be turned away.

As before, the old woman, dressed head to toe in black bombazine, was sitting in her parlor. She looked up and spotted Sara. Her expression grew hard.

"I thought I told you never to come back here."

Girding herself with all the strength she could muster, Sara walked all the way into the room and faced Clarice. Despite not being invited to take a seat, Sara sat on the large settee facing Clarice. "You did, but I have some questions for you. Questions I know you have the answers to."

"And if I don't want to supply you with the answers?" Her eyes were hard and cold.

"Then I will sit here until you do." Resolutely, but

with butterflies filling her stomach, Sara leaned toward the old woman. "Rest assured, I am not leaving until you answer my questions."

Clarice's maid stood behind Sara like a hovering bodyguard. "You want me to call Josiah, Miss Clarice?" she asked.

The old woman studied Sara for a very long moment. Hoping she wouldn't be ejected from Candlewick, Sara forced herself to meet Clarice's intimidating assessment head-on. The woman's dark-eyed gaze dropped for a second to the carpet at their feet, as though Clarice were recalling the crow that had flown through the window on Sara's last visit. A chill shimmered over Sara. Considering that the bird's appearance had coincided with the mention of Katherine's name, Sara understood. Especially after her near drowning in the Mississippi, and the cracked mirror in her room. Clarice had every reason to be so frightened. Katherine Grayson was a formidable woman to anger.

Finally, Clarice waved her fingers at the maid. "No need to call Josiah, Cherry. I'll speak with Miss Wade." She turned to glare at Sara. "You *will* make this brief."

"Should I bring refreshments, Miss Clarice?" Cherry threw Sara a look that said she didn't think she deserved such a show of good hospitality.

"Miss Wade won't be here that long," Clarice said,

her dark eyes snapping her ill feelings at Sara. "Now, what is it you want to know?"

Summoning her courage to face off with the daunting older woman, Sara cleared her throat, stiffened her courage, and got straight to the point. "Why was Katherine so determined to marry a man she didn't love?"

Clarice laughed derisively. "Oh, my dear, naïve woman. It's really quite simple. It's as I told you before. Because she hated her sister. Maddy was everything she wasn't . . . pretty, funny, well-liked, smart. All the men in the county were after Maddy's hand."

"Why didn't her family let her marry one of them?"

"Back then it was the custom that the oldest marry first. Besides, from the day of the twins' birth, there was never any question who Katherine would marry."

Sara shook her head. She'd never understand the archaic views some families had about marriage. Thank goodness her father wasn't one of them.

"Katherine's father had made sure that, should the child be a female, her future was assured by agreeing with Henry Bradford to betroth their children the moment she came into this world—and Katherine came first." She smiled slyly and laughed. "He had no idea his wife would give him two daughters. It was rumored that the betrothal would pay off a long overdue debt Bradford owed Katherine's father. The girl came with a sizable dowry. So when Katherine became a Bradford, not only would her dowry settle the debt, but Bradford would also have a ready supply of more cash if he needed it . . . and he always did." She raised her hand to cup her mouth, and then lowered her voice. "Everyone knew he spent more time in the gaming dens and brothels of the French Quarter than he did running his shipping business."

"That doesn't make sense. Why would Mr. Grayson marry his daughter into a family that was on the verge of destitution? How would that assure her future?"

Clarice sipped her lemonade. "Because Grayson knew that when Jonathan reached twenty-one, he came into the enormous fortune left to him by his grandfather, Lord Bradford. Bradford was some kind of nobleman in England. Had a lot of land and owned a large shipping concern over there. Jonathan didn't get on with his father, so there was no hope of the old man getting his hands on a penny of the money."

Sara frowned. "I don't understand what any of this has to do with Katherine hating Maddy."

Clarice sat straighter in her chair. "Oh, my dear, Katherine didn't just hate Maddy. She was insanely jealous of her twin to the point of an obsessive need to deprive Maddy of anything she wanted. Maddy never asked for the things her mother gave her or for men to fall at her feet. There was only one thing Maddy really wanted—Jonathan." She sighed as if talking was taking all her energy. "By marrying him, Katherine made sure her sister would never have him. Katherine had been willing to live her life with a man who detested her as much as she detested her sister only to wreak her ultimate revenge."

Sara had no idea Katherine's hatred for Maddy ran so deep and so strong. Even in death, Katherine fought to keep Maddy from the man she loved. That certainly answered one of her questions, but there was still one more, and she hesitated to ask it. How could she ask this woman if her son killed Jonathan?

"Well, now you know, so you can leave." Clarice waved her hand dismissively.

Sara ignored her hostess' rudeness. Instead of leaving, she faced off once more with the formidable Clarice. "Not yet. I have one more question. When I get the answer, I'll leave." Sara read interest in the wrinkled face. She had chosen just the right words to encourage Clarice to tell her what she wanted to know.

Clarice immediately rearranged her features, raised one impatient eyebrow, and frowned. "Well?"

Taking a deep fortifying breath, Sara decided asking outright was the only way to approach the subject that would no doubt bring pain to this poor woman.

"Did Phillip kill Jonathan Bradford?" Just saying

the words sent a sharp pang through Sara's heart.

Clarice's stern expression melted like hot wax. Sorrow so deep and so ravaging shone from the woman's rheumy features that Sara regretted asking. She knew the answer before the woman spoke a word. Nevertheless, she waited.

The silence stretched out interminably. Then a lone tear trickled down Clarice's pale, papery cheek. When she spoke, her voice didn't come close to resembling that of the vindictive, angry woman who had addressed Sara moments earlier.

"That's what they said." Clarice swiped at the tears with a white handkerchief she'd pulled from the sleeve of her dress. "Phillip never talked to me about it."

"He was in love with Katherine, wasn't he?"

Clarice nodded. "He'd been totally bemused by her from childhood. God only knows why. There wasn't a thing about the girl that was likeable. But then, I guess there's no accounting for what the heart decides."

Sara couldn't argue with that. Given the choice, she wouldn't have aspired to fall in love with a ghost. But she *had* fallen in love with Jonathan, and now that very love fueled a need to know the whole story behind that terrible night in the Garden of the Moon.

"Their betrothal must have been devastating for him." Sara could recall the anguish she'd heard in

Phillip's voice.

With effort, Clarice pulled her arthritic body from the chair and hobbled to the mantel, where a miniature of Phillip resided in a gold frame. She ran her fingertip over her son's face. "Devastating? More like plunging a knife in his chest. No matter what I said, he was inconsolable." She turned to Sara. "I can't tell you exactly what happened that night. Since Phillip never tried to defend himself, all I have to go by is what they brought out at Phillip's trial, which, along with his confession, seemed to be irrefutable proof of his guilt." She took a deep breath. "He left here after dinner with a gun and went to Harrogate to confront Jonathan. They faced off in the garden, and Phillip shot him." She dabbed at her eyes again. "They arrested him the next day. He was tried and convicted. My husband was able to use his standing in the community to prevent Phillip from being sentenced to the gallows. But he might as well have been put to death. He's in prison at the Cabildo in New Orleans for the rest of his life. Two months later, his father died of a broken heart."

She turned back to Sara. "I always felt that the house slaves at the Graysons' plantation knew more than anyone, but who would take the world of a nigra before that of a white man? Those servants knew a lot more than any of the men who testified against my son. I always regretted that I never questioned the servants at Brentwood myself. Perhaps, if I had, my son would be here, instead of . . ."

By the time Clarice said the last words, tears spilled down Sara's cheeks. Her heart went out to the poor woman. How devastating to lose your only child because of a selfish woman with no room in her heart for anything but hatred, greed, and revenge.

Sara went to stand beside Clarice. "I'm so sorry to have resurrected all these memories for you. And I'm even sorrier that you lost your son because of Katherine." She laid her hand on Clarice's frail arm. "Will you be all right?"

Clarice glanced at her. "I've lived with this for many years and survived. I'm sure that won't change just because you asked a question and I answered you." She smiled weakly at Sara. "When you have your own children, you'll find that a mother's heart is an amazing thing. It can be broken over and over and still continue to beat."

Warmth poured from Clarice's eyes, the first warmth Sara had ever witnessed in the old woman. Along with it, Sara read a friendliness that had also been missing before. Having formerly judged her as a cold, hard woman, Sara now realized she'd been using her pain as a shield against the terrible memories that haunted her.

Sara's heart softened. "I know you won't come to

Harrogate, but may I come back to visit you?"

A genuine smile erased some of the lines of age from Clarice's face. "I'd like that."

Sara walked back to the settee and picked up her reticule, then started for the door.

"Child."

Sara turned toward her. "Yes?"

"Be careful. Some would call me crazy, but I know Katherine's spirit haunts Harrogate. I could feel it lurking there every time I stepped into that house. That's why I stopped going. She is a hateful, evil woman who is capable of doing anything to reach her ends."

Chapter 12

All the way back to Harrogate Sara thought about Clarice's parting words.

I know Katherine's sprit haunts Harrogate.

Had Clarice experienced Katherine's spirit at Harrogate? Had there been more than that one incident with the crow? She said she never came to Harrogate anymore. Was it because of more than just having felt Katherine's presence in the house? Though many of Sara's questions had been answered at Candlewick, she'd left with many more. She made a vow to discuss it with Clarice on her next visit.

Deep in thought on the ride home, Sara didn't note that anything was wrong at Harrogate until they were more than halfway down the long drive leading to the house. Then she saw it . . . a huge column of black smoke filling the sky and coming from a distance behind the house. It billowed and curled over Harrogate like the hand of a fiery demon throwing sparks into the air with all the abandon of a child in a tantrum.

Samuel must have seen it, too, because he'd whipped the horse into a run. Instead of stopping in front, he drove the horses and carriage around to the side of the house. Only then could she see in the distance the most frightening sight she'd ever witnessed.

The horse barn was a pillar of roaring flames licking at the afternoon sky. Field hands raced from the well to the barn carrying buckets of water to throw on the inferno. Julie tried to organize them into a bucket brigade. Her strident voice could barely be heard above the roar of the fire. Sara jumped from the carriage and ran the rest of the way to Julie. The overwhelming intense heat from the fire slapped her in the face.

She gasped for air, and then sped toward Julie. "What happened?"

Julie continued to direct the field hands. "Get more water on the doorway. We have to get the horses out." She turned to Sara. Beads of sweat ran down Julie's cheeks, mixing with the soot that streaked her face. "I don't know . . . what happened. Chloe . . . spotted the flames from the kitchen . . . window and alerted me."

Julie's breathless voice was growing raspy from yelling orders and breathing in the smoke. "By the time . . . I got here, the barn . . . the barn was engulfed in flames."

Sara couldn't believe what she was seeing. Losing the barn would be nothing compared to losing the live-stock trapped inside. No sooner had the thought passed through her mind than the door burst open. A dozen plow horses and four riding mounts raced from the fire, screaming in terror, and disappeared into the trees bordering the road.

Heaving a relieved sigh, Sara's attention went back to the burning structure. At the top of the barn, flames licked out the hay hole like a dragon belching fire. Their long, orange fingers curled around the old wood, igniting it in seconds.

Sara jumped into the fray, grabbed a bucket, and passed it on to the line of men and women leading to the well. Bucket after bucket passed through her hands until her shoulders burned with the exertion and her palms were almost raw. Still the fire raged. The hay and the dry wooden walls continued to fuel the fire, and the pitiful amount of water they were able to pour on it had little effect on the inferno.

"It's no use," Julie screamed from beside her. "We may as well just let it burn until it goes out."

Sara nodded and set the bucket she'd been holding

on the ground.

Suddenly, a deafening crash rent the night air, and the barn collapsed in on itself. Burning embers shot into the sky and fell on the ground around them. Sara and Julie screamed for everyone to back away. Here and there a few flames licked at the remaining unburned wood. A pile of bright red ashes covered the ground where the barn had once stood.

She stared at the structure now completely obliterated by the hungry flames. A flare-up shot flames in the air again, and Sara thought she saw the outline of a woman's figure inside them.

She blinked several times, certain that her eyes were playing tricks on her. Then the figure vanished as if it had been gobbled up by the flames, evaporating into thin air. Sara looked around to see if perhaps Julie had gone into the fire to rescue an animal that hadn't escaped, but Julie was standing beside her. And, although Julie's gaze was trained on the rubble where the figure had stood, she showed no signs of having seen it.

Sara opened her mouth to ask Julie if she'd seen the figure, but she stopped when a lone sheet of paper shot out of the flames and drifted toward her.

Since the entire plantation's records were kept either in the overseer's office in his home or the office in the house, both buildings separate from the barn, it was highly unusual for paper of any kind to be inside the barn. And even if the paper had been inside the barn, how had it survived this wall of flame when it appeared nothing else had?

Sara watched the paper as it floated on the air currents generated by the fire. Finally, it settled to the ground a few feet in front of her. She looked around. As with the ethereal figure of the woman, no one else had noticed the paper.

She hurried to it and snatched it up. The edges were blackened and partially burned, but the writing on it was still visible. In what she immediately recognized as Gran's elegant handwriting, it read: *There's a letter.* Then the paper crumbled into nothing but powder.

By the time the fire was out, black soot coated Sara's and Julie's clothes and skin. The field hands showed signs of physical exhaustion, and many of them were coughing from the smoke they'd inhaled while rescuing the livestock. The men not being treated for injuries rounded up the livestock and led them safely inside a makeshift corral near the orchards. A dense cloud of black smoke, a product of the still smoldering remains of what once were stables and a barn, still hung over Harrogate like a specter of doom. Both structures were lost, but thankfully the same did not hold true for any lives. In the corner of the yard, Chloe and Raina had set up a first aid area and were busy treating burns and scratches sustained by the field hands. Litisha was handing out food and drinks.

As Sara walked back to the house, in her mind's eye she could still see the angry flames licking at the structure. Lady Luck had been on their side—this time.

Once again, unanswered questions began to swim through Sara's mind. Who was that figure she'd seen inside the barn? Could it have been Katherine? But the letter had been in Gran's handwriting. But did that mean anything? Sara knew what Katherine was capable of, and she would not have been surprised if Katherine had forged Gran's handwriting. But would Katherine help Sara by telling her about some letter? She would only if it served one of her nefarious purposes. Sara decided that, until she got further proof of the actual existence of this letter and its contents, this was probably nothing more than Katherine's attempt to lure her into a dangerous situation.

By the time Sara made it to the house, her temples throbbed in protest. Of one thing she was sure: Katherine had set the fire as one more warning to stay away from Jonathan. More alarming, however, was the realization that Katherine's warnings were becoming more serious with each event.

On the heels of that realization came a horrible revelation. Because of her obsession with Jonathan, she had put many lives in grave danger. Katherine was no longer content with threatening her. Now she was threatening those around her.

For Julie and Sara, dinner that evening was a quiet affair with neither of them saying more than a few words. Aside from exhaustion, guilt was eating at Sara. She couldn't get it out of her head that she'd put the lives of everyone on the plantation at risk because of her blind pursuit of Jonathan. People could have died today, and all because of her. The realization made her see the foolishness of her total preoccupation with a ghost.

Though she knew she would always love Jonathan, she also had to admit to herself that there was no future for that love. He was a ghost, and she was very much alive. Logically, aside from all else, this not only left them with no hope of a future, but it also made them totally incompatible. It made no sense to risk lives in the face of Katherine's vindictive need to wreak revenge on her sister.

Though her heart felt as if it had been sliced into tiny

pieces, she made the decision to lock the diary away and give up on her quest to be with Jonathan.

When she reached her room, Sara took Maddy's diary, wrapped it in a shawl, and tucked it into the very bottom of Gran's old steamer trunk. Hopefully, if she didn't see it, Sara could dismiss it and Jonathan from her mind. Exhausted and heartsick, she fell into bed and quickly drifted off into a troubled sleep.

The next morning, Sara rose early, determined to take over as mistress of Harrogate, something she should have done long ago instead of leaving it on Julie's capable shoulders. Donning one of her older dresses, she swept back her hair into a bun and headed downstairs to breakfast.

As she entered the sun-dappled dining room, she had to smile. At the table, Julie was digging into a plate loaded with eggs, slices of pink ham, and biscuits drenched in white sausage gravy. Evidently, she'd been too quick to believe that Julie's appetite had started to decrease.

"Morning."

Julie stopped eating, fork halfway to her mouth, and turned toward Sara's voice. Her eyes widened in shock. "Well, this is a surprise. What got you out of bed so early?"

"I decided it's time I became the mistress of this plantation. I've left it for you to do for too long."

"I don't mind. I like taking care of the place for you, and I feel like I'm earning my keep."

Sara laid her hand on Julie's shoulder. "I know, and I thank you for all you've done, although you were never expected to earn your keep. It's just past time I did my share of the work."

Julie laid her fork aside. "Does this mean that you've stopped trying to find a way to get back to Jonathan?"

Sara's heart twisted in pain. She swallowed hard. Instead of answering right away, she helped herself to the eggs on the sideboard, added a slice of ham and a gravy-covered biscuit, and took the chair at the head of the table. "I never told you, but I found the way back. It was actually very easy. Maddy's diary is the way it happens. When I read it, it takes me back in time."

Julie stared at her, openmouthed.

"I know. It's not easy to accept. It wasn't for me at first either."

"And you actually went back in time and saw Jonathan?"

Saw him? Instantly, Sara recalled the feel of his embrace and his kiss and how close they'd come to making love. "Yes, I went back to 1805 and saw him."

She could say no more and Julie, bless her, didn't

push for more information. It hurt too much to even think about never seeing him again, much less talk about it. Nor could she explain that Katherine's ghost was putting everyone in danger because Sara wouldn't give up on having a man who belonged to the past. Not because she felt Julie wouldn't believe her. Simply because talking about anything remotely to do with Jonathan just brought too much pain.

Forcing a smile, she picked up her fork. "So what do you have planned for today?"

Julie didn't speak. She continued to stare at Sara, brows furrowed. "Are you sure you want to do this?"

Sara knew Julie was not referring to her taking up her duties as plantation mistress. She was certain Julie was recalling Sara's brokenness when she'd been unable to go back to Jonathan before. She'd have to give her friend some kind of an explanation to reassure her it would not happen this time.

For a moment, Sara considered lying, but decided against it. "No, I'm not, but it's something that has to be done. The past is the past and should be left to rest in peace."

"But what about what your grandmother told you?"

Sara opened her mouth to tell Julie that her grandmother wanted her to be happy, and that over the past weeks she'd learned living in the past was not the way to do it.

But the dining room door opened, and a grinning Raina entered, accompanied by a tall, distinguished gentleman wearing a dark frock coat and trousers, a snowy shirt, a sparkling twinkle in his eye, and a neatly trimmed Vandyke concealing his chin.

There was no need for Raina to announce who he was. Sara would have recognized Preston Wade in her sleep.

"Papa!" Sara bolted from her chair and rushed into her father's open arms. "I've missed you so much." She hugged him so tightly, he groaned in protest.

Grinning, he set her at arm's length. "Well, that's odd because I haven't missed you at all." Then he kissed her cheek soundly and laughed that robust laugh that always made Sara giggle like a little girl.

"What are you doing here?" she finally asked.

"Do I need a reason to visit my only daughter and her friend?"

Reminded of her manners, Sara indicated Julie. "You remember Julie?"

His grin widened. "I certainly do." He bent and placed a kiss on Julie's cheek. "How are you, my dear?"

"Fine, Mr. Wade." Having finished her breakfast, she rose. "Will you be staying for a while?"

"For a day or two, if my daughter will have me."

"Of course I'll have you, silly." For the first time in weeks, Sara felt giddy. It was wonderful to see her father.

"In fact, I just may keep you here permanently."

"Well, your mother might have something to say about that."

Some of the shine went off Sara's happiness. "How is Mother?"

"She's well. She told me to tell you she's sorry she couldn't accompany me, but she had some prior commitments she couldn't cancel."

"I'm sure she did," Sara said. Her *prior commitments* were no doubt an excuse to keep from having to be embarrassed by being seen in the company of her crazy daughter. "Perhaps next time."

Oddly, her father frowned. "Yes. Of course. Next time."

Julie pushed her plate aside and stood. "Well, if you'll excuse me, I have some things to look after. I'll leave you two to catch up." She slipped from the room.

Sara linked her arm through her father's and led him to the buffet. "Have you eaten, Papa?"

"No, and I could use some of Chloe's cooking. Our new cook is good, but her biscuits don't equal Chloe's." He picked up a plate and began loading it with food.

When her father had finished eating, he and Sara strolled into the Garden of the Moon and sat in the gazebo in the center. The sweet aroma of the many blossoms filled the air, making Sara feel happy and lazy. Warm rays of morning sun beat down on them and made the dew glisten on the leaves, turning the entire place into a garden seemingly bedecked with sparkling precious gems.

Despite the beauty of her relaxed surroundings, Sara was uneasy. She could detect tension in her father's body as he settled beside her on the bench. "What's bothering you?"

He smiled and patted her knee. "What makes you think there's anything bothering me, sweetheart?"

"Papa, I know you." She kissed his cheek.

He frowned and then sighed. "Would it surprise you if I told you that your grandmother paid me a visit?"

Considering that her father shared her gift for seeing dead people, it didn't surprise her at all. What did surprise her was that Gran had chosen to appear to him and not to her. "Gran?"

He nodded. "It was two nights ago."

"Why didn't she come to me?"

"She did come to you, but you chose to ignore her."

"What? I would never ignore Gran."

He took her hand. "Remember the fire and the note?"

Sara's mouth fell open. "That was Gran. I wasn't sure." She didn't bother telling him she thought Katherine was up to another of her tricks. That would have required an explanation of the times when her life had been in jeopardy, and she was unwilling to share that with her father.

She couldn't have known it was Gran, but how foolish of her to dismiss the note without proof that it was Katherine.

High overhead a hawk squawked. For a long time, it circled, gliding on the air currents and gazing down at the earth. Then it suddenly swooped down into the flower bed and instantly rose again, a squirming, tiny gray body clutched in its sharp talons. Sara watched as the bird disappeared into the blinding blue sky. She felt like that poor little mouse, trapped in Katherine's talons and unable to free herself.

"She told me to tell you that, before she died, Katherine wrote a letter to Maddy—"

With a start, Sara said, "You know about Katherine and Maddy?"

He nodded. "Your grandmother told me the whole story."

"What's in this letter?"

Shrugging, he turned on the bench to face her. "Gran only said it's important that you find it and read it."

"Did she say where it is?"

"No. Just that it's in the house, and that it's very important you find it. She probably would have said more, but your mother woke up and wanted to know who I was talking to. I told her she must have been dreaming." He snickered. "I'm not sure she believed me, but she went back to sleep."

Sara was only half listening. Her mind had centered in on the letter. What could possibly be in it that she needed to know? And what new torture would Katherine devise to punish her if she decided to seek it out? This complicated her decision to let this whole thing rest. Still, she was not convinced that she shouldn't.

"Papa, I've decided that I'm not going to pursue any more of this . . . this mystery surrounding Maddy, Katherine, and Jonathan."

He stared at her, wide-eyed. "Why?"

Dare she tell him she was sure Katherine was trying to hurt her and to continue with this whole thing would mean putting the rest of the plantation, as well as herself, in danger?

Chapter 13

Sara's father took her hand and squeezed it. "I don't understand. Why aren't you going to pursue this? Gran indicated you were very anxious to find out the truth of what happened here and the people involved."

"I am . . . I was." She stood and walked to the railing of the gazebo. "Things have gotten . . . complicated."

Her heart twisted. The truth was not the only thing she wanted. She wanted even more to go back to Jonathan, to feel his arms around her, to feel his lips on hers, to hear his love words. But at some point, she had to start thinking of someone other than herself. If her happiness meant those she cared about would be hurt, then she could not do it.

"Complicated how?" Her father had come to stand

at her side. He rested a hand on her shoulder.

How could she tell him she'd fallen in love with a ghost? Her father was very understanding of her gift, but this would tax even his imagination. She couldn't bear the idea of having her father look at her with the same disdain her mother had all her life.

Avoiding a direct answer, she struggled for the right words. "It's hard to explain, Papa. All I can tell you is that this doesn't concern just me anymore. So I'll think about it."

He drew her into his embrace. "Very well. All I've ever wanted for you is that you be happy." He kissed her hair. "I have a feeling that finding this letter will help explain a lot of things."

Like why Katherine wants me dead?

For the rest of the day, Sara found herself preoccupied with the letter her father had told her about. Though she wanted to dismiss it from her mind and stand by her decision to not enter this spiderweb of mystery surrounding people who had lived fifty years ago, she couldn't.

Where could the letter be? Harrogate was huge and had many rooms and potential hiding places for something so small and easy to conceal. It could be anywhere. Then she recalled how she and Raina had found Maddy's diary hidden behind a picture frame. Could the letter be in such a place as well? Or what about the harpsichord where she'd found Maddy's necklace?

All through dinner with her father and Julie, she tried to be attentive to their conversation but found herself drifting off into thought. Methodically, she mentally combed through each room, looking for a possible hiding place. But it just got more and more confusing. There were far too many possibilities. Maybe—

"Isn't that right, Sara?"

Her father's question roused her from her mental search. "I'm sorry, Papa. I'm afraid I was wool gathering. What was it you said?"

He frowned at her, and she was certain he knew what had occupied her mind so much she'd missed what he'd said. Then he smiled and patted her hand. "No matter. I was just recounting for Julie some of my boyhood memories of Harrogate." He tilted his head as if to better see his daughter's face. "You look tired. Perhaps you should retire early."

Happy for the excuse to go to the privacy of her room, Sara took her napkin from her lap and then laid it beside her barely touched dinner plate. "I am a bit tired. And I have to admit that, right now, the thought of snuggling down under Gran's quilt holds great appeal." She stood, kissed her father's cheek, and smiled at Julie. "I'll see you both in the morning."

Preston Wade lit his cigar and settled onto the bench in the garden. Cicadas filled the night with their music, but just as he'd begun to enjoy their song, they suddenly went silent. Deciding that something, a raccoon or a possum, had scared them into silence, he leaned back and gazed at the full moon hanging like a large lemon in the sky. He soaked in the silence with a contented sigh. It was good to be back here where he'd grown up, where his dear mother had lived. Until this very moment, he hadn't realized how much he'd missed not only his daughter but also Harrogate.

Thoughts of Sara brought a crease to his smooth brow. Something troubled her deeply. He could feel it. But until she chose to talk to him about it, he could do nothing. Perhaps when she found the letter—

"She has vowed not to look for it."

The man's voice yanked Preston out of his relaxed state and brought him to attention. The abrupt silence of the night creatures should have told him all was not as it should be and he was not alone. He swung toward the voice. Standing a few yards away was a man dressed in clothes from a bygone time, and nearly transparent.

Having seen apparitions like this before, Preston calmly stood, then descended to the pathway and faced him.

"And you are?"

"Jonathan Bradford."

"Ah. At last we meet." Preston stubbed out his cigar on the stone path and discarded the butt into a clump of azaleas. "What makes you think Sara won't look for the letter?"

"She's convinced Katherine will do harm to her or those close to her."

Preston frowned. So that's what Sara meant about this involving more than just her. "And will she?"

The ghost walked closer. "No one can predict what Katherine will do. If that were possible, then this might have been avoided." He pulled back his coat to reveal a bloody shirt and a gaping hole in the center of his chest.

Knowing the story of Jonathan's demise, Preston only started slightly at the grisly spectacle. His interest lay elsewhere. "Who did this to you?"

Jonathan shook his head. "I don't know. All I remember is the flash of the gun, a woman's scream, and then a searing pain in my chest. Then nothing. Next thing I knew, I was like this." He spread his arms to encompass his translucent body, then dropped them back to his sides and looked imploringly at Preston. "You must convince Sara not to give up. She has to find the letter."

"And if I can't?"

Jonathan's expression crumpled. "Then I will have lost her again."

"And do you love her?"

"More than life itself."

Preston thought for a moment, unsure if he should say what sat heavily on his mind. "She is not Maddy Grayson," he finally said. "You know that."

Jonathan made no reply. He just smiled and then bowed. "I believe that is for Sara to decide."

Before Preston could say more, the apparition faded and the cicadas began to sing their night song again. Preston sat heavily on the bench. Acute heartache infused his very bones.

Had Gran been speaking the truth? Did Sara's destiny lie with Jonathan? And, if that destiny were fulfilled, Preston knew he would never see his beloved daughter again. But in his heart he knew that even if he lost her forever, he could not deny Sara her happiness.

All the next day, Sara fluctuated between wanting to search the house for the letter and telling herself such a move could incite Katherine's wrath again, with awful consequences . . . possibly not just to her. By the time her father's departure rolled around, she still hadn't made a decision about what to do.

With his arm securely around her shoulders, Preston walked with Sara to the front steps of Harrogate. Fighting back tears, she turned to kiss him good-bye.

"Promise me you'll search for the letter," he said, his face grimly serious.

He had no idea what he was asking. "I . . . can't do that." Her voice, choked with tears, emerged weakly.

Framing her face in his big hands, Preston looked deep into her eyes. "You must."

"Why?"

"Jonathan." With that one word, he kissed her cheek and said, "Goodbye, my lovely child. Remember I love you . . . always, no matter what happens." Then he climbed into the carriage and motioned for the driver to leave.

Sara stood on the front portico and watched until her father's carriage disappeared around a curve in the drive. His last words seemed so . . . final. As if he'd expected to never see her again. A cold cramp clutched her heart. First she'd lost Jonathan, and now she sensed that in some strange way, she'd also lost her father.

As she turned to walk back into the house, Sara remembered how excited and full of plans she'd been when, such a short time ago, she'd climbed these very steps for the first time as the mistress of Harrogate. Happiness had filled every fiber of her being.

The way things had been going recently, she was beginning to wonder if she'd ever feel that kind of happiness again. Right now, she doubted it. With the weight of the world resting on her slim shoulders, happiness seemed very elusive.

Since Julie had gone into town to do some shopping and planned to stay overnight rather than making the long trek back to Harrogate after dark, Sara ate alone that evening. Once she'd been served and the dishes cleaned up, Raina and Chloe had gone to the slave quarters to visit with Litisha and her new baby.

With no reason to stay downstairs, Sara retired to her room early. Purposefully, she avoided even a glance at the trunk at the foot of the bed that held Maddy's diary hidden away in its depths. Instead, she sat in her favorite chair overlooking the Garden of the Moon. All around her, the room was bathed in darkness, but outside, the garden was alive with light. The moon had turned the flowers to an iridescent white, and the moonflowers had opened their hearts to the rays. Some of the magnolias had dropped their creamy leaves on the grounds, looking like circular tuffs of cotton sprinkled over the grass. Even the white stones in the pathway seemed to gleam with the moon's light, transforming them into scattered pearls.

As the serenity of the garden and the silence of the house settled around her, Sara's mind drifted off to the very place it had spent most of the last two days—the letter. How she wished her father had never told her about Gran's visit to him or her message. But he had, and now Sara had to make a decision.

Should she look for the letter, or should she keep her vow to end her quest for answers to the dilemma in which Gran had left her immersed? What would happen if she did nothing? But more importantly, what would happen if she took action?

Unable to ignore the urge, she turned to Jonathan's portrait.

"Help me, Jonathan. Tell me what I should do." She waited for some sign, but none came. His expression remained frozen in the smile the artist had painted on it. Evidently, she would have to find her own answers.

Then her father's words echoed through her head. *You must.* He'd been so emphatic, so forceful. And then his answer to her query as to why she had to find the letter . . . *Jonathan.*

That one word, more than anything else her father could have said, had the power to make up her mind for her. For Jonathan, she would walk barefoot to the ends of the earth. She would look for the letter. But where?

After having circuited the entire problem several times over the past days, she found herself back at the beginning. Where in this vast house could the letter be hidden? Mentally, she had searched everywhere from the basement to—

The attic! Of course. Wasn't that where she'd found Maddy's diary? Didn't it make sense that she would have hidden the letter there as well?

Sara sprang to her feet and rushed from her room. She hurried down the hall to the attic door. When she realized she'd have to go up there alone, she hesitated. Then, before she could lose her nerve, she threw open the door and hurriedly began to climb the staircase.

She stumbled over the hem of her dress and went down to her knees. Hoisting her dress, she continued to the top. Not until she stood inside the attic's dank heat and gazed around at the inky darkness did she realize she'd been so eager to begin her search that she hadn't brought any source of light. Cursing her own stupidity, she retraced her steps. Just as she reached the bottom of the attic stairs, the latch sprang back into place with a loud *click*. Sara grabbed the door latch and pulled, but no matter how hard she tugged at it, it wouldn't budge.

She was locked in.

Chapter 14

Pounding on the door, Sara screamed for help. "Someone? I'm locked in the attic. Help me."

But no help came. With a sinking heart, she realized no help would come. Everyone had left the house. Julie wouldn't be home until tomorrow morning, and there was no guessing when Raina and Chloe would return from the slave quarters. Even if they did, they'd never hear her at the back of the house in their unattached house slaves' quarters.

The seclusion she'd been thankful for not minutes before, now punctuated the hopeless situation she'd gotten herself into. Fighting down panic that would serve no purpose, she sank to the dusty stairs and prepared herself for a long night of waiting to be found.

Then that familiar high-pitched laugh resounded off the walls. Sara jerked her gaze to the attic platform above her. Two disembodied, large, evil eyes swooped down on her, then receded, then swooped again and receded. The laughter grew so loud, Sara had to cover her ears.

Katherine.

Anger boiled up in Sara. She'd had enough of this woman's games. The time had come for her to stand up to Katherine Grayson and let her know she wasn't going to win this time. "Do your best, Katherine. Jonathan is mine, and I *will* find the letter." Her angry voice reverberated off the attic walls.

The laughter stopped, and the haunting eyes faded into the dusty air.

Then, just above her, Sara caught sight of a small oak chest of drawers teetering on the edge of the opening to the stairs. It swayed back and forth as though attached to a string that kept retrieving it just before it toppled over. In horror, she watched as it continued its macabre dance, unsure what frightened her most—the possibility that the dresser would fall on her or the bizarre spectacle itself. Fear choked her breathing. Despite the smothering heat in the attic, chills raced over her entire body.

Keeping her gaze fixed on the dresser, she waited for the worst.

Still the dresser continued to teeter back and forth.

Each time, it leaned farther over the stairwell.

She curled into a ball, her hands over her head to protect it. Just when she'd begun to wonder if it would fall, the stillness of the attic was fractured by the loud screeching of wood on wood. Unable to keep her eyes closed, she peeked above her just as the dresser tumbled over the edge. She braced for the impact, but it never came.

After a loud *thunk* some inches above her head, she chanced another look. The dresser, too big to fit into the narrow opening, had become wedged in the stairwell about two feet over her head. She waited to see if it would drop more, but it didn't move. Fate had been on her side for a change.

Content with her safety and suddenly very tired, and feeling very foolish, she sat down on the stairs, cradled her head on her arms and waited for morning and someone to rescue her.

As she lay there, mentally chastising herself for coming alone on her mission to find the letter, anger boiled inside her at what Katherine had intended. Despite being exhausted, courage born of her love for Jonathan grew inside her.

Raising her head so she could look into the inky darkness above her, she vehemently mumbled, "I *will* find the letter, and you should be warned: I won't die easily."

Cool air roused Sara from her fitful sleep. Forcing her eyes open, she could see the attic was bathed in soft light from the one attic window. She greeted the morning with a cry of delight. The dresser was still wedged in the stairwell above her.

It took her a moment to uncurl her body and stretch her cramped muscles. Tentatively, she pulled herself to a half standing, half stooped position with the help of the wall for leverage. Very slowly the flow of blood restored sensation to her numb limbs, and along with it came the memory of her situation.

Quickly, she tried the door latch and found it still refused to budge. Her only hope of getting out of here was to get someone's attention from the window.

Gathering her grimy skirts around her, she slid beneath the dresser and crawled up the stairs until she could stand upright. Then she climbed to the attic landing and hurried to the window. Using the hem of her dress, she scrubbed one of the small panes clean and peered below at the front yard. No matter how much she craned her neck and searched, as far as she could see, not one person was visible anywhere. She sighed and leaned back against the window frame. Tears of frustration blurred her vision.

Reminded again of her own stupidity, and unmindful of the grime from the pane coating her hands, she swiped the tears from her eyes.

But tears would not unlock the door, and neither would frustration.

You made it through Katherine's attempts to crush you under a dresser and spent the night curled up on the stairs because you were locked in here. Certainly you can hold yourself together until you can catch someone's eye and you're let out.

Pulling a moth-eaten chair to the window, Sara sat down and prepared to wait until she spotted a rescuer.

Sara had no idea how much time had passed. To her it seemed like days. From the position of the sun in the east, she guessed the time to be a few hours past daybreak. Julie would be home soon. Raina would be serving breakfast and wondering where her mistress was. Hope blossomed inside her. Certainly Raina would come looking for her.

But that hope died as quickly as it was given birth. Aside from the attic being the very last place anyone would look, both Raina and Julie normally let Sara sleep until she woke up on her own. If she wasn't down in the dining room, Raina would assume she was just sleeping late. And, since Julie wasn't even home yet, neither of them would come looking for her if she wasn't downstairs for breakfast. They had yet to get over the time when Sara roamed her room until the wee hours of the night trying to find a way back to Jonathan, and they still felt she needed her sleep.

Just when she began to sink back in hopelessness, movement on the lawn below caught her eye. Raina was coming up the path from the garden with a basket of vegetables for Chloe.

Hope rising in her, Sara pounded on the window. Though Raina looked around for the source of the sound, she never looked up at the window. Sara pounded again—harder this time, and with an added cry for help.

"Up here, Raina. I'm up here."

Raina again glanced around, but still didn't look up.

Desperate to gain Raina's attention before she disappeared inside the house, Sara grabbed a tarnished silver candlestick and swung it hard at the glass. The resulting explosion rained glass all over the floor and down on Raina. Cool, fresh, clean air rushed in at Sara through the broken window.

The falling shards of glass had finally drawn Raina's attention, and she looked up.

Sara stuck her hand through the opening and waved

it. "Up here, Raina."

Shading her eyes against the glare of the sun, the maid stared up at her, mouth agape. "Miss Sara, whatcha doin' up there? You should be in the dinin' room havin' yo breakfast."

Sara couldn't very well tell her she'd been up here all night looking for a letter from a ghost. Not Raina. She had to think fast. "I . . . I came up here last night to see if I could find . . ." *Find what?* She struggled to finish the thought. "I was looking for a mirror to replace the one on my dresser," she finally blurted. "Mine got broken."

Raina shook her head.

"Ain't fittin' fo you to be doin' dat. Samuel take care of it. Now, you come down from there right now an gits yo breakfast."

"I can't. I'm locked in," Sara called back. "Come open the door for me."

"How you do dat?" Raina, one hand on her hip, craned her neck to see Sara.

"Just come let me out." No need for further explanation that would more than likely scare the bejesus out of the poor girl. "Now, please!"

Raina nodded and ran toward the house.

A few minutes later, the door opened to reveal Raina, a puzzled expression on her face. "Door wasn't locked, Miss Sara."

"Yes, it was. I tried to open it over and over, and the latch wouldn't budge."

Raina looked down at the latch, then back at Sara. "Can't be. Dey's no way to lock dis here door."

Julie joined Sara on the veranda, where she'd retired to sit in the shade of the huge Corinthian columns to think about the mess she'd ended up in the evening before. How did a door that had no lock get locked? She didn't have to wonder *who* did it, just *how*. She couldn't think of a logical explanation. Then again, Katherine had managed quite a few things that didn't come with rational explanations.

"Raina tells me you locked yourself in the attic last night." Julie sat in the wicker chair beside Sara and folded her hands in her lap. A half smile curled her lips. "Mind telling me how you managed that?"

Casting a sidelong glance at Julie, Sara centered her attention on the young black boy sweeping the drive with a bundle of twigs. Dust clouds rose in the air, reminding her of the choking dust in the attic. A chill chased down her spine.

"I don't care what either of you think. I *was* locked in. It was not my imagination."

She hesitated for a moment. "Katherine did it."

Julie's expression lost any hint of amusement. Her gray eyes grew to the size of lemons. "Katherine?"

Sara nodded, and then turned toward her friend. Leaving nothing out, she told her the events of the night before.

"You're very fortunate the dresser got wedged in the stairwell. But how can you be certain it was Katherine?"

Sara frowned. "Who else would want to hurt me?"

Obviously having no reply to that, Julie just shook her head. "Why did you go up there anyway?"

"To look for a letter."

"A letter? From whom?"

"From Katherine to Maddy. My father said Gran told him about it and that I had to find it."

"Did he say why?"

"No. He said Gran never told him."

A thoughtful silence grew between them. Finally, Julie spoke again. "What made you think it was in the attic?"

"That's where I found Maddy's diary." Sara shrugged. "It just seemed like the logical place to look."

"Maybe it seemed so, especially since Katherine went after you again. But I have to wonder if it is up there. If she didn't want you to find it, why would she lock you inside the very place it was hidden?"

Perhaps being frightened out of her mind had impeded Sara's cognitive thinking. She hadn't considered that, but what Julie said made a lot of sense. If the letter had been up there, it made more sense for Katherine to lock Sara *out* of the room, not *in* it.

She sighed resignedly. So that meant she was back to the start. Where else could the letter be?

That night, pushing the letter from her thoughts with the hope that looking at the mystery of its whereabouts with a fresh eye in the morning would help, Sara considered this last attack by her nemesis. The thing that stood out in her mind was that, this time, she'd been the only one in danger. After weighing the events of the last few days, she decided that Katherine's wrath had been aimed at only her all along.

She had no proof that Katherine had set the fire. Barn fires were not an uncommon occurrence on plantations. A careless slave, dry hay, the sun focused through a window pane, lightning—all caused fires. The barn fire may well have been coincidence but because of the strange happenings at Harrogate, Sara had automatically relegated the blame to Katherine.

She glanced at the portrait of Jonathan above the mantel. His dear face made her yearn to be with him. It had been so very long since she'd seen him—really seen him. Oh, she'd sensed his presence, but she wanted to *see* him, to be held by him, to feel his lips on hers. Until this very moment, Sara hadn't realized how empty she was inside, how lonely her soul was without him, how very much she missed him.

Unable to look at his dear face any longer, Sara turned away, tears streaking down her cheeks. She bent double to ease the pain slicing through her heart to its very core. Sobs issued from her in a deep choking outpouring of her sorrow. Despite her vow to end this, she could not remove the thorn of desolation from her soul.

A long time later, the sobs ceased, leaving her drained and empty. The tears had done no good. The pain of this separation from the man she loved—ghost or mortal, it made no difference—just could not be assuaged.

Sara dried her eyes and laid the handkerchief on the table at her side. As she did so, she saw something that stopped her heart cold—Maddy's diary. Suddenly, as though mobilized by a strong wind, the book flopped open and the pages began flipping wildly. When they finally stopped, Sara stared at the date. It was the very day after the date of the entry she'd read last.

But the diary had been locked in her grandmother's trunk. *How did it . . .*

She turned to Jonathan's portrait. His smile had deepened. Returning his smile, she picked up the book and began to read.

> *June 21, 1805*
>
> *The days have passed slowly, the nights even slower. I lay awake at night thinking of Jonathan, of his arms about me, his kiss pressing on my lips, his gentle voice whispering words of love in my ear. At times, I think I shall die of wanting him. At others, I try to believe that Katherine will relent and free him. I think I shall never know what it is to be truly happy again.*
>
> *This morning, no longer able to stand the ache in my heart, I made a decision. I went to Katherine's room to beg her to release Jonathan from their betrothal, but she would hear none of it. She actually glared at me with an expression that chilled me to the bone and said, "He will never be yours." There was something ominous in the tone of her voice, as though she'd do anything to keep him from me. I continued to try to persuade her . . .*

The room began to spin, and Sara gladly gave herself up to it, eager to reach the end result.

Maddy stood just inside the doorway to her sister's bedroom. Katherine sat at her dressing table, still clothed in her filmy, white nightgown and calmly running a brush through her waist-length, brown hair.

"You demean yourself with all this begging, Maddy."

She stared at her sister's back, her mirrored expression sending fear filtering through Maddy. She'd seen Katherine at her worst, but even that did not reach the level of the evil she saw in her sister's eyes and heard in her tone at this moment.

Still, Maddy pressed on. "You don't love him. Why are you doing this?"

Katherine scoffed at Maddy's question as if it were some kind of joke. "Love is for fools. Love has nothing at all to do with why I'm marrying Jonathan." She smiled malevolently at Maddy's refection in her mirror. "I'm doing it, *sister* dear, because at last I have the very thing you want most in the world, the thing you would give your life to possess." She swung around, her brown eyes glittering as she glared at Maddy. "And I fully intend to keep him, so don't pin your hopes on him ever being free to marry you. Jonathan Bradford is mine."

Maddy's heart sank. She'd hoped against hope that she could talk woman to woman and change her sister's mind. Obviously, she'd been blowing smoke in the wind. Katherine was taking an inordinate amount of pleasure from Maddy's heartbreak and wasn't about to set Jonathan free.

"Now, if you'll excuse me, I have to get dressed. Mother and I are going to the dressmakers for a fitting on my wedding gown. That is, if that lazy maid ever gets in here to help me dress." She threw the brush down, stomped across the floor, pushed Maddy aside, and leaned out the door. "Floree! Get your black ass in here, now!"

Maddy cringed at Katherine's verbal laceration of the gentle black woman who had taken care of both of them since birth. Many times she'd begged Katherine to treat the maid better, but she knew that, as with her insane hunger to hold onto Jonathan, nothing Maddy said would make Katherine develop a gentler attitude toward Floree. Even though their mother and father had objected to Katherine's lack of feelings when dealing with their slaves, she continued to treat them callously.

Moments later, Floree bustled into Katherine's room. Her breathing was labored from running up the long flight of stairs. "Sorry, Miss Katherine. I's tendin' a birthin' in the quarters. Chile came behind first. The po momma—"

Katherine threw up her hand to stop the flow of words. "Shut . . . up! I don't want to hear about some worthless nigra's childbearing problems. Lay out my dress and do my hair. Now!"

"Yes 'um." Floree's entire body seemed to melt into submission to Katherine's demands. She picked up the brush and began brushing Katherine's hair.

"This midwife nonsense is interfering with your household duties, Floree. I intend to speak to Momma and Papa about stopping it. You have enough to do right here in the house."

Floree turned to Maddy with pleading eyes.

"Katherine, Floree takes care of all her duties quite well. There's no reason she should not continue to be our slaves' midwife. It takes a lot of extra burden off Momma's shoulders."

Katherine's lips were moving, but Maddy couldn't hear what she was saying. The room began to spin. Her head felt light. Her mouth wouldn't work. Something was sucking her into a spinning tunnel.

Chapter 15

Sara had barely slept the night before. All she could think about was getting to Floree and finding out more about the letter and her nemesis, Katherine. As soon as she'd returned from Maddy's world, she'd recalled Floree being present at the birthing of Litisha's child that she and Julie had attended in the slave quarters. Given the advanced age of the freewoman Negro midwife, Sara had no doubt she was the same slave who had taken care of Maddy and Katherine as children and then as young women.

Not wanting either Julie or Raina to come with her, she had sent word through one of the other house slaves for Samuel to saddle a horse for her. Donning Gran's old riding breeches, which she'd found buried in Gran's trunk, she hurried through the house and out the back door. Samuel waited just beyond a crop of oak trees with two horses. One horse sported a side saddle for Sara; the other, a standard saddle.

"I asked for one horse to be saddled, Samuel. Who's the extra horse for?" she asked when she got close enough to be heard.

His eyes widened at the sight of her breeches, but he said nothing. "Horse fo me, Miss Sara."

"I'm going alone." She took the reins of the horse with the standard saddle from Samuel.

"No, you isn't. Yo momma would swoon at the sight of ya in dem pants, and yo daddy would skin me alive if he knew I let you ride astride dat horse by yoself."

"Momma and Papa aren't here, Samuel, and I'm mistress of this plantation. I'll decide what I wear when I ride and what horse I'll ride. Now, help me up."

"Yas, 'um. But it ain't fittin'. No sir, ain't fittin' at all." Shaking his head, Samuel cupped his hands and leaned forward. "Put yo foot here."

Sara did as he instructed. He hoisted her up, and she settled into the saddle. Taking the reins in her hands, she looked down at him. "I should be back before anyone knows I'm gone." She started to move away, and then stopped. "And if you're worried about Papa finding out, my advice is . . . don't tell him." She swung the horse away from him and then quickly prodded it into a full gallop and disappeared down the drive.

Through some discreet questioning of one of the house servants, Sara had found out that the little cottage Seth Grayson had given Floree when he'd freed her was located on River Road, halfway between Harrogate and Brentwood, the Graysons' plantation. The girl hadn't known exactly where—only that it was past the second bend in the river. As Sara passed the second bend, she slowed her horse and scanned her surroundings. Even as careful as she had been in her search, she nearly rode right past it.

The little weathered shack in which Floree lived lay nearly hidden by a dense grove of cottonwood trees. Although the rundown house appeared to be something most people would have torn down and used for firewood, the pride the old woman took in having a place to call her own was obvious in the neat, well-kept yard. Wildflowers had been transplanted into a small garden bordering the one rickety stair leading up to the porch. A black and white cow grazed a few feet from the house, and a butter churn and a rocking chair sat side by side near the door, which, though now faded, apparently had been at one time a garish shade of red. White muslin curtains fluttered through the open, glassless windows.

Sara slid from the horse's back and tied him to one of the oak trees. Glancing around for any sign of life, she made her way to the front door and knocked. The sound of shuffling feet could be heard coming from inside. Moments later, the door opened to reveal a small, slender, black woman with snowy hair pulled back in a tight bun and several teeth missing from her welcoming smile.

But very quickly, the smile melted like hot wax. Her eyes grew large and fearful. Color drained from her face. Mouth agape, she clamped a hand to her breast and took a step back. "Lord Almighty!"

Sara didn't have to wonder what had caused Floree to look so startled. The day she and Julie had attended the birthing, Sara hadn't gone inside the cabin where the midwife was attending the new mother, so Floree had never seen her. Now, face to face, the poor woman had to think she was gazing at Maddy Grayson's ghost.

"Floree, I'm Sara Wade from Harrogate." She waited for her words to sink in. "Alice Wade's granddaughter."

"You're not—"

Sara smiled kindly. "No, I'm not Maddy's ghost. I just look a lot like her."

"Enough to be more her twin than Katherine," Floree stated emphatically, the color slowly returning to her cheeks.

Sara was suddenly struck by what good English Floree spoke. When she'd gone back in time, the woman had spoken with the same broken patois of Raina and Chloe. "You speak so . . ."

"Good?" Floree finished for her. "Miss Katherine said she didn't like my *darky* talk. Said she couldn't understand that gibberish. So she talked her daddy into letting me have lessons to learn English. Course, it had to be done in secret, 'cause it's against the law to teach any Nigra anything but how to pick cotton or clean a house. I got so used to speaking proper to keep her from flying into one of her fits that pretty soon it was as natural to me as falling off a log." Then without further explanation, she opened the door wider and stepped to the side. "Don't suppose you came here to stand on the porch and talk. Come in and sit. I'll make us some tea."

While Floree bustled about getting their tea ready, Sara watched her and marveled at her agility. She had to be in her eighties or even her nineties. For a woman of her advanced years, she was in remarkably good health. And her little house was immaculate. No dirt on the floor. A colorful patchwork quilt neatly covering the single bed in the corner of the one room.

Suddenly, Floree began to chuckle to herself, and then she turned to Sara. "I remember your grandma riding astride across the fields in breeches just like those. Hair blowing loose in the wind. A big smile on her face. Horse just about flying across the ground. Lord, but she was a sight to behold!" Her smile deepened. "Scandalized all the ladies on the neighbor plantations to within an inch of their lives, she did."

"The breeches are hers, and, just between us, I think she secretly enjoyed shocking the ladies almost as much as she enjoyed riding that horse." They both laughed. Sara found she liked Floree a lot. Considering Floree's quick wit and ready smile, she couldn't understand how Katherine had been so disagreeable with the woman.

"Yes, she sure enough did. She was a fine lady, your grandma." Floree sighed deeply, and her shoulders slumped, as though the memories were too heavy for her to bear. Then she shrugged and finished preparing their drinks. "You drink this, and I guarantees you'll feel like a new woman."

She set a cracked cup in front on Sara and placed another one on the other side of the table for herself. No doubt the china cups and saucers were castoffs from the big house, but she could see that Floree prized them as though they'd just arrived on the boat from Europe's best china maker.

Then Floree lowered her body slowly into the chair. "Now, child, what is it that brings you to visit an old Nigra lady on a fine day such as this?"

Unsure, now that she was here, what she'd come for,

Sara stalled for time by sipping her tea, surprised at the hint of peppermint in it. "This is delicious."

Floree smiled. "Knew you'd like it. It was Miss Maddy's favorite."

"I'm not Ma—"

Floree grinned. "You sure?"

No, she wasn't sure of anything anymore. Even so, Floree's question took her by surprise. However, she gave no answer.

Floree nodded. "Now, what is it you want to know?"

For some reason, Sara relaxed. "Tell me about Maddy and Katherine."

For a moment, it was as if Floree hadn't heard her. Memories clouded her eyes. "I was just five when they were born. I wasn't there for the birthin', but I got to hold them later. Two beautiful little girls. Missus was so happy. Directly after the births, Master Seth sold the gal who attended Miss Grayson at the birth to a fella from Tennessee, and then he rode right off to the Bradfords' to let them know their future daughter-in-law had been born. Before he left, he and the missus had some angry words. After he left, Missus didn't say anything, but you could tell she didn't like the idea of the betrothal. She said babies need time to be babies, but Master had made a promise, and he was honor bound to keep it. Miss Katherine would marry Jonathan Bradford."

Sara knew most of that. She wanted to hear something Clarice hadn't already told her. "What about when they got older?"

Floree shook her head. "I should have knowed when they were babies what we'd be in for with the two of them. Miss Maddy was as sweet a baby as the good Lord ever put on this here earth. Smiled and cooed and just loved everybody. Miss Katherine was just plain cantankerous from the start. Colicky, didn't sleep more'n an hour or two at a time, didn't want nobody but her momma to hold her." Floree shook her head and made a *tsking* sound with her tongue. "That one sure was a handful. Yup, she sure enough was."

She refreshed their tea from a teapot that matched the cups. "And she got worse as she got older. I never saw anybody who could fly into a rage so fast or who could hate another person like she hated her sister." She stopped talking and stared hard at Sara. "But I don't need to tell you that, do I? You got the sight, don't you? Just like your grandma." Floree didn't seem frightened by this revelation. As a matter of fact, she seemed pleased.

Sara didn't hesitate to affirm Floree's statement. "Yes, I do. How did you know?"

The old freewoman smiled knowingly. "Cause we have a look about us, don't *we?*"

"We?" Sara's mouth fell open. "You're . . ." Floree

simply smiled and nodded. Was that why she wouldn't go inside the big house? "Have you seen Katherine's ghost?"

"I don't need to see her. I know she's there. I can feel her when I go inside that house." She shivered. "That woman's as evil dead as she ever was alive." She shook her long finger at Sara. "What with you looking like Miss Maddy, you best be careful."

Memories of her run-ins with Katherine sent a chill down Sara's spine. She nodded, not about to go into all that had happened in past weeks. "I will, but I need you to tell me if you know anything about a letter that Katherine wrote to Maddy and what happened to it."

Floree stiffened. "I know Miss Katherine wrote a letter when she was in the Ursuline Convent, 'cause I delivered it to Miss Maddy. She said I was to give it to only Miss Maddy, that it was a secret only Miss Maddy could know. I did what she told me, but I don't know where it is now. I expect Miss Maddy burned it, being it was from her sister and all."

"The Ursuline Convent?" Somehow, Sara had a hard time believing someone like Katherine had turned religious and become a nun. "What was she doing there?"

Floree lowered her gaze and shook her head slowly. "It's not a pretty tale, Miss Sara. Nope. Not pretty at all." Floree took a deep, fortifying breath. "After Mr. Jonathan was killed, Miss Katherine started drinking heavy, that green stuff, abs . . . absin—"

"Absinthe?"

"Yes. Seems the more she drank the worse she got until she went a little . . ." Floree stopped talking and tapped her finger against her temple. "Her papa finally sent the poor thing off to the convent. I think it was to hide his shame about having someone in their family who wasn't right. He sent me to see to her. That's why he give me this house and set me free—to thank me for taking care of his child. He told everyone she'd got that yellow jack fever and had to be nursed by the nuns." She shook her head as though to clear her thoughts. "She was there for nearly three years before she died. But just before she passed on to wherever it is that souls as black as hers go, she wrote the letter and made me swear to take it to her sister."

"You don't know what the letter said?"

"No. I just delivered it. With Miss Katherine not being in her right mind, no telling what she put in that letter." Floree frowned thoughtfully. "Lord only knows. She never told me, but I was sure it was just one more evil thing she was bent on doing before she died. Even then, she couldn't leave poor Miss Maddy alone."

Floree's explanation did nothing to either help Sara find the letter or hint at what could have made it so important for her to read. What was the secret Katherine wanted only Maddy to know?

Chapter 16

Sara was beginning to feel like a member of the newly formed Pinkerton Detective Agency she'd heard about. The problem was that with further investigation, whereas the agency probably got answers, she just faced a bigger dilemma and more unanswered questions.

Floree knew about the letter, had even delivered it, but had no idea what it contained. Though she hadn't thought so at first, Sara was beginning to believe something in it was vital to her solving this puzzle.

Mentally and physically exhausted, she arrived home only to be met by an indignant Raina, who, though she didn't say it, was visibly upset that Sara not only had left the house dressed in breeches but also had gone riding without an escort. Julie just snickered behind Raina's back. Probably because she knew whatever reprimand the maid could rain down on Sara's head would do no good. Just like her grandmother, Sara had a mind of her own, and if she wanted to do something, neither hell nor high water would stop her. Too tired to give the maid the satisfaction of an explanation, Sara went straight to her room and changed for dinner.

Later, after dinner, while she and Julie sat on the veranda sipping Chloe's strong Creole coffee, Sara was not surprised when Julie began to question her about where she'd been all day.

"I went to talk to Floree about that letter Papa mentioned."

"And?"

"Nothing. She knew about it and even delivered it to Maddy, but she has no idea what was in it."

For a long time, Julie said nothing. Then, finally, she turned in her chair and faced Sara. "Why don't you give up this whole business about Jonathan and Maddy and Katherine? It's done nothing but disrupt your life, put you in danger, and keep you so distracted that you can't concentrate on anything else."

"I wish I could. I've truly tried, but I can't." She took Julie's hand and squeezed it. "Have you ever been in love? I don't mean just an infatuation. I mean really, truly in love."

Julie shook her head, and Sara saw a fleeting sadness come into her eyes. "No."

"It's unlike anything else I've ever experienced. Like living in another world where everything centers around the person you love. Every thought, every move, every moment of every day is filled to overflowing with him. I wake up thinking about Jonathan, and I go to sleep thinking about him." Her cheeks grew warm, and she dipped her head to hide her blush from Julie. "I know, since he's a ghost, that it's crazy, but I don't feel like he's a ghost. To me he's as real as you are."

Julie sighed. "But that's just it, Sara. He's not real, at least not in the sense of being alive. What kind of future will you have loving him? You won't be able to have children. You certainly can't introduce—"

Sara sprang to her feet. "I know all that," she said hotly, more angered at the truth of Julie's words than at Julie. "I know all that," she repeated more calmly. "But it doesn't change anything. I still love him."

How could she explain to Julie that Jonathan was as much a part of her as the air she breathed? That she could no more forget him than she could forget to take her next breath or ignore the next sunrise.

"There's nothing I can do to change your mind?"

"No." Sara turned to face her. "But there is something else you can do for me. You can be my friend, support me, and try to understand I *have* to do this."

For a long moment, Julie said nothing, and Sara thought she would refuse her request. Then she stood, hugged Sara, and put her at arm's length. "I'll always be your friend, no matter what. I will support whatever decision you make, even if I don't agree with it. And I will try my best to understand why you're doing this." She kissed Sara's cheek. "Now, I'm going to bed. How about you?"

Smiling, Sara linked her arm in Julie's, and together they entered the house and climbed the stairs.

Maybe it was because of the talk with Julie. Maybe it was because, no matter how much she denied it to herself, missing Jonathan had become a constant agony gripping her heart like a fist. Whichever it was, Sara knew tonight she would go back to see him again.

When she reached her room, Sara took out Maddy's diary and settled in her chair by the window. She glanced out at the garden and inhaled deeply. The mixture of perfumes emanating from it brought a profound peace to her soul. Then, as she always did before going back in time, she cast a glance at the portrait over the mantel.

Jonathan was smiling. Not the smile the artist had

portrayed, but the smile that was just for her . . . for Maddy. She smiled back and then opened the diary to the last entry she'd read, June 21. Then, taking a deep breath, she turned to the next page, but the date stopped her dead.

July 3, 1805.

Sara turned the pages back and checked to make sure they hadn't stuck together, but they hadn't. Maddy had skipped two weeks of entries. Why? Until now, she'd entered something every day for the past year. Why, now, had she not entered anything for so long?

Perhaps she'd explain in the entry. Sara leaned back and positioned the book so the light from the oil lamps beside her fell on the pages. Undeniable excitement flowed through her like syrup on a hot day. Totally aware that the sensation came from her excitement at once more seeing Jonathan and with the anticipation growing inside her like rising bread in a warm kitchen, she began to read.

July 3, 1805

For a time, it seemed the days passed with all the speed of a tortoise. But now the time has passed quickly, too quickly, and the wedding is nearly upon us. Depression has taken its toll on me. I haven't seen Jonathan and, as a result, have not had the heart to write anything until now. His absence from my life is a ball and chain around my heart.

But tonight that will change. For a few fleeting moments, I will be with him. I'm wearing the blue gown he likes so much and have brushed my hair until it glows. I've left it around my shoulders. Jonathan likes it that way so he can run his fingers through it.

As I write this, I am waiting for the rest of the people in the house to go to sleep. Once I'm sure they will not discover my absence, I will slip out to meet Jonathan in the grove of trees beyond the barn. He sent word that he has something very important to tell me, something that will make me very happy. I'm hoping it will be that Katherine has come to her senses and broken their betrothal. But, in my soul, I have little hope of that happening. Had she released him from their betrothal, it would have been big news around the house, and no one has said anything of the kind.

My heart is beating so hard, I fear it will burst right out of my chest. Just the thought of being in his arms again is exhilarating. Whatever he has to tell me cannot be as important as being close to him again. I have missed him so very, very much.

Yesterday, when we went to Brentwood to see the Bradford's to finalize plans for the wedding, which Katherine showed little or no interest in being a part of, I expected to see Jonathan. However, he wasn't there. The disappointment was stifling. His father said Jonathan had gone to New Orleans the week before on business. The misery that took a hold on me from the news was almost paralyzing. I want to take advantage of every moment we still have. Once he's married, I will no longer be able to make excuses to see him, to be alone with him.

But I must not dwell on what can't be and what has passed. I must look forward to tonight. It has been hours, and I'm sure the house is asleep. It is time . . .

The room began to spin, and soon Sara was whirling through that familiar tunnel to Jonathan.

Maddy made her way through the thick grove of cottonwood trees. Her breathing came hard, partially due to the exertion of fighting her way through the trees and underbrush, but mostly due to the prospect of seeing who waited for her at the end.

As she rounded a particularly large tree, a hand covered her mouth and stifled the scream that rose in her throat. Then someone dragged her into the thickening shadows. Fear filled her to the exclusion of all other emotions. Had Katherine decided to abduct her? She struggled to get free.

"Shh, my love. It's me." Warm breath fanned her ear. Then gentle lips caressed her cheek.

All struggle stopped. She spun in his arms and then snuggled against his broad chest and looped her arms around his neck. "I missed you so much. I'd so hoped to see you yesterday."

He set her back from him. She could barely see his face in the darkness, but she didn't need to. Every line, every wrinkle, every pore was written indelibly on her memory.

"I was in New Orleans making plans for us."

She stared at him. "Us? I don't understand. The wedding—"

Gently, he stopped her words with fingers to her lips and then moved her next to a fallen tree trunk and pulled her down beside him. "Forget the wedding. There's not going to be a marriage . . . at least none between Katherine and me."

"Katherine called off the betrothal?" Her heartbeat raced with excitement.

"No. She's still determined to go through with it."

"Then how—" Again he stopped her words, but this time with his lips. Fiery sparks sang through her blood. She clung to him, absorbing the sweetness of his mouth on hers. Her heart beat triple time. She buried her fingers in his silky hair and held his mouth to hers.

But he pulled away and cupped her face in his hands. "I would love to go on kissing you for all eternity, but we have to make plans." Once more he touched her lips briefly, and then dropped his hands to grasp hers.

"When my grandfather died, he left me a fortune, but he also left me a shipping business. His manager in London runs the business. One of those ships is soon due to leave the Port of New Orleans for England, and we're going to be on it, my love."

"London? We're going to London?" Sara held her breath. Could this be true? She and Jonathan together forever? "Am I dreaming?"

He scooped her back into his arms, crushing her against his chest. "No, my love. You aren't dreaming. I've already made arrangements not only for our passage, but also for our wedding. The captain will marry us aboard the ship. By the time we reach England, you'll be my wife, and no one can change that."

Jonathan lowered his head and covered her lips with his. His mouth was warm and hungry, and the intensity of the kiss would most certainly have been a shock to anyone seeing them. But Maddy didn't care. She drank in his passion like a flower drinks in a spring rain. She'd waited so long to feel his touch, and now soon he would be hers. All hers.

She wrapped her arms tightly around his neck, unwilling to allow anything to separate them even for a second.

Then her surroundings began to spin out of control. She fought against it, but to no avail. As the spiraling tunnel sucked her in, Sara could hear the hissing laughter of a woman coming from deep in the copse of trees.

Chapter 17

With a sudden jolt, Sara was in her room at Harrogate. The details of the scene she'd just lived ran rampant through her mind. Jonathan and Maddy had been planning to run away and get married. Obviously, since Jonathan had been killed, that had never happened. But why would Phillip kill Jonathan and prevent that? With Jonathan out of the way, that would have left the way clear for him to pursue Katherine.

Unless . . . Phillip hadn't known about the elopement plan.

That had to be the answer. He would have assumed the wedding would take place as planned. Clarice did say he was blindly in love with Maddy's sister. Killing Jonathan was the only way he could prevent losing the woman he loved. It's just too bad that Katherine never appreciated his love and devotion and that something which should have been so wonderful could have caused something so very tragic.

Sara couldn't believe how many people Katherine had infected with her hatred for Maddy, how many lives she'd touched and destroyed, and how she continued to terrorize from the grave.

But Katherine wasn't the only one to blame for Jonathan's death. Maddy had her own guilty cross to bear. If she hadn't encouraged Jonathan, continuing to show her love for him and to meet him and to voice her hope that Katherine would relent and set him free, he might not have gotten desperate enough to arrange the elopement. Then he wouldn't have been in the garden with Maddy. Had Katherine overheard the conversation that would eventually drive Phillip to commit murder in her name?

The more Sara found out about this twisted, doomed triangle, the more she felt the burden of Maddy's guilt. Weighted down by this new bit of information, she made her way to her bed and, without undressing, collapsed on it.

Sara awoke choking and coughing. She pushed herself up and, through her watery gaze, was able to see that smoke filled her bedroom. Frozen in fear, Sara watched as the flames curled around three sides of her bed. Some reached up to ignite the lace canopy. Others licked up over the sides of the mattress as they consumed the eiderdown quilt.

Slowly, the flames crept around the bed and would soon cut off any means of escape. She had to get out of here before she was burned alive, but every time she tried, she felt as though something held her back. Again and again, as the flames came ever closer, she attempted to get out of bed. Again and again, she was held immobile.

The flames crept closer. The heat was almost unbearable. The stench of burning material filled her nostrils. She covered her mouth and nose with her hand to block the smoke. But it didn't help. The acrid smoke continued to sear her throat and eyes. A spasm of coughing overcame her, and her throat felt raked raw.

God help me, I'm going to die!

Then, through the flames, she made eye contact with Jonathan's portrait. Somehow, that gave her the strength to break free of whatever held her down.

Panicked, she bolted from the bed, picked her way around the encroaching flames, and raced to the door screaming, "Fire! Fire! Wake up! My room is on fire!"

Running into the hall, she kept up the steady stream of warning cries to the rest of the house. Another coughing fit ripped from her throat, and she leaned against the wall to catch her breath and wipe the smoke-induced tears from her eyes with the hem of her dress.

"Sara! What is it?" Julie came running at her from the other end of the hall, her nightgown flapping crazily around her legs. Behind her came Raina, Samuel, and several other house slaves.

Unable to speak, Sara pointed at her room and squeaked out, "Fire!"

Julie ran past her to look in the room. The others followed. For a moment, Julie stared into the room. Her face twisted in confusion. She turned back to Sara. "There's no fire in your room, Sara. You must have been dreaming."

"But there is," Sara argued.

Summoning what was left of her strength, she pushed past Julie. Astonished, she gaped at the interior of her room. Julie was right. There had been no fire. Where flames had devoured the bed moments before, there was nothing more than a fluttering of the perfectly intact coverlet in the breeze blowing in through the open window. The clean, fresh air held no trace of the smell of smoke that had awakened her and filled her mouth and throat moments before.

"I don't understand," she mumbled, vaguely aware that her throat no longer hurt and her eyes no longer watered.

Julie slipped her arm around Sara's shoulders. "You

can all go back to bed," she told the others who had gathered in the hall. With confusion in their expressions, they did as they were told, but not without a few backward glances at their mistress. "Come on. Let's get you back to bed," Julie told Sara, concern filling her voice. "It was a dream."

Sara shook her head violently. "No! I saw the flames. I smelled the smoke. It was not a dream." Was she going mad? No! She *had* seen the fire, *had* smelled the smoke. She grabbed Julie's arms. "I swear the fire was real—as real as you are." She tried to keep the fear out of her voice, but was unsuccessful.

Poor Julie just stared at her, her eyes full of all kind of emotions—compassion, doubt, worry, bewilderment, uncertainty—but not belief. Not that Sara blamed her. If the tables had been turned, she wouldn't have believed it either.

Flopping down on the side of the bed, Sara glanced around her, astounded that everything was intact. How could that be? Then she recalled the bloody words on the wall that had been there, and then gone. Was this fire another of Katherine's ominous warnings?

As she dressed the next morning, Sara looked into her mirror. Reflected back at her was someone she barely recognized. The mirrored woman's image could have been a stranger. Deep purple circles ringed her haunted green eyes. Her pallid complexion made her appear almost ghostly. Her chestnut hair hung dull and lank around her face.

This couldn't go on. Before long she'd be sick again, and that wouldn't help her or Jonathan. But how could she stop Katherine from torturing her? One answer was to give up her love for Jonathan. The pain that shot through her heart at the very thought made it clear that this was not the answer she sought.

What, then?

Perhaps if she got away from Harrogate for a while, cleared her head, regrouped . . .

Suddenly, without explanation, Sara knew she must go to New Orleans and visit her parents for a few days. She had no idea why or how, but something told her she would find answers there.

Without hesitation, she pulled the bell rope beside her bed. Moments later, Raina appeared in the doorway.

"You called, Miss Sara?" Raina didn't even try to conceal the concern in her face when she saw Sara.

"Raina, please pack a few clothes for us. We're going to visit my mother and father."

"How long we gonna be gone?"

Sara shook her head. "I don't know. A few days? Please have Samuel get my trunk down from the attic; then ready the carriage. We'll be leaving right after breakfast."

"Yas, 'um." Raina turned to leave, then stopped and turned back, concern written clearly in her features. "You gonna be okay?"

Sara forced a smile to her lips, then surprised herself by saying, "I think I will be soon. Now, please do as I asked."

Never in her wildest dreams did she ever think she'd be happy to leave Harrogate. But she knew in her heart that if she stayed here, she'd never be able to think clearly; Katherine would see to that. If she was ever to find the answers about what had happened here, she had to start thinking with her head and not her heart. But even more strongly, she knew that answers awaited her in the Crescent City—answers she would never find at Harrogate.

The Garden District regaled Sara with all its summer splendor. Thanks to a flood in 1816 and the resulting deposit of nutrient-filled sediment, the district had the perfect soil to help the section live up to its name. Giant, ancient oaks, pecans, and leathery leafed magnolia trees surrounded and caressed the rooftops of the homes, while a myriad of flowering shrubs and meticulously tended gardens circled their feet. Only the perfume emanating from the landscaping exceeded the richness of the residents of the neighborhood.

As her carriage made its way down St. Charles Avenue, Sara reacquainted herself with the splendor of each house. Antebellum mansions lined the street and boasted architecture reminiscent of Italy, Spain, France, and Greek Revival. Each house stood apart from the others in its uniqueness and overlooked the street like a reigning monarch. Although a deep-seated hatred existed between the Americans and the Creole's, it didn't stop the American's from adopting the Creole's ornamental ironwork on their galleries and railings and the intricately designed wrought iron fences.

As one of the largest on the street, the Wades' home, a classic Greek Revival style called Azalea House for the many flowering shrubs in its gardens, stood out as one of the most resplendent residential achievements of famed architect James Gallier Sr.

The front, with its upper and lower porticos topped off by a pediment at the top, towered high above some of the trees. Four columns marched across the façade, and planters spewing forth multicolored flowers were positioned between them.

Sara had to tilt her head back to see one of the many chimneys reaching above the roofline. It was a good thing the chimney tax had been revoked in the 1700s, or her father would have been digging deep into the Wade coffers to pay for the many chimneys that topped his home.

Samuel maneuvered the carriage through the high wrought iron gates and eased it to a stop before the lower portico. The front door flew open, and Josiah, the Wades' butler, stepped out to greet the callers.

When he saw Sara, total surprise washed over his features. "Miss Sara. Wasn't 'spectin' you."

He hurried forward to help her down from the carriage and, at the same time, instructed the two young black men who had followed him out to take Sara's luggage to her room. They did as instructed and disappeared back into the house with Raina on their heels to supervise.

"It was a spur-of-the-moment decision, Josiah." She shook the travel wrinkles from her skirts. "Are my mother and father here?"

Before the butler could answer, a shout came from behind him. "Sara!" Her father rushed to her and scooped her into his arms. "What a lovely surprise." Looping his arm around her waist, he guided her into the house.

The inside of Azalea House was, if it was possible, grander than the outside. With its eighteen-foot ceilings; twenty-five rooms, each with its own fireplace; walls covered in hand-painted murals; crystal and bronze chandeliers; marble mantels; and ornate frieze work ceiling medallions, it far outshone the elegance of many of the street's counterparts. Of course, Sara's mother,

Patricia Wade, wouldn't have it any other way. She'd always demanded the best of everything and usually got it. Flaunting their wealth was among her favorite pastimes. Sara was convinced she felt it her duty to society.

"Is Mother here?"

Preston Wade stopped smiling. "Yes, but she's having her hair done upstairs. You'll see her at dinner. You are staying for dinner, aren't you?"

Heat rose in Sara's cheeks. Her mother would look very dimly on her unannounced arrival. It was just not done in polite society. The routine was to send word ahead to prepare the hostess for the visit. Nevertheless . . . "I had hoped to stay for a few days . . . if that's all right with you and Mother."

He laughed. "Of course it is. This will always be your home." Moving toward the wide Y-shaped marble staircase, he urged her forward. "Now, you freshen up, and then we'll talk."

Sara hadn't come all this way to rest. "I'd rather talk first, if that's okay."

For a moment, her father studied her. "Very well." He turned to the butler, who had just come down from upstairs, presumably having delivered Sara's luggage to her room. "Please bring refreshments to the drawing room, Josiah."

"Yassur." He stepped past them, then paused and

252

grinned at Sara. "It's mighty nice havin' you back at 'Zalea House, Miss Sara. Mighty nice."

She smiled. "Thank you, Josiah. It's good to be back."

She wished she meant that. Oh, she loved seeing her father, but along with seeing him came the daunting prospect of also coming face to face with his most stringent critic —her mother—something Sara was not anticipating with any degree of eagerness.

Preston eased Sara across the hall and into the drawing room, a more informal room used for family. He slid the pocket doors closed behind them. She took a seat on the settee and waited for her father to join her. When he did, he took her hand and enveloped it in his much larger one.

"Now, what brings you to New Orleans?"

Sara looked at their linked hands. "To be quite honest, I'm not sure why I came. I just felt like . . . I had to come." She wasn't worried that her father would look at her reasoning with skepticism. He'd always understood her more than anyone else had.

Preston nodded. "I'm sure the reason will be made clear soon. Have you found the letter yet?"

Before she could answer, the drawing room door opened, and Patricia Wade entered in all her glory— gown immaculate and in the latest style, hair coiffed to perfection. But her tightly drawn mouth marred the picture of a beautiful woman. The reprimanding look she sent

Sara told her that her impromptu visit was going to be received exactly as Sara had anticipated . . . with indignant displeasure.

"Hello, Mother."

"Sara," she said with a cold tone that hardly reflected that of a mother happy to see her only child. "How delightful to see you." Stiff insincerity dripped from the words. "However, it would have been nicer if you'd prepared me for your visit. Haven't I taught you better than to just drop in on people?"

Sara's nerves coiled into tight springs. Could her mother never just be happy to see her?

Patricia sat and spent several minutes arranging the folds of her gown around her.

With her mother out of the way, Sara could see beyond the drawing room door. Staring intently at her from the hallway was a very beautiful, statuesque mulatto woman who seemed vaguely familiar to Sara. A bright yellow *tignon* covered her head, and a brilliant red shawl embraced her shoulders. Clutched in her hand was a small carpetbag. The woman continued to study Sara with an intensity that made her squirm in her seat.

Despite the discomfort produced by the woman's scrutiny, Sara couldn't seem to tear her gaze away, nor could she hear what her mother was saying. The mulatto woman stepped inside the room, walked directly to Sara, and took her hand. Patricia stopped speaking and looked from her daughter to the back woman.

Then the woman smiled. "You must come see me at my home. I can help you." She dropped Sara's hand and then left the house.

Sara stared after her, mouth agape. "Who was that, Mother?"

"My hairdresser, the so-called voodoo priestess, Marie Laveau."

Chapter 18

When Samuel guided Sara's carriage down Bourbon Street the next day, they found the streets of the French Quarter teaming with people. Peddlers hawked rice cakes on the sidewalks. Flower vendors passed their wares under the noses of couples strolling down the street, tempting the gentlemen to buy their ladies a bouquet. Rich aromas of freshly baked bread, cakes, and pastries wafted from the bakeries and saturated the humid air, making Sara's mouth water despite her recent breakfast. From the direction of the docks came the singsong chant of the workers unloading cargos of cotton and sugar cane from a line of snow-white riverboats.

Having been at Harrogate for the past few weeks, Sara had forgotten how much she loved the French

Quarter and its exciting, never-ending, diversified activity. By day, the French Quarter was the proper lady; by night, the bawdy woman of the streets.

Samuel skillfully maneuvered the carriage down Bourbon Street, through the throng of conveyances ranging from street vendors' carts to the carriages of the Creole elite. Just as the steeple of St. Louis Cathedral came into view, he turned left onto Saint Ann Street, where he stopped before a two-story, red adobe cottage surrounded by a partially broken-down courtyard fence with trees that had spent many years peeking over it. At one time, the cottage must have been lovely. Now it was just rundown, neglected, and sad.

Sara took Samuel's hand and climbed down from the carriage.

"Wants me to come, too?" Samuel asked, casting the house a wary glance.

As frightened as the Negroes were of the woman who professed to be a voodoo queen, Sara didn't have the heart to have him accompany her. "No. Wait for me here."

"You sure, Miss? No good for you to be goin' in der alone. I can come with you."

Samuel's willingness to join her despite his fear touched Sara immeasurably. She patted his hand. "I'll be fine. You wait here."

"Yas, 'um." He climbed back into the driver's seat, relief obvious on his face, though his gaze remained fixed on the cottage as though a demon would emerge and gobble them both up.

Sara pushed open the rickety gate, its hinges announcing her arrival with a high-pitched squeal. Picking her way amid the overgrown vegetation half covering the walkway, she moved quickly to the front door, which, even judging from her diminutive height, seemed too low for a person to pass through without ducking. Tentatively, she knocked.

Through one of the tiny panes in the small windows, she caught sight of someone peeking out, and then quickly vanishing behind the curtains. Moments later, the door opened.

Framed in the doorway, a dim light behind her, was the lovely mulatto woman Sara had met in her mother's drawing room. Today, a bright green *tignon* concealed her hair and a rainbow-colored shawl covered the bodice of a plain blue dress. Gold hoop earrings hung from each ear. Her dark brown eyes, set in a face the color of *café au lait,* studied Sara.

"Hello. I'm—"

"Sara Wade. Come in, Miss Wade." Marie stepped to the side.

Sara bowed her head and entered the cottage. She

could see nothing. She paused for a moment to allow her eyes to adjust to the contrast between the bright sunlight and the dimness inside the cottage. When she could see again, she found herself in a narrow room lit by a few meager candles. In the center of the room was a table covered with a variety of objects. Behind the table was a chair with a thick red velvet cushion. The aroma of something like incense filled the air with a rather overwhelming, sickening odor.

Turning to her hostess, she gasped and stepped back. Marie stood beside her with a large snake draped around her shoulders. The head swayed a foot or so above Marie's head, and its slitted, cold eyes focused on Sara. Her skin crawled. She shivered and took several steps backwards.

"Do not be afraid. Zombi is quite harmless and will not bother you." As she spoke she lovingly caressed the length of the snake's back. "Please, have a seat." She motioned to the table littered with things the identity of which Sara could only guess at.

After Sara was seated, Marie took the snake from her shoulders and placed it on a cushioned seat behind her, where it coiled and surveyed them, then Marie sat down facing Sara. "It was good of you to come."

Had she a choice? After their strange meeting in her father's house, Sara could scarcely stay away, especially now when her life had turned into one series of strange occurrences after another. Added to that was the fact that she'd felt inexplicably drawn to New Orleans. Perhaps Marie could tell her why.

"I still don't understand why you asked me to come here."

"Nevertheless, you came." Marie's dark eyes bore into her much the same as those of the serpent hovering over her shoulder.

"Yes. I came." Sara chomped at the bit to get to why Marie had asked her to visit.

As if reading Sara's thoughts, Marie said, "You are being haunted."

Astonished, Sara nodded.

"You must continue to fight her. She will not give up. Your will to live and fulfill your destiny will be your salvation." For a moment she closed her eyes. When she opened them, she smiled. "As will your love for this man Jonathan. But neither will save you from this woman's wrath. She does not want him, but neither does she want you to have him."

Sara gasped. "How do you know about Jonathan?"

Marie said nothing. She just smiled.

"Is that all you have to tell me?" Sara knew all this or had guessed at it. She'd really hoped to learn something new.

"No. I will give you a gris-gris to protect you from the malevolent spirit of the woman who haunts you." She reached into a bejeweled box on the table and extracted a small cloth bag.

In awe, Sara watched as Marie placed a variety of objects in the bag: pieces of colored stones, bits of what appeared to be bone, salt, and red pepper. Then she added a large pinch of dust. Sara recalled Raina telling her about a gris-gris a slave on one of the neighboring plantations had made to give her master. The addition of a dust known as "goofer dust" or "graveyard dirt" was what the slaves believed had killed the man the following day when he fell on a hay fork.

"I'm not trying to kill anyone," Sara protested.

"On rare occasions, goofer dust also protects, Sara." Marie said a few words that Sara didn't understand over the bag, but that the snake, from his angry *hiss*, seemed to find irritating. Then she handed Sara the bag. "Keep this with you always. It will protect you from this Katherine woman." Sara took it, but she must have let her skepticism show. Marie smiled knowingly. "She has already tried to kill you, has she not?"

Sara nodded.

"She will try again. The time is drawing close when she must defeat you or lose everything."

As her carriage began to pull away from Marie Laveau's cottage, Sara fingered the strange little bag, doubting how something so small could protect her from Katherine's wrath. Nevertheless, she tucked it in her reticule. As they pulled into Dauphine Street, Sara spotted a nun hurrying along the street.

The little nun reminded Sara that Katherine's parents had sent her to live at the Ursuline Convent after Jonathan's death. Could the nuns shed some light on this relationship between Maddy, Katherine, and Jonathan? Were any of the sisters who had been in the convent when Katherine was living there still alive? It was worth a try.

"Samuel, take me to the Ursuline Convent."

"Yas, 'um."

Dutifully, Samuel turned the carriage toward Chartres Street and brought it to a halt before the doors of the convent. He tied the horse to the hitching post and then helped Sara down.

"I won't be long," she said and, hoisting her skirts a few inches so as not to trip over them, she hurried up the front walk. At the door, she lifted the heavy knocker and let it fall. The hollow *thunk* seemed to echo through her bones.

A short time later, the heavy cypress door swung open. An unusually petite woman, dressed in a black habit and veil with a white wimple framing her angelic face, smiled up at her.

"May I help you?"

Now that Sara was here, words failed her. How could she express what she wanted? She couldn't very well say she was being haunted by a woman who used to live at the convent.

"I'm not sure," she finally said. "I need to speak with someone who was here a while ago."

The nun smiled. "How long ago is a while ago?"

Feeling a bit foolish, Sara returned her smile. "1820."

The little nun thought for a moment. Sara held her breath and prayed someone who tended Katherine would still be alive.

"That would probably be Sister Agnes. She was here when the old convent was being used. Perhaps she can help you." She stepped to the side to allow Sara entrance, and then led her through a maze of hallways to a gallery overlooking a beautiful courtyard. "Sister Agnes has been quite ill, but if you'll wait here, I'll see if she is up to a little company."

Leaving Sara, the nun hurried off down a long walkway and then disappeared inside one of the doors leading off the gallery. A long time later, that same door opened and the little nun reappeared, pushing a wooden wheelchair. In the chair sat another nun. Her hands and face, which were the only parts of her body visible from her nun's robes, were withered, wrinkled and deformed from advanced arthritis.

As she drew closer, Sara could see a kind twinkle in her pale blue eyes. "Sister Valerie tells me you want to speak to me." Belying her physical condition, her voice was strong and affirmative, though a little breathless.

Sara sat on a nearby bench to be on the same eye level. "Not you precisely, but someone who was here when Katherine Grayson was confined at the convent."

The old nun nodded. "That would be me. I tended Katherine for most of her stay with us." She shook her head sadly. "A very troubled young woman." Then she waved Sister Valerie away. "Go about your duties, Sister. I'll be fine."

Sister Valerie patted her shoulder. "I'll come back in a little while to see if you're ready to go back to your room." Then she looked at Sara with silent pleading in her eyes. "She tires easily." Sara nodded to let her know she understood, and then followed the retreating form of the young nun as she walked away.

"Now, what is it you'd like to know about Katherine?"

Sara took a seat on a wooden bench facing Sister Agnes. "Why was she brought here?"

"Something had happened to her, something tragic. Neither she nor the black woman who came with her ever spoke of it."

"Her fiancé was shot and killed by a jealous neighbor on the eve of their wedding." As always, speaking about Jonathan's death sent a pain shooting through Sara's heart.

The shock of Sara's astounding statement left Sister Agnes speechless for a few minutes. Then she sighed. "Well, I'm sure that would account for why she started drinking. I believe her choice of liquor was absinthe. Her father brought her here when her indulgence began to take a toll on her physical and mental health. She'd become irrational and uncontrollable." The old nun stopped and took a deep breath that rattled in her chest. "For her first few weeks here, we kept her heavily dosed on laudanum. But I'm afraid it was too late. The absinthe had already robbed her of her sanity." She took a deep, shuddering breath, then continued.

"Toward the end, she became obsessed with writing a letter to someone. Actually, it was one of her few lucid moments. She was determined to write the letter, and I couldn't control her until I brought her pen and paper. She scribbled away constantly for days, throwing away one draft after another until she was finally satisfied. Then for weeks after the servant had delivered the letter, she kept asking over and over if it had been taken to the recipient."

Sara's ears had perked right after the first mention of the letter. "Did she say who the letter went to or what it contained?"

The old nun shook her head. "No, and I never asked. Right after that, she seemed to decline quickly. Now that you've told me of the tragedy, I understand why. She talked on and on in disjointed thoughts that ranged from childhood memories to statements such as the moon being too bright. One morning, I found her in the garden, just over there." Sister Agnes pointed toward a small, gurgling fountain tucked in the corner of the courtyard. "We carried her inside, and a few days later, she died." She crossed herself. "Lord bless her tortured soul. May God forgive me, but I think her daddy was relieved when she passed away."

Aghast at the nun's conclusion, Sara had to ask, "Relieved? Why in heaven's name would a father be relieved when his daughter died?"

Sister Agnes frowned at her. "Well, isn't it obvious, my dear? He wouldn't have to hide her illegitimate birth anymore."

Sara was confused. "Illegitimate birth? But she and Maddy were twins."

The nun's mouth fell open. "You don't know." Then she patted Sara's hand. "Of course you don't. It was a closely guarded secret."

"Secret? What secret?"

For a moment Sara thought Sister Agnes wasn't going to tell her. But then she shrugged. "Since everyone concerned has passed on, I don't think they can be hurt by me telling you about it." She looked around and then lowered her voice. "She and Madeline were not twins. Mrs. Grayson was not Katherine's mother."

Chapter 19

Now it was Sara whose mouth dropped open. "Katherine and Maddy not twins? I don't—"

"Understand why they passed the girls off as twins?" The nun smiled, but without humor. Rather, her smile looked like relief and perhaps, surprisingly, just a touch of disdain.

Though she obviously disapproved, perhaps the Graysons' secret had been too burdensome for her, and she was as relieved as Mr. Grayson had been to finally remove it from her mind. Or perhaps she just liked to gossip. Sara didn't know, nor did she care. What she wanted to know was the story behind this astounding bit of information.

"Society, my dear girl. Society. It seems that for a

few years, Mr. Grayson had indulged in a brief . . . indiscretion with a lady from a good family that resulted in his . . . liaison . . . becoming with child. She died in childbirth, leaving her tiny daughter without any relatives. Whether from a guilty conscience or fear that word of his affair would leak out, Mr. Grayson took the little girl home." She leaned back in her chair. "It just so happened that Mrs. Grayson was also pregnant and about to deliver her first child. Somehow Mr. Grayson convinced his wife to take in his mistress' motherless babe and let the world think his wife had given birth to twins." She tilted her head. "Have you ever seen pictures of the girls? Do they look alike?"

Sara shook her head, her mind whirling with the information Sister Agnes had just disclosed. "I've only seen their portraits, and they look nothing alike. In fact, I look more like Maddy than Katherine does, but I thought that—"

"It was not unusual for twins not to resemble each other? That's true, which made it easy to pass them off to everyone as *fraternal* twin sisters."

Sara was half listening. This explained why Maddy's mother had doted on her and not Katherine. She obviously had resented raising her husband's illegitimate offspring and had taken it out on the child. How terrible to have to face a reminder of his betrayal every day.

If Katherine was not the child of both the Graysons, then technically, Maddy was their firstborn and should have been the one betrothed to Jonathan. But if they had admitted to that, then their secret would have come out. So they had to let Katherine pass as the oldest and the one who would complete the bargain made between Mr. Grayson and Mr. Bradford. One more thorn in Mrs. Grayson's side. No wonder Mrs. Grayson fought against announcing to the Bradford's at Maddy's birth that their baby girl, Katherine, would wed the Bradford's son. She knew that her blood child should have been the one entering into a betrothal.

So many lives destroyed by one indiscretion. But worst of all was what it had done to Maddy and Jonathan. Through a horrible twist of fate, Maddy and Jonathan were cheated out of the life they should have had together. A life they deserved to have together. Sara's insides curdled with anger. Her hands balled into impotent fists in her lap. She wanted to scream out at the injustice of it all. Her heart wept for what could have been, but never was. At last, she knew the full measure of the intense frustration and pain that, without even knowing the facts, Maddy and Jonathan must have endured.

She lifted her gaze to meet Sister Agnes'. "If it was all kept so secret, how did you learn about it?"

"When Mr. Grayson brought Katherine here, he

was so distraught that it just seemed to pour from him. I would imagine carrying that burden for so long had been far too much for the poor soul to stand any longer. Of course, none of this got out. Everyone was told Katherine had suffered from an acute case of yellow jack fever. Since that scourge plagued the city on a yearly basis, no one questioned it."

Just then, Sister Valerie stepped onto the gallery, walked to where they sat, and laid her hand on the old nun's shoulder. "Sister Agnes, are you ready to go back to your room?"

"Yes, I believe I am," Sister Agnes said softly, the strain of the last hour plainly audible in her voice.

"Thank you," Sara said, feeling a bit guilty when she noted the lines of fatigue showing around Sister Agnes' eyes.

"You're welcome." She reached for Sara's hand. "Don't distress yourself over this. It's in the past, over and done, a wrong that can never be righted, child."

Sara watched her being wheeled away. *In the past, perhaps, but Katherine is making certain it is not nearly over and done.*

"So where was it you went today?" Sara's mother never lifted her gaze from her embroidery, which told the young woman the question had been asked only to fill the silence in the drawing room.

For a second, Sara thought about being evasive. But then she reminded herself she did not live under her mother's thumb any longer, and she could speak the truth without fear of reprisal.

"Into the Quarter to see Marie Laveau."

Her mother lowered her embroidery to her lap. "Silly, Marie would have come to the house to dress your hair. Ladies of refinement don't go to her home."

"I didn't go to get my hair styled, Mother."

"No? Then what on earth could you possibly have gone for?"

Sara fumbled in her dress pocket and pulled out the small cotton bag Marie had given her. "For this." She swung the bag between two fingers.

"And what, may I ask, is that? It looks rather . . . nasty." Patricia's nose curled in a most unladylike fashion. "I suppose it's got something to do with the strange religion Marie practices. Voo— voo— something."

"Voodoo," her husband put in, laying his book aside and showing interest in their conversation for the first time.

"Yes, that's it." She glanced around, and then lowered her voice. "I've heard Marie claims to be some kind of queen and at midnight they all dance naked out by Lake Pontchartrain." Derision dripped from her voice. She shook her head, her expression haughty and repulsed. "Those Nigras have the strangest practices." She picked up her embroidery again. "And exactly what is that . . . that thing she gave you, Sara?"

"It's a gris-gris, Mother, to protect me against the ghost haunting Harrogate."

Patricia's embroidery dropped to her lap and then slipped unnoticed to the floor. Her mother's face went sheet white. "G— g—"

Sara got a certain amount of pleasure from watching her mother's reaction. "Ghost, Mother. It's quite all right to say the word. Nothing will happen to you."

Sara's mother laid her head back against the chair, pulled a lace handkerchief from her sleeve, and began fanning herself. Sara made no move to comfort her. She'd seen her mother pull her fainting spells many times before. Ninety-nine percent of the time they were fake and used to draw attention. When no one rushed to her side and Sara noted her mother's clandestine peek from beneath fluttering eyelids, Sara surmised this was as fake as the rest. As soon as Patricia realized no one was coming to her aid, she recovered far too quickly by herself.

"A ghost? Ridiculous. There are no such things as ghosts."

"I'm afraid you're wrong. Harrogate is haunted, and not by just one ghost." Sara knew her perverse pleasure in watching her mother's building outrage was shameful, but, oh, was it satisfying. Her pleasure doubled when, out of the corner of her eye, she saw her father fighting to contain a smile. "There's a woman and a man. Oh, and Gran comes from time to time as well."

This was the end of the line for Sara. Either Patricia Wade would accept her daughter's *affliction* as something real, or she would disown Sara completely and send her packing back to Harrogate. Sara didn't care much one way or the other. She just wanted it over and done.

"So what was it Marie told you?" Her father leaned forward, eager to forestall the inevitable confrontation between Sara and her mother by asking to hear the recounting of her visit with the voodoo queen.

"Preston! Do not encourage this outrageous behavior." They both ignored her outburst.

"Actually, she didn't tell me anything, except that Katherine . . ." She turned to her horrified mother. "She's the female ghost." Her mother's horrified expression grew more intense. Sara turned back to her father. "She said Katherine is evil, and I need to be careful. She gave me this." She held up the little bag again. "This will protect me," she said, and then put the bag back in her pocket.

"Rubbish!" Her mother bolted to her feet. "I won't stay here and listen to another word of this complete and utter nonsense, and I'll thank you not to repeat it where the servants can hear it and peddle it all over the Garden District to my friends." She stormed from the room, her skirts swishing angrily around her, her nose tilted into the air as though she smelled something putrid.

Preston and Sara watched Patricia's departure, and then turned back to each other as though the interruption had never occurred.

"Actually, I learned a great deal more at the Ursuline Convent from Sister Agnes." She told her father the story of the Grayson twins. "If Katherine knew, it would explain why she hated Maddy so vehemently."

Preston stood and walked to the sideboard beneath the bay windows. He took a pipe from the rack and then lifted the lid from a humidor and filled the pipe's bowl with a fragrant tobacco. Then, still without speaking, he went to the fireplace and withdrew a piece of wood with a flame curling up on the end and lit the pipe. When the contents of the bowl glowed to his satisfaction, he threw the piece of wood back into the fire and retook his seat across from Sara.

"Word of something like that doesn't die, even after years. I'm sure if it had leaked out, the story would have been told again and again. I never heard it, and your grandmother never mentioned it. So, my feeling is Katherine never knew either. However, if she had known, that would have explained a lot." He glanced at

Sara and puffed thoughtfully on his pipe.

Sara had to smile. It wasn't considered good manners for a gentleman to smoke with a lady in the room, but Sara had never minded. She loved the smell of her father's pipe tobacco. Somehow, it always made her feel closer to him. Had her mother remained in the room, he never would have lit a pipe. The fact that he did now made her realize again what a wonderful, relaxed relationship she had with him.

He cleared his throat and went on. "Her hatred of Maddy was so strong and unreasonable. According to your grandmother, no one really ever understood it. This explanation would certainly make sense." He studied the glowing embers in the pipe's bowl. "Mother always said Katherine had a very vindictive disposition."

"Oh, she does, Father. She's very evil." Sara didn't bother to recount the incidents when Katherine had shown just how evil she could be.

"And now, because Maddy had so much that she could never have, you seem to be after the one thing she had the power to keep from Maddy: Jonathan. Since you look like Maddy and have contacted Jonathan, she's made you the object of her displeasure."

Sara nodded. "That was my guess, too." She remained silent for a few seconds. Dare she tell her father why she continued this duel of wills with Katherine? Deep in her heart, she knew he'd understand. "I won't give him up to her, Papa. As insane as it sounds, I love Jonathan."

Preston displayed none of the surprise Sara had expected to see. Instead, he looked very sad, but he nodded. "I know." He took her hand and looked deep into her eyes. "I want more than anything for you to be happy. If Jonathan is what it takes, then you have my blessing. But I will miss you terribly, my darling daughter."

Miss her?

What an odd thing to say. She wasn't going anywhere except back to Harrogate and an occasional trip back in time. But the intensity of his emotions seemed so out of place simply for her return home. Sara stared at him. How very sad he looked. His sorrow seemed to blanket him like an impenetrable fog.

Sara spent the carriage ride back to Harrogate the next day thinking about her fathers' strange words and what Sister Agnes had told her. What he'd said sounded so . . . final. Almost as though they would never see each other again. Was he ill and keeping it from her? He hadn't looked ill. The idea of losing her father nearly broke her heart, so she pushed it from her mind, refusing to consider it.

Instead, she centered her thoughts on Sister Agnes. The circumstances surrounding Katherine's and Maddy's births still preyed heavily on her mind. Her father hadn't really been able to shed more light on the event. By telling him, she'd almost felt like she was betraying Sister Agnes' trust, but she knew he would keep the secret.

The fact that the Grayson family had managed to keep their secret so well hidden for so long amazed Sara as much as it had her father. If no one else, the servants should have known. They always knew what transpired within the walls of the big house and had no compulsions about sharing it with each other. Eventually the news had to reach the residents of the big house and neighboring planters.

And what about Floree? Had she known? Probably not. She'd only been five at the time of the births. She'd never said she was actually there when the babies were born, only that they were beautiful little girls and that the servant who had attended Mrs. Grayson had been sold to a man from Tennessee the next day. *Probably to ensure she wouldn't have a chance to tell anyone.*

Had Katherine found out about herself? Was that why she hated Maddy so intensely? Sara decided that wasn't probable, considering the lengths to which Mr. Grayson had gone to hide it. He never would have allowed Katherine to find out about her illegitimacy.

Katherine's hatred of Maddy had to be rooted in the fact that Mrs. Grayson resented raising her husband's mistress' child, and as a result she must have taken it out on Katherine. Maddy had mentioned her mother's ill treatment of Katherine in her diary.

What a tangled web this whole thing had turned out to be, and Sara was no closer to untangling it than she had been at the start. If anything, it had grown more complicated. But maybe she wasn't supposed to untangle anything.

Now that she'd had time to think about it, she couldn't help but wonder if maybe Sister Agnes was right. Perhaps she was fighting a losing battle. Perhaps she had irrevocably lost Jonathan a long time ago, and reliving Maddy's last days with him would do no more than allow her to go through the pain and agony of the tragedy of his death again.

Logically, the chances of her and Jonathan's ever being together were very low, maybe even nonexistent. He was a ghost, and she was a mortal. Because of past events, she was destined to never feel his touch as his wife.

That night, exhausted from her long trip, Sara fell asleep quickly. But not for long. After what seemed like only a moment of sleep, she felt a hand caressing her cheek. Fighting eyelids that felt weighted down with large, heavy rocks, she forced her eyes open. She blinked several times to focus.

When the sleep had cleared, she found Jonathan sitting beside her on the bed. His smile seemed to light up the room. She was instantly wide awake. Her heart swelled at the sight of him. "Jonathan?"

"I had to come. I missed you. It's been too long since you came to me." He gently kissed her. "Are you sorry I came?"

"No." She cupped his dear face in her hands. "Never. I've missed you so very much." How strange it was that he didn't look at all ethereal, but rather as solid and mortal as she. Sara could feel the firmness of his muscle and bone beneath her fingers.

He smiled, and she felt like hot wax all over. "Would you be scandalized if I told you I want you?"

Heat rose in her cheeks, and she was thankful for the darkness surrounding them. Words refused to pass her lips. She shook her head.

"Good, because I do. I ache with the wanting, my love."

His lips slid across her collar bone, then on to her shoulder, where he ran his tongue over the strange little mark she'd been born with. He pulled away, then slid his hand down her throat and stopped just above the swell of her breast. He paused, his gaze fixed on hers, as though waiting for her permission to go farther. Taking his hand, she guided it down to cup her breast. He sucked in his breath. Smoky passion filled his dark eyes; then they heated with the desire his touch told her boiled just below the surface of his deceptive calmness.

"Are you sure?"

Sara pulled his head down and pressed her mouth to his, leaving no doubt of her answer. Putting every bit of her pent up longing into it, she kissed him. His mouth opened beneath hers, and he slipped his tongue inside, tasting her, devouring her, telling her in his actions that his longing was as deep and as powerful as her own. His hands moved over her breasts, kneading, caressing, coaxing.

She couldn't catch her breath. Her lungs burned. Her body ached with a new hunger she couldn't name, but knew had to be fed to ensure her survival. Of its own volition, her back arched to press her even closer to him. His tense muscles strained against hers. She felt his arousal pressing against her leg.

This was insane, dangerous. She should stop him. But she could no more tell him "no" than she could stop the sun from rising. Needing to be closer to him, she kicked the covers aside and pulled him down beside her.

"I never thought that we . . . that I . . . that—"

He silenced her with his lips. It seemed like his

hands were suddenly everywhere, stroking her breasts, caressing her thighs, smoothing her stomach—exciting her to heights beyond anything she'd ever dreamed of before. This was nothing like the *woman's duty* her mother and her friends had whispered about with such distaste. This was . . .

Oh, God, she couldn't think.

Everywhere he touched, new fires ignited in her body. The flames licking at her belly grew until she had to bite her tongue to keep from screaming and bringing everyone in the entire house down on them.

Then he pulled away. Sara cried out at the loss and reached for him. "No, don't leave me."

"I would never leave you." He stood beside the bed, his heated gaze never leaving her face. Very slowly, he took off his jacket, and then his waistcoat, and threw them aside. Piece by piece, his clothes disappeared until he stood before her like a beautiful bronze god.

Sara couldn't speak. She could only stare at him, amazed at his arousal and a bit afraid. Though she wanted him desperately, she had never lain with a man before and had no idea what was expected of her. Sex was not something her prudish mother felt should be talked about. Sara often wondered how she had come into being at all.

Jonathan returned to his place beside her, but he didn't take her into his arms. Instead, he slowly peeled her nightdress up her body and over her head, and then threw it to join his own clothes on the floor.

For a long moment, he stared at her, his eyes burning pathways over her flesh. "My God, you are even lovelier than I'd imagined."

In an almost worshipful manner, he ran the tips of his fingers over her collar and down to her breasts. She sucked in air at his touch. Never had she felt anything like the myriad of sensations rushing through her every nerve ending. The muscles in her stomach clenched. Her hands balled into fists. Sparks ignited behind her closed eyelids.

Then his hand traveled over her hip and across the V of hair at the apex of her thighs. Very tenderly, he stroked the heated flesh between her thighs. As his finger penetrated her, he covered her lips with his.

At first, it hurt. She tried to cry out, but the sound was lost inside his mouth. Then, as he stroked her faster and faster, the pain vanished and in its place came that strange, unfamiliar hunger again. This time it burned with an intensity that left her weak, unable to control her body movements. Surprised to find herself thrashing beneath his hands, she tried to stop, but her body seemed to have a mind of its own.

Her back arched. Her hands dug into the bunched muscles in his upper arms. Something was happening to her. Something she couldn't control and, in all truth, didn't want to. The hunger had increased until she thought she would die of it.

Then it happened. Lights burst behind her eyelids. Her body was no longer hers to control. She longed for these feelings to never end. But they did. Eventually, the cataclysmic rush eased away, leaving her lethargic and drained.

Sara opened her eyes and looked up at Jonathan's dear face. He was smiling down at her. "You're ready for me now," he whispered.

He moved so that his strong body covered hers and spread her knees with his. Then he settled in the cradle of her parted legs. She felt something hard nudge her there. Suddenly, he was filling her, and the pain came back, worse this time. She dug her nails into his back to keep from crying out. It seared through her thighs like a hot poker.

He paused, waited, and then began to move very slowly. Then, like magic, the pain was gone, replaced by an incredible hunger much stronger than anything she'd felt before. He began to move faster. She matched his rhythm as if she'd known what to do all along. Barely aware that the covers had slipped to the floor, Sara wrapped her legs around his hips and opened herself fully to his love.

They moved together in perfect time until their movements became faster, more frantic, more insistent. Suddenly, the world around her exploded. Sensation after sensation rushed through her. Jonathan cried out her name over and over. Not until her lungs seared with pain did she gasp for breath.

Jonathan collapsed on her and buried his face in her neck. Their labored breathing filled the silence in the room. Then, when he was able to speak again, he propped himself up on one elbow and smoothed the hair from her face.

"I love you. I have always and will always love you. We were meant to be together, and we shall. I promise."

We were meant to be together.

His words cut through the fog of spent passion blanketing her brain. Did he know? Was he aware of what they'd been cheated out of because of the lies perpetuated by the Graysons?

Sara opened her mouth to ask him, but the room began to spin. She closed her eyes. Her stomach heaved with the motion. Then it stopped.

Dazed, she looked around. She was lying in her bed wearing her nightdress, the bed linens neat and covering her to her chin. Outside, the light from the morning sun was just peeping over the treetops.

Had it all been a dream?

Tentatively, she ran her fingertips over her mouth

and found her lips tender from his kisses. Her thighs felt moist. Her body more alive than ever before. None of it the product of a dream.

Finally, she irrevocably belonged to Jonathan, body and soul.

Chapter 20

As they picked their way through the underbrush growing beneath the pomegranate trees, Julie threw a sidelong glance at Sara. "I missed you at breakfast, but Raina said you slept in this morning. I must say it did you good. You're looking better than I've seen you look in days."

Sara smiled, but refrained from commenting. Instead, she hugged her new secret close and steered the conversation to an entirely different subject. "Did you know these trees are said to have come from ones Thomas Jefferson grew at Monticello?" She pulled two ruby red pomegranates from a low hanging limb and added them to the picnic basket they carried between them. "Gran said my grandfather loved them made into syrup and poured over fruit compote."

Julie stopped and placed a hand on her hip. Squinting into the sun, she studied Sara. "Am I to gather from the change of subject that you're not going to talk about whatever it is that has put that sappy smile on your face?"

Unable to contain her joy any longer, Sara let go of the basket's handle and threw up her hands, as though reaching to touch the clear blue sky, and then danced in circles. Her dress billowed out around her like a colorful mushroom. "I'm in love, Julie. Gloriously and wonderfully in love."

Julie didn't speak or join in Sara's happiness. Instead, she frowned. Taking Sara's arm, Julie guided her to a large grassy area shaded by the spreading limbs of an oak tree draped in silvery beards of Spanish moss. "Let's eat here."

Julie spread the tablecloth Chloe had tucked around the basket's contents and kneeled down on the edge of it. Sara set the basket on the tablecloth and began unpacking their lunch of fried chicken, sliced tomatoes, fresh baked biscuits, two glasses, and an old wine bottle Chloe had filled with lemonade and re-corked. Along with the food, she'd added plates, napkins, and silverware.

They filled their plates and ate in silence, enjoying the company and the balmy river breeze that cooled the afternoon heat. Neither of them spoke, each lost in her own thoughts. When they'd finished, they stowed everything back in the basket.

Sara lay back and stared up at the azure sky. A hawk traced slow circles above them in its quest for an unwary field mouse. The treetops danced high above them, catching the breeze off the river. Butterflies paraded their vibrant colors before her as they moved from flower to flower. The faint buzz of bees gathering honey lent music to the day.

Could a day be more perfect than this one? *Only if I could share it with Jonathan,* she thought.

"Sara?" Julie had reclined beside her. She propped herself on one elbow and peered down into Sara's face.

"Hmm?"

"I'm not going to tell you that I understand any of what's been happening with you for the past few weeks, because I can't even begin to pretend that I do. But I do know that, even though at first I didn't believe any of it, I have never seen you as driven about anything as you have been about Jonathan." Julie laughed lightly and plucked nervously at the blades of grass overlapping the edge of the tablecloth. "Of course, that's not counting your efforts to free yourself of your mother." She raised herself to a sitting position. "Despite the fact that I can't see him, nor do I think I ever will, in my heart I truly believe that you do. Nothing else could bring the kind of happiness to your face that I saw a little while ago."

She touched Sara's arm where it lay over her stomach. "If there is anything I can do to help, you have only to ask."

Sara covered Julie's hand with her own. "You just did." Tears burned her eyes. "You are the best friend anyone ever had. How many people would blindly accept that their friend was in love with a ghost and offer to help?" She sat up and pulled Julie to her in a tight hug. "Thank you, my friend."

Julie sighed, drew away, and righted herself. "Just allow me the right to worry about you."

"There's nothing to worry about. Katherine wants to scare me, not hurt me. If she'd wanted to hurt me, she would have done it by now." Not for a moment did she believe her own words.

Julie looked at her with skepticism written all over her face. "Hmm. Let's see . . . pushing you into the river, almost crushing you with a dresser, setting your bedroom on fire . . . all done because she didn't want to *hurt you*, right?"

Sara turned away, unwilling to allow Julie to see the fear she knew was plainly visible in her eyes. If Katherine could prevent her from having Jonathan by hurting her, Sara had not a doubt that she would. But just because she lived with that constant fear didn't mean she had to inflict it on Julie.

With memories of what she'd shared with Jonathan the night before running through her mind, and dreams of it happening again during the hours of darkness to come, Sara strolled along the upper balcony of Harrogate and stared off into the beauty of the impending sunset. The sky above the oak trees lining the drive to the house glowed with streaks of orange, purple, salmon, and gold. Fluffy clouds gilded in the colors of the setting sun hovering over the horizon to the west. A mockingbird sang out its monotonous call somewhere down the drive. The early evening twilight hung heavy with the perfume of the flowers in the garden. In every respect, a perfect ending to a lovely day. Perhaps an even lovelier night was yet to come.

Memories of Jonathan's visit to her bed brought a smile to her lips. She ran her hands down her arms, recalling the feel of Jonathan's skin next to hers, the gentleness of his touch, the tenderness of his exquisite lovemaking. She'd heard the girls at boarding school whisper about *doing it* with a man, but from their crude descriptions of the pain and humiliation they expected to experience, they had no idea what a beautiful, spiritual thing giving yourself to someone you love could be. They'd probably been indoctrinated by women like her own mother who believed it was something a woman did out of the necessity to produce an heir and not something that any self-respecting woman would actually enjoy.

Sara didn't care what society thought. She would not exchange that one night with Jonathan for anything, not even immortality.

Her smile deepened. How could she feel so content when so much of her life was in turmoil? But she did, and she had a good idea why. Jonathan was forever hers in every way possible, and Katherine would never have him in that way no matter what nefarious scheme she came up with to stop them.

Almost as satisfying was the knowledge that Julie finally believed her. That one fact meant more to Sara than she could express. Julie had been her dearest friend for . . . forever, and for her to doubt her and be at odds with her was something Sara hated. But no more. Even though there were still many unanswered questions for both of them, the fact that Julie believed Sara and would help her made the burden seem much lighter.

Turning her body in to the breeze, she rested her palms on the railing and raised her face skyward to inhale the aromas of the waning day. Because of the work of the field hands her father had sent to her, Harrogate had come into its own, a home she could be proud of, the showplace Sara remembered from her childhood visits to her grandmother's.

Below her perch on the gallery high above the lawn, the tangle of grapevines that had choked out the shrubs and flowers had been removed, leaving them free to bloom, to spread their branches unhampered, and to cast their perfume into the humid air. The drive, once cluttered with fallen twigs, dried leaves, and small limbs, was now cleared, opened to welcome all visitors. The Garden of the Moon had been weeded and trimmed, the gazebo painted and repaired. Both temple dogs had been scrubbed free of the lichen and moss that had coated them, and they now stood as proud sentinels guarding against evil outside the moongate.

Harrogate itself had been whitewashed and gleamed snowy white in the sunlight like a virgin bride on her wedding day and golden under the setting sun like an old matron. To anyone coming down the drive, Harrogate greeted them in all her finery, as stately, serene, and welcoming as Jonathan had meant it to be. Oddly content, Sara let her mind drift to the night to come and Jonathan's possible return.

Before she could fully form the thoughts, hands pushed at her back. Shock, panic, and absolute terror ravaged her body and mind. In terror, she seized the railing. She tried to turn to see who it was, but the hands against her back kept her from moving anywhere but toward the long drop to the ground below.

To prevent herself from tumbling over the side, she clutched the railing ever more tightly. The insistent hands continued to shove at her back. Splinters dug painfully into her palms. Pushing the pain to the back of her mind, she strengthened her grip. But sweat coated her palms, and her grasp slipped.

Her upper body began to pitch forward. Her feet began to slide out from under her. She fought to keep them securely on the floor, knowing if she lost her balance, she would go over the railing. But the hands at her back were stronger and more insistent.

Sara looked down through fear-widened eyes. The ground, though covered in grass, seemed miles away. If she fell, she'd surely die or, at the very least, end up with a variety of broken bones. Terror gripped her with icy manacles. The tips of her fingers began to tingle from the pressure being exerted on them. Then, slowly, they began to go numb. She had to concentrate on keeping them bent to maintain her hold on the railing.

The pressure at her shoulder blades increased. She felt herself leaning out over the ground below.

A cold, maniacal voice filtered into her thoughts.

You think you have him, but you don't. He's mine, and he'll always be mine. Even though you spread your legs for him like some Bourbon Street whore, he's still mine, bitch.

You should have stayed in New Orleans. Now you will die.

The voice was terrifyingly familiar. There was no mistaking the derogatory sarcasm that imbued each phrase. It was the same voice that had berated Floree for being late.

Katherine.

Cold horror such as she'd never known seeped through Sara's body. She opened her mouth to scream for help, but no sound emerged. It was as though the same cold hand at her back had grasped her vocal cords, freezing them and rendering her incapable of communication.

On her own, she could do nothing but fight for her survival. But the hands at her back were relentless and pushed harder. Terrorized, she gazed over the railing, knowing she was powerless to stop the inevitable.

Then her feet lost their traction and slipped from beneath her. Her hands ripped loose from the railing. Suddenly, she catapulted over the side and plummeted in slow motion toward the ground. Her scream echoed through the humid afternoon. A sharp pain cut through her head, and then there was no more.

"My love. Are you all right?"

Jonathan's voice came to Sara from a distance. She

tried to move, but her entire body ached. Forcing her eyes open, she stared up at his dear face hovering above her. Gasping to reclaim the air that the force of her landing had pushed from her lungs, she attempted to sit up, but he stopped her with a gentle hand to her arm.

"Don't move. You don't want to do more damage than has already been done."

She struggled against the restraint. "I . . . I'm fine. I ache . . . a bit, but I . . . don't think anything is broken." Finally, he relented, and she eased herself to a sitting position. Painful needles attacked every part of her body.

Experimentally, she flexed her arms and legs and, although the pain shooting through them told her that tomorrow she would have bruises aplenty, they all worked as they should. Something warm ran down her cheek. She wiped at it, and then looked at her fingers to find them smeared with blood.

"You struck your head when you went over the railing. I believe it knocked you out. There's a rather nasty-looking cut on your forehead." Jonathan wiped at it with his handkerchief.

She glanced at the railing high above them. That she hadn't broken her neck, which was probably the intended end to this event, could be nothing but a miracle.

"It was Katherine, wasn't it?"

He nodded. "She's gone now."

"Why would she do something like that?"

"Your determination. I don't think she expected it, but now she can see that you're not going to give up, and she's desperate to stop us from being together before . . ." Though he'd left the rest unsaid, Sara knew he was thinking about his and Maddy's plan to run away and get married. His beautiful brown eyes grew sad. "I'm worried about you and what she'll do next. The last thing I want is for something terrible to happen to you." He paused. "Perhaps you should give up."

"No!" More terrified than she had been gazing over the balcony railing and knowing she was about to plunge to what could be her death, she clutched at his jacket lapels. A sharp pain shot through her arm. She cried out and let go. "I will . . . not give up. Let her do her best to stop me, but I will not give you to her." She gazed up at him. "I love you, Jonathan. Katherine cannot change that, not after last night. I am yours. Forever."

He opened his mouth to speak, but his attention was caught by something behind them. Sara turned to see Julie. Her face was very pale. Her eyes were large. When Sara turned back, Jonathan was gone.

Julie rushed toward her. "Are you all right?"

She put her arm under Sara and helped her to her feet. With much wincing and groaning, Sara stood erect. It surprised Sara that Julie hadn't asked what happened first. Perhaps it was the excitement of the moment.

Nothing could be gained from keeping Julie in the dark. This time, she didn't try to hide what had happened from her friend. "Katherine pushed me off the balcony."

Julie glanced up at the gallery, then back to Sara. "I know. And Jonathan broke your fall."

Sara stared at Julie, searching her face. That would account for Julie's pale complexion and surprised expression. "You saw him this time, didn't you?"

Chapter 21

Julie nodded. "Yes, I saw Jonathan. I heard you scream, and just as I came out of the house, I saw him rush toward you and use his body to protect you from hitting the ground." She frowned. "Why do you suppose I can see him now?"

Sara had no idea, but she suspected it was because Julie had finally accepted his existence. "I don't know. I'm just glad you can so you know I haven't lost my mind." She forced a smile, despite the pain in her forehead from the cut.

"I never thought you were crazy, just unreasonably obsessed. After seeing your Jonathan, however, I can fully understand your fixation with him. His portrait does not do him justice." She grinned, wiggled her eyebrows, and then grabbed Sara's arm. "Now, let's stop all this chatter and get you inside so I can put something on that cut."

For the next few days, Sara's body served as a painful reminder of her fall. Smears of black and blue covered both arms and legs. Her right shoulder, which, despite Jonathan's attempt to soften her landing, must have taken most of her weight when she'd hit, ached horribly when she moved her arm. Her head pounded from the cut she'd received and, as a result, encouraged Raina to, on a daily basis, fuss over her endlessly while brushing her hair.

"Beats me how yo's fell over dat rail, Miss Sara. Lord above, you coulda died." Then she'd cluck her tongue in her normal *you -just -can't -be -trusted -alone* tone. This had been going on every morning since the accident.

But it hadn't been an accident. Julie knew it. Sara knew it. Katherine had pushed her. Her nemesis was no longer trying to scare her off. She wanted Sara dead, and she had no idea why the game had suddenly turned deadly.

But perhaps Maddy could tell her.

Sara retrieved Maddy's diary from the trunk and then settled on the chaise. She opened the book to the page she had last read and then turned to the next entry. Again, Maddy had skipped a large portion of time. It was a week later.

July 10, 1805

I've spent the week preparing for Jonathan's and my elopement. I have been especially careful not to give away anything, but it's difficult not to shout my joy from the roof-tops. I had lost all hope, and now the thought of being with Jonathan forever makes me smile. I still have to pinch my-self to make sure it's not all a dream and I'll awake to find he still belongs to Katherine.

I've had to hide everything from my family, especially the servants and Mother. Just yesterday, Mother inquired about my perennial good mood. I can't even recall what I told her, but whatever it was, it seemed to assuage her curiosity.

I don't think anyone else suspects, especially Katherine. If she found out, I would not put it past her to do some-thing drastic to stop us. Sometimes, though, I wonder if she's guessed something is amiss. She looks at me in that strange way she has, as though she can see through me to my very thoughts. But she says nothing. Knowing my sister as I do, I know she would not let an opportunity to deride me for something pass unnoted.

If Mother would just treat her better, perhaps Katherine would change. Father dotes on her, but Mother barely speaks to her. I don't understand it, but I'm sure it makes Katherine feel bad. Sometimes, I find myself on the edge of feeling sympathy for her, but she usually does something ugly and any sympathy I felt dissolves into anger. Off and on I've seen Katherine look at Mother with something akin to hatred in her expression.

Oh well. Very soon now, I'll have the Atlantic Ocean between my sister and me, and how she acts will no longer affect me. My heart flutters at the mere thought. Jonathan and I alone and together at last. Can it be true? Can such happiness be only days away?

This is not the time for daydreams. It's nearly midnight, and I'm to meet Jonathan to make our final plans. The house is asleep, and it's time for me to sneak down the stairs, out the back kitchen, and across the field to the orchard. He'll be waiting for me beneath the oak tree that marks the edge of the fields. I can already picture his dear face in my mind's eye, feel his lips on mine and his arms holding me close . . .

The room began to spin. Sara closed her eyes and let herself be swept into the vortex.

Moments later, Maddy stood in the orchard. The half moon's silvery light illuminated the figure of a man standing a few yards away. She ran into his open arms.

"I've missed you so," she mumbled against his warm

lips while she soaked in the feel of his solid body aligned closely with hers.

"And I you," he said, devouring her with heated kisses. Then he raised his head and cupped her face in his strong hands. "Soon, my love, nothing will part us again. Until then, let our night of love sustain us both." His arm encircled her waist, and then he drew her down beside him on a large outcropping of rocks.

Maddy rested her head on his shoulder. Where her hand lay against his shirt front, she could feel the accelerated beat of his heart against her palm. "I have everything packed and ready."

"And no one is wise to what we're doing?" His voice was thick with his denied passions.

"I'm sure no one knows. I've taken extra care to pack only at night after they've all gone to sleep. Then I've hidden the carpetbag inside a trunk in the attic."

He kissed her forehead. "It's important they think everything will go on as planned. If they even suspect we're up to something, Katherine will find a way to stop us."

"I know."

Before she could pull away, he turned his head and kissed her full on the mouth. All the passion they'd been tamping down for so long threatened to explode into the open.

Jonathan pulled away first, gasped for breath and stood. He moved a few feet away. "You are a dangerous woman, my love. A little more, and you would not leave this orchard as you came into it." He chuckled low in his throat. "But that will happen soon enough. It won't be at all easy, but we can wait until we've exchanged our vows to lie in each other's arms again."

Maddy nodded, straightened her rumpled gown, and then folded her hands in her lap.

He laughed, the sound low and sexy in his throat. "You look so demure, but I know the fires that burn deep inside you." Jonathan's face was obscured by the deepening shadows, but she felt if she reached for it, she could touch the passion saturating the air between them. Heat rose in her cheeks.

He cleared his throat. "We leave on the eve of the wedding. Can you manage to get your bag to Harrogate by midnight?"

She nodded. "If I can't, I'll leave it behind, and you can buy me a whole new wedding trousseau when we get to London. Nothing will prevent me from being there."

"Nor I. I love you so, my Maddy. I know that fate meant us for each other." For a long time, he simply stared at her. "At this moment, I want nothing more than to hold you and kiss you and make love to you until neither of us can breathe, but that would not be wise."

She said nothing. She couldn't get a word past the emotion filling her throat. Instead, she looked at him, knowing her expression told him she would not object. A breeze blew across her face, cooling her heated skin. "I live for the day when I will belong to you completely."

Something nudged at her memory. Something that told her they had already . . .

The orchard began to spin. Jonathan's face blurred out, then disappeared completely, along with her surroundings. Something was wrong. This time she spun more violently than ever before, and the brilliant colors that usually accompanied the transition in time had turned gray and ugly. Sara's stomach heaved. Her head began to pound painfully.

Suddenly, the spinning stopped. She reached out to steady herself and touched cold glass. The dread gathering in the pit of her stomach told her this was not her room. Not the place where she normally found herself after a trip back in time. Instead, she was trapped between a window and a thick drapery. The heavy material threatened to suffocate her. She struggled to free herself, but the fabric clung to her, imprisoning her in the thick folds. Curiously, this time she had not taken on Maddy's persona and was Sara Madeline Wade.

Then she heard voices.

"How can he do this to me?"

Katherine.

Sara peeked around the edge of the drape. Katherine was sitting on a settee in what Sara recognized from one of her previous trips back as the drawing room at Brentwood Plantation. This was where Phillip Degas had broken down after the engagement announcement. Beside Katherine was a brown-haired man Sara recognized as Phillip Degas. His head was bent toward his companion.

Before Sara could duck behind the drape, Katherine raised her head and stared straight at her. Sara held her breath. Katherine should have seen her. But when she said nothing, Sara realized that though their gazes should have met, Katherine seemed to look right through her. Could it be that they couldn't see her at all? Stranger things had happened.

She continued to stare at Katherine, but the woman showed no sign of having seen her. Knowing Katherine as she did, Sara knew she would not pass up an opportunity to attack her sister for spying on her. Convinced that Katherine couldn't see her, Sara took a deep, fortifying breath and stepped out from behind the drape and into full view of both of the people on the settee. Neither of them as much as blinked.

Slowly, still fearing she might be discovered, she made her way to the chair across from them. Still, neither of them showed a sign that they were aware of her presence in the room.

She sat and listened.

"Jonathan is betrothed to me. Me! Does he expect me to live with a man for the rest of my life who would rather be with another woman?" Katherine sniffed loudly. Then she dabbed at her eyes with a lacy white handkerchief. Giving another loud sniff, she peeked over the edge of the handkerchief at Phillip. Her eyes were as dry as Sara's.

It's all a masquerade.

Phillip patted her hand. "I'm sure you're imagining this, my dear. What man would not be honored to have you as his wife?"

You certainly would, Sara thought.

Katherine forced a smile. "You're so sweet, Phillip. I wish Jonathan thought as you do."

"I'm sure he does."

Another theatrical sob issued from Katherine. "No, he doesn't. He's lusting after my sister. My own sister! I saw them kissing in the garden the very night of our engagement." She leaned her head on Phillip's shoulder. "He's broken my heart." Several more well-orchestrated sobs followed.

Phillip's complexion reddened with rage. "That bastard doesn't deserve a woman like you." He gathered Katherine in his arms. "Were it me, I would cherish you for all time."

"If it weren't for my betrothal to him, I would welcome

your suit, Phillip. Any woman would be lucky to spend her life with you." She inserted another well-executed sob for effect. Sara wanted to scream at Phillip not to believe her, but she knew he couldn't hear her. "I've asked him over and over to release me, but he refuses. He wants my dowry to save his father from disgrace." Another sob and a dramatic dab at her eyes added emphasis to her blatant lie. "He says I'll only be released if he dies."

Phillip raised his head. The look of intense hatred in his eyes frightened Sara. But as quickly as it had come, it disappeared when he bowed his head and looked at the woman leaning against him. The same love Sara had seen in Jonathan's eyes when he looked at Maddy filled Phillip's.

"Perhaps we should oblige him," he said softly against her hair.

Over his shoulder, Sara could see a dry-eyed Katherine's mouth turn up in a satisfied smile.

My God! Katherine had planned this all along. She'd coerced poor, unsuspecting Phillip into becoming a murderer by playing on his love for her with the use of fake tears and outright lies.

Sara was stunned. She couldn't believe what she'd just overheard. Having been the victim of it many times, she knew Maddy's sister's cruel side well, but she never realized Katherine's vindictiveness knew no bounds.

Anger, hot and intense, roiled inside Sara. No longer

able to remain silent, Sara opened her mouth to refute Katherine's lies.

Again the room began to spin but, as before, the colors were dark and dreary. The motion was violent, and Sara's stomach heaved in revolt against the ferocious rotation.

This time, when the spinning finally ceased, she didn't recognize anything about her surroundings. And because the people around her didn't react, she knew she was once more invisible, just as when she'd eavesdropped on Phillip and Katherine.

The stench, a product of either the unwashed bodies of the men engaged in everything from gambling with small round objects to sewing rips in their clothing or the excrement scattered around the ground, made her cover her nose with her handkerchief. High stone walls surrounded them, and other men with guns stood watch over the motley group. The men seated around the courtyard were dressed in clothing so dirty she couldn't tell the color of the material.

Prison. She was in The Cabildo prison yard. But why?

Then, in the far corner, she saw a man who was very familiar to her. Phillip Degas. Like his clothes, his hands were encrusted with filth. His brown hair, which had been neat and trimmed to above his collar when he was speaking to Katherine, now hung in long, grimy tangles around his shoulders. He was gnawing on what looked like a chicken bone that had long since given up any semblance of meat.

Sara wondered if he had any idea what his life would become when he decided to kill Jonathan for Katherine. And poor Clarice. Had she seen her son here? Sara fervently hoped not. It would kill her. Losing him would be easy compared to seeing him living like this.

Picking her way carefully, lifting her skirt high enough to keep it from dragging in the garbage on the ground, and clamping the handkerchief securely over her nose, she moved closer to him.

Just as she reached him, a man with a long, straggly beard flopped down beside Phillip. From inside his shirt, he pulled out two more chicken legs. These still retained a bit of meat. Both men attacked them with unrestrained relish. When they'd finished, they put the bones in their pockets, no doubt for later.

Phillip dragged himself to his feet and walked away. Sara followed him down a long corridor to a dank cell, hardly big enough for him to move around in. The odors in this tiny place of confinement were worse than in the open courtyard.

Phillip stretched out on a pile of dirty rags that

served as his bed. He threw his forearm over his eyes and sighed. Sara stood silently in the corner, trying to figure out why she was there.

Suddenly, Phillip bolted upright and stared straight at her. "Maddy?"

Rather than correct him, she allowed him to believe she was Katherine's sister. "Hello, Phillip."

He peered around her, no doubt searching for Katherine. Disappointment washed over his expression. "She hasn't come with you?"

Sara shook her head, her throat full of sorrow for this poor deluded man. "I'm sorry."

He buried his face in his hands and then raised his gaze to her and shook his head. "You have nothing to be sorry for. It's been two years, and she has never come to see me. I thought maybe this time—" Sara reached out to touch him, but he pulled away. "As you can see, my toilet has not been at its best in here. I find my hair is full of bugs and my skin sometimes peels off in layers that I'm not sure are actually skin or just the filth I live in every day. I am far from acceptable company for a lady."

"Phillip, Katherine is never going to come here," she said in an effort to stop his rambling excuses for his appearance.

He nodded. "I know."

But he didn't know. He had no idea that she tricked

him into this. That she didn't care a jot for him or what happened to him as long as Katherine got her way. He at least had the right to know that much, instead of spending his miserable life here waiting for someone who would never come.

"No, you don't know, at least not everything."

His gaze narrowed. "What are you talking about?"

"That Katherine tricked you. That she used your love for her to get you to do exactly what she wanted you to do. She's evil, Phillip, and totally unworthy of your love and devotion."

For a moment, she expected him to argue with her, but then his face crumpled. "Having little else to think about in the past two years, I think I've come to know all of that, but as long as no one actually said the words, I could talk myself into believing she'd really cared about me."

"Katherine cares for no one but herself." The hatred she held for Maddy's sister colored Sara's voice. "You don't deserve this. If there were justice in this world, and she could be punished for using you and your love, it would be Katherine sitting here in this hell hole and not you." She shook her head. Her next words were more Sara's thoughts than Maddy's: "Is there no limit to the lengths to which she'll go to achieve her goals and with no thought of the consequences to others?"

He raised his head and met her gaze. The eyes that

had been dull and lifeless suddenly came alive; his features beneath the mane of dirty, tangled hair animated. "There's something you don't know. She—"

Suddenly, the walls of Phillip's prison cell blurred, and the spinning began again.

Sara cried out. "No! Not yet!"

She wanted to hear what Phillip was about to say. But the spinning grew faster, and this time the colors were bright and beautiful as always, the spinning less violent than it had been when she'd ended up in the Brentwood drawing room or in the Cabildo. This time, in her heart, Sara knew she was on her way back to Harrogate.

Chapter 22

Sara bolted upright in the chair. She waited for the intense melancholy at the loss of Jonathan's presence that always accompanied her return from the past. But it never came. This time, she was overcome by anger at Katherine's manipulation of Phillip, and fear for Jonathan's life.

As she recalled the conversation between Maddy and Jonathan in the orchard, she almost wept with the realization that their plans would never see fruition. They'd had such high hopes for their future and such deep love for each other, and it had all come to a bitter end with one bullet from a jealous man duped into committing a terrible crime by a woman who thought only of herself.

If only she could have remained there long enough

to hear what Phillip would have told her. What was it she didn't know? Did he know the secret of their births? Or was there something else?

"Sara?"

She glanced up and found Julie sitting on the bed, her face twisted with worry. "I've been waiting for you. You were gone a very long time. Does it always take so long?"

Sara shook her head, closed the diary, and laid it on the table. "I don't know. It doesn't seem long. However, this time was very different from the others."

"How?"

"In the past, I've gone back to one place and then returned. This time, I went to three different places. First I was Maddy with Jonathan, but then I was myself and I overheard Phillip and Katherine talking about . . ."

"About what?"

"About killing Jonathan to release Katherine from the betrothal."

Julie gasped, and then frowned. "But didn't you tell me Maddy had asked Katherine to release Jonathan, and she refused?"

"Yes, Maddy asked her, and Jonathan asked her. But that's not what she told Phillip. She let him believe she had asked to be released from the betrothal and Jonathan had refused because he wanted her dowry. It was all a lie. She was never going to let him go."

"If she'd been so determined to hang onto him, she must have had some feelings for him. So why would she want to kill him?"

Sara scoffed. "She had feelings for no one but herself. She wanted him dead because she saw Maddy and Jonathan kissing, and if Jonathan lived, Maddy won. If he died, Katherine won. Through his death, she would make sure Maddy never had him."

"So she got Phillip to do it for her. The woman really is evil. Not to mention conniving and cowardly."

"Then I was whisked away to the Cabildo. Phillip was there. He said that Katherine—"

A ceramic statue on the mantel suddenly flew through the air, barely missing Julie's head. Both women turned and followed its flight. Then it smashed against the wall, shards of glass spraying all over the floor.

Though slightly pale and visibly shaken, Julie smiled weakly. "Add ill-tempered to that, too."

A high-pitched scream rent the air, and a white misty figure sailed across the room and through the wall behind the bed. It was only the second time Sara had actually seen Katherine's ghost. She shivered.

Julie, complexion snow white, eyes as large as dinner plates, stared in frozen awe at the wall. "Was that—"

"Katherine," Sara finished for her. "She doesn't normally appear in full apparition. Gran told me it takes a great deal of energy for a ghost to materialize. Katherine's rage at what you said must have made it possible."

Throwing a wary glance at the wall where Katherine had vanished, Julie sighed. "So what are you going to do?"

Sara looked at Julie. She couldn't believe her friend would have to ask. "Stop him."

"You'll be playing with history, Sara. Do you think that's a good idea?"

She picked up the diary and ran her hand over the cover. This book had connected her to a love she had never hoped to find. She could not turn away from him. "I can't let Phillip kill him again. I can't." Anguish filled her voice, and the familiar melancholy descended on her.

"But he's already—"

"Dead," she snapped. Then more softly she said, "I know." She laid the book aside and went to sit beside Julie on the bed. "You don't understand. When I go back there and become Maddy, Jonathan is as real as you are. I can feel his touch, his kiss; hear his voice telling me he loves me; caress his dear face. I can't just stand by, knowing what I know now, and do nothing to stop it."

True to her word, Julie laid her hand on Sara's. "What can I do to help you?"

Sara stood and began pacing the floor. "I need time to think, to plan. If you can just see to Harrogate, as you've been doing, that would be a big help."

"How long do you have?"

Sara stopped and faced her friend. Her heart pounded against her chest. "The wedding will take place in a few days. I have until the night before."

"Very well." Suddenly, Julie's face changed. Her expression became heartbreakingly sad. But she said nothing.

Sara didn't need to ask what Julie was thinking. If Sara were successful and saved Jonathan's life . . .

Suddenly, the same high-pitched wail that had preceded Katherine's previous appearance filled the room. Her specter floated through the wall, passed both women as though they weren't there, and then grabbed the diary, and vanished.

The diary, her means to returning to Jonathan, was gone.

During the next days, which seemed at times to stretch out far beyond their twenty-four-hour time frame and at other times to pass by far too swiftly, Sara lived in constant fear of not being able to go back to save Jonathan. Where could Katherine have put the diary? Had she taken it back into the past with her? If she had, there would be no way for Sara to go back again.

By the end of the second day, her nerves were so raw, she was hardly able to concentrate or hold a conversation with anyone. Every time a board creaked or a shutter banged, she jumped. Her appetite diminished in direct contrast to her rising anxiety. Sleep eluded her. It was a miracle that the rug in her room didn't have a path running through it from the many hours she'd spent pacing the floor, thinking. Over and over she checked the trunk, just in case Katherine's twisted sense of humor had prompted her to replace it in the last place Sara would look, but it was always empty.

Once again, worried concern reflected from Raina's and Julie's faces. Of course, Julie knew why, but Raina didn't and compensated by fussing over Sara until she thought she'd go crazy.

"Yo's gonna make yourself sick again, Miss Sara. Yo gots to eat somethin'."

Every meal was the same ritual. Julie watched her shove food around her plate, and Raina hovered off to the side, frowning at her. Once the meal ended, the two of them fussed over her and tried to get her to go to bed early. Little did they realize that going to bed early served no purpose. She would either lie there, staring at the ceiling, or pace the floor trying to think where the diary could be. Either way, sleep remained elusive.

This night was no different. As she paced the confined space between the window and her bed, Sara increasingly feared she would not be able to get back to save Jonathan.

By now, she'd become convinced that Katherine had taken the diary back in time where, since she could no longer go back, Sara would never find it. Without it, Jonathan would die again and Maddy would die a desolate, sorrowful old maid.

Despondent, she threw herself on the bed. "There has to be a way I can do this without the diary." Tossing and turning, she racked her brain for an answer.

Finally, she settled on her side and stared out the window at the full moon hanging in the sky. It reminded her of the ball of light that had accompanied Gran on her first visit to Sara.

Then it came to her. Gran's advice.

Be careful, my darling girl, and be happy. Above all else, trust in the power of love.

Trust in the power of love.

Why had she had to be reminded of how strong her love for Jonathan was? If there was anything in this world that would take her to him it was her love.

She lay on her back and stared at his portrait above the mantel. From deep inside, she summoned her love.

It began as a small, warm ball in the pit of her stomach. Slowly, it grew and blossomed with an intensity that nearly stole her breath away. Still it kept growing, expanding, sending a need through Sara that defied description.

Need became longing.

Longing turned to devotion.

Devotion turned to love.

The love swelled inside her like a rising tide, growing and filling every part of her being with a fiery warmth and peace that left her limp. Closing her eyes, she allowed the love to take over her body and fill it with purpose.

Then the spinning began, swirling and twirling Sara through the rainbow vortex to Jonathan. But it was different this time. This time it was frantic and more violent than ever before, as though it had to get her there with as much expediency as possible.

Maddy finished putting the last of her clothes in the carpetbag. She shoved it under her bed. Later, when everyone was asleep, she'd take it back to the attic, where it would stay until tomorrow night.

"Why are you still awake?"

Maddy spun guiltily toward the voice.

Victoria Grayson stood in the bedroom door smiling at her daughter. "You should be in bed. You have to look your best for the wedding tomorrow."

"I was just going to ring for Floree to help me get ready for bed," Maddy said, hoping she sounded convincing, but sure her guilt was written clearly on her face for her mother to see.

"No need to call Floree. I'm sure she's retired for the night. I'll help you." Her mother caressed her cheek, then went to her dresser and withdrew a nightdress. She laid the nightgown on the bed, and then she turned Maddy so she could undo the buttons down the back of her dress.

Maddy stepped out of her dress, and then stood still while her mother helped her remove her undergarments. Her mother slipped the nightdress over her head and tied the ribbons that held the front closed. Maddy allowed her mother's ministration, knowing this would be the last time in a very long time that she would be able to be this close to her mother.

Leaving her mother would break her heart. But not leaving her would crush her soul.

"I haven't helped you dress in a very long time." Victoria's voice caught. "I remember when you were a little girl and I would brush your hair at bedtime." She chuckled. "You'd insist on taking the brush from me to brush mine. Then it would take my maid hours to get out the tangles."

Maddy turned to her, kissed her cheek, and gazed into her mother's dear face. "I remember that. It's one of my favorite childhood memories."

Her mother's eyes grew moist with unshed tears. Quickly, she pulled a lacy handkerchief from beneath her cuff and dabbed at her eyes. "Look at me getting all weepy over helping you get ready for bed."

"Momma, I love you."

Victoria cupped Maddy's cheeks in both hands. "I love you, too, Maddy." For a long moment, her mother stared into her eyes, and then she pushed a hair from her forehead. "Come sit on the bed, and I'll brush your hair."

Maddy sat with her back to her mother. Very slowly, her mother ran the brush through her daughter's loosened hair. Neither of them said anything. Maddy wasn't sure how much time had slipped by before her mother spoke again.

"It should have been you, you know."

Puzzled, Maddy turned to face her. "What should have been me?"

"You should have—" Suddenly her mother dropped the brush and rushed sobbing from the room.

Puzzled, Maddy consigned her mother's strange outburst to nerves. After all, it wasn't every day one's daughter got married. The time leading up to the wedding had been a hectic whirl of arranging the wedding, ordering flowers cut from Brentwoods' gardens, choosing a menu for the party afterward, sending invitations, last-minute fittings of all their gowns, and more. Since Maddy had been preoccupied with her plans to run off with Jonathan, she had been little or no help to her mother, and Katherine had simply sat back and let everyone else do all the work.

Was it any wonder then that her mother's nerves had caught up with her?

As she did every night, Maddy prepared to make her daily entry into her diary. When she went to her dresser to get it, it wasn't there. With panic licking at her nerves, she searched everywhere: in her dresser, under her bed, in the armoire, behind the books she kept on her shelves, and even on the balcony outside her room. But it was nowhere to be found.

Where could she have left it? She was always careful to put it somewhere where no one could read it. If it fell into Katherine's hands . . .

Katherine!

Maddy slipped from her room and tiptoed down the hall to her sister's room. Making as little noise as possible, she turned the knob, opened the door, and stepped inside. A shaft of moonlight fell across the bed, illuminating the sleeping form of her sister. Looking at the peaceful expression and the hint of a smile on her sleeping face, Maddy would never have guessed that true evil resided inside this woman. But Maddy wasn't fooled. She knew what Katherine was capable of.

Shifting her gaze from her sister's face, she scanned the room. Then she gasped. On the table beside the bed lay the diary. Though she'd hoped to find it here, she'd also dreaded it.

If Katherine had read it, she'd know of the elopement she and Jonathan planned to carry out tomorrow night. She could not believe her sister had such a treasure and had not read the words with relish. Was that why she smiled even in her sleep? Had she already hatched a plan to stop them?

Paralyzing fear took hold of Maddy's limbs. The sickening knowledge that Katherine knew everything forced her to move. Along with it came the surety that she would do everything in her power to make sure the elopement never took place.

Limbs quaking and nerves as tight as a bow string, Maddy crept to the side of the bed and picked up her diary. Cradling it against her pounding heart, she quietly backed out of the room and closed the door.

Back in her own room, she sat on the bed, opened the diary to read her last entry, and, even though she already knew she had, prayed she hadn't written too much. But it was all there, every detail, and after reading it, she knew that if Katherine had read it, and Maddy had little hope of that eventuality, her sister also knew every detail.

Worst yet, she couldn't even warn Jonathan. He'd gone to New Orleans to make the final plans for the voyage to England and wouldn't be back until tomorrow evening.

She'd just have to hope they could make their getaway before Katherine could stop them.

Maddy leaned back on her bed, held the diary against her heart, and allowed the tears to fall. Had they gotten their hopes up for naught? Would Katherine win again? Would she ever have a life with her beloved Jonathan, or were they destined to never be together?

Before she could form any answers, the room tilted off center and then began to spin crazily.

Sara stared down at the diary lying on the bed beside her. Hopelessness overwhelmed her. Katherine's ghost had stolen the diary and delivered it into the hands of the one person who could use it to her advantage. The person who would persuade Phillip to kill Jonathan. And she could do nothing about it except wait for the next night and try to get to the garden before Katherine and Phillip did.

Chapter 23

Julie fanned herself with a copy of *Harper's New Monthly Magazine,* from which she'd been reading aloud to Sara from a poem entitled "Ode to the Sun" by Leigh Hunt. As she tried to stir the heavy air, she gazed languidly out over the manicured lawn of Harrogate.

Julie said the poem fit the sweltering July day perfectly. For Sara it only underscored the way her damp clothes stuck to her skin and the perspiration beaded on her forehead and upper lip, all things of which she needed no reminder, even in lyrical poetry.

She sighed and leaned her head back against the rocking chair, impatient for the sunset to hurry on so the heat of the day would dissipate and relief would come through the cooling evening breezes off the river. Even more urgent was the fact that, as the night deepened, it would be time for her to go back to Maddy's time to stop Phillip.

It seemed she'd waited forever for this day to come.

The squeak of Julie's rocker ceased. "Are you still bent on doing this?"

Sara had no need to ask what her friend referred to. "I love him, Julie. Do I have a choice?"

Julie shook her head. "I suppose not."

Sara stopped rocking and stared in awe at her friend. "You suppose? Julie, if it were you, and you knew the man you loved was going to die, wouldn't you do everything in your power to prevent it?"

Julie looked confused. "I honestly don't know if I could love anyone so much that I could do what you have been doing . . . and will do tonight."

Sara touched the back of her friend's hand. "I truly hope and pray that the day will come when you do know this kind of love."

Neither of them spoke again for a long time. The shadows on the veranda began to lengthen, and the sun slipped lower and lower in the sky. A lone star twinkled against the fading light.

Finally, when the sun had been long gone and a sliver of moon hung high in the sky, the time came for Sara to retire to her room. She stood.

Julie took her hand. "Be careful, Sara."

So many emotions—fear, apprehension, anticipation, and eagerness—blocked Sara's throat so that she couldn't speak. So she simply nodded and squeezed Julie's fingers.

As she climbed the stairs, she was very aware that everything that had happened in the last few weeks had been leading to this night and the terrible events about to unfold. Aside from the ever present worry for Jonathan's life, she was also ambushed by the unmistakable sensation that she was about to walk into her destiny.

In her room, she tucked into her pocket the cotton bag Marie Laveau had given her for protection, sat in her usual place, and opened the diary.

The day has dragged on stubbornly slow feet. But the time is drawing near now when I will leave Brentwood forever. I'm going to try to get to the garden before Katherine so I can warn Jonathan that she knows about us and will probably try to stop us. I have no idea what it will be; I just know my sister, and she will not let this slight go unpunished.

My carpetbag is packed and waiting in the attic trunk. I can't believe that by tomorrow at this time I will be Mrs. Jonathan Bradford. My only regret is that I'll be breaking my mother's heart. All my life, she's been my friend, my confidante, and my champion. It seems heartless to run off and not tell her, not have her at my wedding, but I must. I can't take the chance that anyone will stop us.

The clock on the mantel seems to have slowed to almost a standstill. It feels like hours have gone by, when it's actually only been minutes. Soon, very soon, the clock will chime and . . .

This time when the vortex began to spin, Sara felt a distinct finality about it. For a moment, she wanted to stop it and go back. But then she was reminded of why she *had* to go back this time. Jonathan's life depended on it. No one else but Phillip and maybe Katherine knew what was about to happen, and neither of them would prevent it.

She relaxed and allowed the churning tunnel to take her wherever it would.

Sara paced in the strangeness of Maddy's bedroom, waiting impatiently for the house to fall silent so she could sneak out and make her way to Harrogate. Hopefully, no one had discovered the horse Maddy had saddled and left tied in the orchard, and it was still there.

She walked to the window. The sky was black with stars scattered over it like raindrops on a windowpane. No bright moonlight illuminated the grounds surrounding the Graysons' Brentwood plantation home. Though it would make it harder for her to see where she was going, lack of moonlight would cover her flight.

The clock on the mantel chimed the half hour. Eleven thirty. Time for her to go. Sara knew that right after dinner Maddy had excused herself early and retrieved the carpetbag she'd packed and hidden in the attic and stashed it beneath her bed. Grabbing the bag, she crept carefully from the room and, without questioning how she knew, wound her way down the stairs and through the unfamiliar rooms to the kitchen.

As she reached for the kitchen door, she heard voices beyond it. She jerked her hand back and pressed her ear to the door. One of the voices sounded like Floree, Katherine's maid.

"Daniel, you best be watching where you puts your hands, boy."

"Aw, Floree, you know you likes me to touch you."

"If one of the Graysons finds us, ain't gonna make no never mind what I like. They'll have our hides." A feminine giggle, no doubt Floree's, filtered through the door. "Now, you best stop that." The sound of flesh hitting flesh came next. "Glory be, boy, you got more hands than a spider got legs."

"If you's so afraid of dem catchin' us, let's get ourselves to the barn. Ain't nobody gonna find us there at this time a night."

A short silence followed. Then Sara heard scurrying feet, a door opened and closed, then silence. They were gone. She slipped through the door and into the kitchen. At the back door, she paused and looked out to make sure they wouldn't see her and were indeed heading for the barn; then she dashed from the house and across the yard toward the barn, her skirts tucked high on her thighs to prevent tripping over them.

On the other side of the barnyard, she slipped into the shadows of the trees and tripped over a bucket. It clattered across the yard on its side. She waited, and when no one came, she breathed a sigh of relief that she hadn't been detected. Then the barn door squeaked open.

"Who's there? Miss Maddy, Miss Katherine, that best not be you."

Sara held her breath and ducked behind the large trunk of a spreading oak. The frightened voice was Floree's. She must have heard the bucket's racket and come out of the barn just as Sara entered the shadow of the trees. She said nothing and hoped Floree would decide she'd been hearing things.

"Floree, what dems gals be doin' runnin' 'round out there at dis hour? Dey's all in bed, woman." Another short silence, then a change of tone. "Come on back here, sugar. We gots business to see to, and I gots us a nice bed made in da hay."

The barn door squeaked and then thudded closed. The latch clattered into place. Daniel's coaxing must have worked. When Sara peeked around the tree trunk, Floree was nowhere to be seen. Sara let out the breath she'd been holding and raced instinctively through the darkness toward where she knew Maddy had left the horse. Oddly, although she didn't feel at all like Maddy, she thought like her. It was as if Maddy was inside her, guiding her movements.

Zigzagging through the trees, she made her way to the far side of the oak grove. As she neared the edge of the clearing that separated Brentwood land from Harrogate land, she heard the soft whinny of a horse. Slowly, she crept toward the sound. If anyone had discovered the horse, they could be waiting for whoever planned to retrieve it.

Peering through the darkness, she could see Daisy, Maddy's mare, standing patiently and tethered to a small sapling, just as Maddy had left her earlier that afternoon. The horse raised her head and sniffed loudly in Sara's direction. Daisy pawed the ground several times and then settled down to wait.

Sara slipped from behind the tree, walked to the horse, petted her nose and crooned to her, and then, hooking the carpetbag on the saddle horn, stood on a nearby stump and climbed into the saddle, her legs astride, her dress hiked up to her thighs. With a gentle nudge to Daisy's flanks, Sara propelled her toward the road leading to Harrogate.

At Harrogate, Sara stopped at the end of the drive, slipped from the saddle, unhooked her carpetbag, and smacked Daisy on the behind. The horse headed back down the road toward Brentwood. She would go home. Maddy had often sent her home when she wanted to walk back from a long ride. Daisy could always find her barn, her cozy stall, and the full feeding bin of oats.

A waning sliver of crescent moon hung in the sky, shedding little or no light on the earth. In the impenetrable darkness, Harrogate stood alone, stately, magnificent, and cloaked in a shroud of mystery. Sara raced frantically up the driveway. The carpetbag bounced off her legs, impeding her progress. Skirting the big house, she headed directly for the Garden of the Moon. Without hesitation, she dropped the cumbersome carpetbag outside, and then hurried down the path.

The darkness in the garden hampered Sara's progress. Here and there a white flower shone through the black night making a feeble attempt to light Sara's way. Blindly, she picked her route through the shrubs, hoping she was heading toward the gazebo where she was to meet Jonathan.

She'd realized hours ago that, unlike most other times when she'd made this trip back into the past, this time she hadn't taken on the persona of Maddy. Although she knew in her heart she *was* Maddy, for some reason, this time she had retained her own identity. Now she had an idea why.

When Maddy had gone to meet Jonathan on that fateful night, she had no knowledge of what awaited them in the darkness, only the supposition that Katherine would stop them if she could. Because Sara knew for sure what awaited the lovers, she had a better chance of preventing Jonathan's death. Whether she did it as Maddy or as Sara no longer mattered, as long as she saved her beloved Jonathan.

Urgency to get to Jonathan in time pushed her on. Anxiety churned away in her stomach. Her hands felt damp, as did her forehead. Her taut nerves kept her stiff and alert to every sound. As she reached out to push aside encumbering branches, she noted that her hands shook. Thorns snagged her dress, almost as though they were in league with Katherine and trying to hold her back. She tore the garment loose, ignoring the sound of the material being shredded.

Pushing on through the jungle of flowers and vines,

she listened intently for anything that would signal someone else's presence. So far, the only other presence in the garden seemed to be the night creatures that crawled through the bushes, invisible to their prey.

Vaguely, in the distance, she could just make out the outline of the gazebo. Standing beside it, tall and confident, was Jonathan. A branch broke beneath Sara's foot, and he swung toward her.

"Maddy? Is that you?"

She opened her mouth to affirm, but stopped when she noticed a shadow moving out of the trees, arm outstretched and holding a dueling pistol. Her heart lurched into her throat. For a moment, her feet were frozen to the ground. A scream of warning caught in her throat.

The shadows were too deep for her to properly identify the person, but in her heart she knew it was Phillip come to do Katherine's dirty work. In another moment, it would be too late.

Without thinking, she dashed forward, throwing herself between the gun and Jonathan.

Everything after that happened in slow motion.

Jonathan dashed toward her.

She could see his mouth moving, but she couldn't hear his words.

A loud explosion rent the night.

The flash of muzzle fire lit up the face of the person

336

holding the gun.

Katherine!

That couldn't be. Phillip. It was supposed to be Phillip who fired the gun.

A white hot pain pierced the left side of Sara's chest. Her body was thrown backwards.

Chapter 24

Sara opened her eyes to find Jonathan bending over her. "My love, how foolish of you." Though his words reprimanded her, his gentle, concerned expression did not. He scooped her into his arms and stood.

Over his shoulder, Sara saw Phillip rush from the bushes and take the gun from a dazed Katherine. He glanced toward where Sara and Jonathan were, and then to the gun in his hand.

"My God, you actually did it." His voice was high pitched, frightened. "I thought you were just talking, that you wouldn't actually go through with it."

"But they were going to leave, Phillip. He was going with her and leaving me all alone at the altar." Katherine's voice emerged a whine. Something that rarely happened to her.

Without a word, he led her a few feet away.

She grabbed his arm and stopped him. "It was supposed to be Jonathan, not her. He was going to run away with her, Phillip. Don't you see? I thought you would do it for me, but you were late, so I had to stop him myself." Her protest hung on the night air. Then her voice turned frantic, frightened, childlike, bordering on crazed. "You can't tell them I shot her. They'll put me in prison. I'd die in prison, Phillip. You have to help me. I love you, Phillip. I've always loved you. I was just marrying him to hurt her."

"I know, *bien-aimé.*" Phillip spoke to her as though she were the child she sounded like. "I'll take care of you. I promise. You won't go to prison."

Katherine's' voice no longer held the strength Sara was used to hearing in it. She sounded more and more like a child begging a parent for help than a grown woman who had just shot her fiancé's lover.

"You can't let anyone know. Please, Phillip. Say you won't tell anyone. Please? Promise, Phillip."

"I promise, *chère.* Don't worry. I won't tell anyone, and I won't allow them to take you away," Phillip said. "Everything will be fine. Just leave it to me." Then, with his arm securely around her, they disappeared into the darkness.

Sara watched them go, and then collapsed against

Jonathan's shoulder.

When Sara awoke, she was lying on the bed in a very familiar, yet strange room. She looked around. It was her room at Harrogate, but not as she knew it. It was as it had been when it was to be the bedroom where Katherine and Jonathan would have spent their wedding night.

She tried to sit up, but a searing, white-hot pain shot through her shoulder. Moaning, she dropped back against the pillow. For a moment, she couldn't understand what was going on, and then she recalled the gun and jumping between the bullet and Jonathan.

"Jonathan?"

"Lie still. I'm right here." Jonathan bent over her with a cloth in his hand. "It's not bad. Thank God, the bullet just grazed your shoulder." He peeled back her gown and washed the blood from her skin. Then he bandaged the wound. "Why?" he asked. "Why would you do that?" His expression crumbled, and tears gathered in his eyes. "My heart stopped when the bullet struck you. I thought you were—"

She laid her finger over his lips. "But I'm not." She smiled through the pain radiating from the wound. "I did it because I love you. Because life without you is not worth living." She slid her hand to the side and caressed his cheeks. "Wouldn't you have done the same for me?"

"Without a second thought." He smoothed the hair from her cheeks, and then kissed each in turn.

"I'm sorry I ruined our plans."

He shook his head. "You ruined nothing. I have a feeling Katherine will not object to our marriage now. She's aware that we know something that can ruin her forever."

Sara frowned. "She tried to kill you. You're not going to tell the authorities?"

He smiled slyly. "I don't plan on telling anyone what happened in the garden tonight, and I will urge Phillip not to as well, but I also don't plan on telling her that. I will ask her to publicly release me from our betrothal, but I will make it very clear that if she refuses, this night will no longer remain our secret."

He sat beside Sara and took her hand. "What matters right now is you're all right, we can be married, and we have a future we can look forward to." He paused. "That is, if you decide to remain *here* with me."

She didn't miss the emphasis he put on the word *here*. She was almost afraid to ask. Her pulse fluttered hard against her skin. "At Harrogate?"

"Yes, but also in my lifetime. Will you, Sara?"

"Sara?"

That was the first and only time he'd called her by

that name. He knew who she was. He'd known all along.

As if reading her mind, he said, "I know who you are. I also know that in here," he laid his hand over her heart, "you are Maddy Grayson, the woman I have loved over many lifetimes." He smiled. "You knew, too, didn't you?"

Sara had known for a long time that Maddy's spirit lived on in her. "Yes, but—"

He stopped her with his lips. They were warm, loving, tender, and insistent. He raised his head and gazed deeply into her eyes. "Will you stay with me?"

Remain with him in 1805? Could she? It would mean leaving her family, Julie, and all her friends behind. It would mean . . . being with the man she loved more than life itself . . . forever.

Although she'd known all along that someday she would have to face this moment, making the choice between Sara's life and Maddy's was no easier.

The last words her father had spoken to her when she had left New Orleans rang through her memory.

I want more than anything for you to be happy. If Jonathan is what it takes, then you have my blessing. But I will miss you terribly, my darling daughter.

A knot of profound sadness formed in her throat. Her father had known before she had what her decision would be. He knew she wouldn't save Jonathan only to leave him. He knew her destiny was to be at Jonathan's side wherever he might be. In all honesty she, too, had known all along where she would choose to spend her lifetime if given the chance.

She smiled up at him. "Your life is mine. I love you, and I would rather that bullet had pierced my heart than leave you."

Jonathan gathered her gently in his arms.

Maddy had finally come home.

But not for good. Not yet. There were still a few things Sara had to take care of before she could begin life with Jonathan as Madeline Grayson-Bradford.

"I must go back one more time, my love." She glanced at the diary where it lay on the dresser. "Please, give me the diary."

Jonathan left her side and retrieved the diary, and then brought it to her.

With his help, she sat up straighter, then laid the book on her lap and opened it to the back, to the pages that had always remained inaccessible to her . . . until now. The diary fell open under her fingers. There, tucked in the fold of the spine, was an envelope. Had Maddy put it there? Was this the elusive letter Sara had searched for? *Miss Madeline Grayson* was written across the front.

Carefully, Sara opened the envelope and slid the paper from inside. Almost afraid of what she'd find, she unfolded it and read it aloud.

My dear, perfect sister,

Long ago, you asked me why I was making Jonathan hold to the bargain Papa made with Mr. Bradford at our birth. Now that my time in this life grows short, I'm ready to give you my answer.

You. You were the reason.

You always had everything: Momma's love, Papa's admiration, the adoration of all the servants, men who came from miles around to worship at your feet. I had nothing. Not even the right to the Grayson name.

Oh yes, I knew. I overheard Papa and Momma arguing, and I found out that I was his mistress' daughter. That makes me his bastard child. Was it any wonder that Momma couldn't stand the sight of me? She knew it was you, as their legitimate firstborn, who should have married Jonathan.

But Jonathan was the one thing of yours that I had, and I was going to hang onto him. Then I saw you kissing him, and I knew I didn't even have him, not really. But I could. There was a way I could always have him for myself . . . a way that not even you could overcome.

When I read your diary and found that you were planning to elope on the eve of our wedding, I was furious and knew I had to find a way to stop you. Then I caught Floree taking your note to him, the note telling him you'd meet him in the garden at Harrogate and would run away with him. I got one of Jonathan's dueling pistols and went to the garden to wait for him.

The fool arrived, satchel in hand, smiling and full of anticipation. All ready to run off to England with my little, perfect sister. I was going to confront him and tell him he would have to make a choice between us. But then I knew he'd chosen you, and I couldn't have that. How would it have looked to all our friends? Jilted the day before my wedding. I wouldn't have been able to live with the humiliation, so I killed him.

Yes, I know everyone thinks that poor, lovesick fool, Phillip, did it. He was supposed to. I was sure he would. But he showed up too late. However, like the simple, subservient, besotted fool that he is, he took the gun from me, along with the blame for having pulled the trigger. I didn't dispute his claim. After all, if he wanted to go to prison for the sake of his "undying love" for me, who was I to deny him that right?

I did, however, miss his little gifts and attention. But that's neither here nor there.

I have little time left. Before I go into death, it is important that you know I was the one who took away the person you loved more than life itself and even more important that you know that in this life or the next, Jonathan will never be yours.

Your bastard sister,
Katherine Grayson

Sara folded the letter and tucked it back into the book. Despite all that had happened, she felt a deep, abiding sorrow for Katherine. Her entire life had been based on a lie perpetuated by the very people who were supposed to love her, and her vengeance had been fueled by a groundless jealousy. In her heart, Sara was certain that Maddy had always accepted Katherine as her sister, and knowing the truth of Katherine's conception wouldn't have changed that. But no one had given them the chance to even develop the closeness and love that should exist between sisters.

Sara looked at Jonathan, his face blurred by her unshed tears. "She knew all along she was not our mother's daughter. How awful for her to have to pretend, to know that each time Momma referred to her as her daughter, it was a lie."

Jonathan took her hand. "Don't feel too sorry for her. She made her life what it was. No one else did."

Sara shook her head. "Not really. Others allowed a lie to form her life. She reacted with vengeance and anger. I can't imagine finding out that everything I believed in was a lie."

Suddenly Phillip's unfinished statement at the prison

came to her. Was that what he was going to say? Or was he going to tell her that Katherine had been the one who killed Jonathan? It really made no difference. Phillip was the one unfairly paying the price for Katherine's jealousy and disappointment in her family.

She glanced at the letter. "I have to take this letter back to Clarice. The time passed long ago for this to be made right. It's unfair for her to go on believing her son is a murderer."

Jonathan nodded. "I understand. I know your compassionate heart, and I would expect no less of you. But . . . you will come back?"

Still clutching the diary, she wrapped her arms around his neck and kissed him hard and hungrily. Then she pulled back and smiled. "I have to come back. I cannot live another lifetime without you."

As the words left her lips, the room began to spin. The funnel of the colorful vortex opened and sucked her in.

"Well? Did you stop him from killing Jonathan?" When Sara arrived back at present-day Harrogate, Julie sat on the edge of Sara's bed, hands folded in her lap, face drawn with worry.

Sara nodded.

"Oh, my God!" Julie's face went white. She covered her mouth with her hands. Sara followed the direction of her stare to the blood-stained shoulder of her dress.

"I'm okay. It was just a surface wound. Jonathan bathed and dressed it."

"Who—" The one word emerged choked, as though Julie couldn't force any others from between her lips.

"Katherine. She shot Jonathan. It wasn't Phillip. He took the blame to keep her from going to prison. I saw her do it, and I heard Phillip tell her she would not go to prison." She raised the diary still clutched in her hand. "I also found the letter my father told me about in the back of this. It's her confession to Maddy."

"I don't understand. Why didn't you find it sooner?"

"I could never open the last pages in the book. I never understood why, but now I have a feeling I wasn't supposed to find it until now."

"Why?"

"Perhaps because I needed to know everything before I read it. Perhaps Maddy needed to know everything before she could forgive Katherine. Perhaps because only Sara Wade could save Jonathan."

"And have you forgiven her? Has Maddy?"

For a moment, Sara couldn't answer. Then her heart told her. "Perhaps not now, but as time goes by and happiness wipes out the pain of all that's happened, I think both Jonathan and I will be able to forgive her. Katherine was a victim of society and a woman who couldn't find it in her heart to forgive a child for her father's sins. Though, to the outside world, she was the daughter of Seth and Victoria Grayson, to Victoria she was a bastard, a daily reminder to her of her husband's betrayal. Had Victoria raised her with the same love and attention she showered on Maddy, Katherine may have grown into a completely different person."

Julie rose. "What now?"

"I have to take this letter to Clarice. She deserves to know the truth about her son."

Cherry led Sara into the drawing room where Clarice sat in her usual chair, sipping lemonade. The older woman looked much frailer than she had the last time Sara had seen her. Her skin seemed more papery, her hair whiter, her wrinkles deeper, and her voice weaker.

Another casualty of the Graysons' deception.

Sara's heart constricted with the realization of how many lives Seth Grayson's indiscretion had destroyed. This woman had done nothing but love her only child. But her life had been turned into one tragedy after another through no fault of her own.

"Sara, my dear. It's good to see you."

Since their last meeting, Clarice had changed in her attitude toward Sara. They weren't close friends, but they were no longer enemies. This time, her smile told Sara she was genuinely happy to see her.

"What brings you to visit this old woman?"

"I have something you need to see."

"Oh?" Clarice sat up straighter in her chair. "And what might that be? Not another mysterious piece of jewelry, I hope." She smiled.

"No. No jewelry this time." Sara hesitated, recalling the time when Clarice had told her the locket she was wearing had been buried with Maddy Grayson. Little had she known then what an adventure lay before her and what a wonderful prize awaited her at the end. "I brought you this." She held out the yellowed envelope to the old woman.

Clarice took it, read the front of the envelope, and then looked questioningly at Sara. "But this is addressed to Maddy. What is it?"

"It's a letter from Katherine to Maddy that you should read."

Clarice slipped the letter free of the envelope and then hesitated for a fraction of a second before she unfolded it. Sara watched her closely, waiting for the moment when Clarice discovered what she'd known all along . . . that her son was not a murderer.

As what she was reading penetrated her mind, Clarice's bottom lip trembled. Then tears gathered in her brown eyes. "I knew it," she muttered. "I knew that woman had something to do with it just as surely as I knew my Phillip didn't do it."

Emotion filled Sara's throat. She swallowed to clear it. Her hand trembled when she reached for Clarice's. The old woman's fingers closed around Sara's, surprising her with the strength of the grip.

Clarice looked away from the letter and locked her watery gaze with Sara's. "Now I can die happy. How can I ever thank you?"

"No need to thank me. Seeing your joy is thanks enough. And I wouldn't plan on dying just yet. This letter needs to be taken to the authorities so they can set Phillip free."

Once she was gone, since the shooting was never reported to authorities, there would be no need for Clarice to prove her son's innocence. History would change, and Phillip would be home where he belonged. Clarice's long held grief wouldn't even be a memory because it would never have happened. But she couldn't tell Clarice that. She could only take solace in the fact that Clarice would never have to endure the heartache of the past years.

A lone tear slid down Clarice's cheek unheeded.

"You're so very kind to me. I'm so sorry that I treated you so badly when we first met."

"No need to apologize. I reminded you of one of the worst pains a mother can endure. I'm not sure I wouldn't have done the same in your stead."

Clarice took Sara's hand in hers. "I cannot imagine you ever being anything but sweet." She tilted her head. "In many ways, including your looks, you remind me so very much of Maddy. That girl wouldn't have brought pain to anyone. Though, God knows, with a sister like hers, she had ample reason."

Warmth spread through Sara. She smiled to herself. If only Clarice knew.

Sara stood. "I have to go."

Clarice pushed her arthritic body from the chair with much more agility than Sara had ever seen her display before. "I always knew Katherine was evil, but I never suspected it was she and not my boy who actually killed Jonathan. I really had no idea who could have done it; I just knew Katherine was involved somehow, and I knew it wasn't Phillip."

Sara took her hand and squeezed it gently. "Someone once told me a mother's heart always knows."

Clarice nodded knowingly, her eyes bright and shining. "That it does, my dear. One day, when you have your own children, you'll understand that, too."

Sara hadn't thought about children since her conversation with Julie on the day Chloe's daughter had given birth. But now she had to wonder if Jonathan would want children. Her cheeks warmed with the memory of his visit to her bed. A man with that much love to give couldn't help but want children, and she would love them all equally.

"Goodbye, my dear. For the joy you've brought me this day, may your life be filled with happiness and love."

Sara kissed her wrinkled cheek. "I'm sure it will."

She would miss Clarice.

Chapter 25

Back at Harrogate, Sara, eager to return to Jonathan, went straight to her bedroom. Sitting down at her desk, she put pen to paper. When she'd finished, she propped the letter up on the mantel just below the portraits of Maddy and Jonathan.

Then she went to lie down on the bed, the diary clutched in her hands. She opened it to the last page she'd read the night before, which had taken her back to Brentwood and Maddy's bedroom. She glanced at Jonathan's dear face smiling down at her from his portrait. Soon, very soon, she'd be back in his arms for good.

Then she turned the page.

The next one was blank.

Sara's heart sank. She sat up and stared at the empty

page. In the past, she'd always read the text Maddy had written to propel her back in time. How could she do that if there was no text to read?

She turned more pages, hoping Maddy had skipped some before she'd made her next entry. Blank page after blank page fluttered through her fingers. With each one, Sara's heart sank a little lower. By the time she'd flipped the last page, she was almost smothered by the veil of despondency hanging over her.

Then she recalled how she'd gone back by drawing on her love for Jonathan. She closed her eyes and called forth all the love she possessed. Though she could feel the love growing inside her, there was no indication she was being swept back to her beloved. For a long time, she continued to summon her love and waited for the sign that she had succeeded. Still nothing happened. At last she gave up.

Gathering up the diary, she made her way downstairs. She found Julie in the library going over the plantation's account books. She dropped the open diary on the desk in front of her.

Julie glanced at it, then at Sara. "What?"

"Look at the last pages."

Julie leafed through the end of the book. "They're blank."

"Exactly." For some strange, totally illogical reason Sara had hoped against hope that Julie would see something

355

she could not. That hope had died with Julie's statement. "I went back to Jonathan by reading what Maddy wrote. She has stopped entering anything into the book. The pages are blank. How can I get back to him now? I promised him I'd come back." She realized she sounded frantic, but she *felt* frantic. Frantic, frightened, and hopeless.

Not knowing what else to do, Sara began pacing back and forth in front of the desk. Her skirts swirled around her as though buffeted by one of the fierce summer storms that tore in from the Gulf. She tried to think, but all that went through her head were her own words promising her return.

Julie laid aside her quill. She stood and came around the desk and caught Sara's arm to bring her frantic pacing to a halt. "I don't know what to do, but wearing out the carpet isn't it. Sit, and maybe we can figure this out."

Though Sara allowed Julie to lead her to a chair, she couldn't remain totally still. Her body had come to a standstill, but she wrung her hands until Julie laid hers on top of them and stopped her.

"What can I do?"

Julie leaned forward. "Are you sure you checked all the pages? There couldn't be one that you missed?"

Sara shook her head. "I looked at all of them, and every one is blank."

Frowning, Julie leaned back in the chair. "I wish I

could help, but I can't think of anything to tell you short of me putting letters on the page for her."

Sara opened her mouth to speak but stopped. Hope rose in her like the morning sun clearing a foggy horizon. "What did you say?"

Looking confused, Julie appeared to search her mind for what she'd said. "I can't help you?"

"No, after that."

She thought for a moment and then shook her head. "I don't know what you're asking for."

"You said you couldn't put the letters on the page for her."

Julie shrugged. "Well, I could I suppose, but they wouldn't be Maddy's words, would they?"

Sara grinned, happiness flooding through her. "But they would be if I wrote them."

This time Julie's expression turned to utter confusion. "I don't understand."

Sara led her to the desk in the corner of the room. She pointed at the diary. "Don't you see? For the past few weeks, I have gone back in time and become Maddy. Jonathan says I am Maddy in my heart, that I've always been Maddy. For all intents and purposes, I *am* Maddy."

Julie still looked confused.

"Have you ever heard of reincarnation?"

Julie shook her head.

"It's the rebirth of a soul in a new human body. I truly believe I was Maddy in another life. So if I wrote the entries, then essentially they would be her words." When Julie continued to look confused, Sara blurted. "Don't you see? *I* can finish the entries." She kissed Julie's cheek and then, grabbing the diary, rushed from the room, her heart singing.

Sara settled herself at her writing desk, took up a quill, and, after studying Maddy's style for a few moments, wrote several words. To her astonishment, the handwriting was not hers, not Sara Wade's. It was Maddy Grayson's.

She began to write. Working meticulously, she recounted everything that had transpired after Maddy left her bedroom on that fateful night. She left nothing out, not even her emotions and the near run-in with Floree and Daniel, the horseback ride to Harrogate, and an accounting of who had actually pulled the trigger. She even added being wounded and Jonathan's ministrations. She signed Maddy's name, just as Maddy had done at the end of each entry.

Then she added the final words.

In my heart of hearts, I believe I am Madeline Grayson. For some reason, fate has chosen to give Jonathan and me another chance at happiness. Perhaps it's because we are soul mates, destined to be together through eternity.

Very soon, as Sara I shall return to Jonathan and become Maddy for the very last time. Although I will forever hold them close to my heart, I am heartbroken at the thought of leaving Father, Julie, and Raina and never seeing them again. I'm sure there will come a time when I can think of them with love and not that terrible starkness of loss that already fills my heart. However, if I do not go back to my love, my heart will break and never mend; my soul will lie in ribbons. The emptiness will never go away, and I shall die alone and lonely, just as Maddy did.

I know now that Jonathan is my past and my future . . . my destiny. I will forever belong to him.

For the last time, I sign myself . . .
Sara Madeline Wade

When she had finished, she laid the pen aside, realizing she had just written the end to her life as Sara Wade. Taking the diary, she went downstairs and outside into the Garden of the Moon. She made her way to the gazebo and sat on one of the benches. With one last look around her, she opened the diary and read her own words.

For the last time, I sign myself . . .

Sara Madeline Wade

As though allowing her one final glimpse of this world, the vortex spun very slowly this time. Colors, vibrant and alive, spun on the outer edges like a large, oval picture frame. Inside the frame, the garden morphed and changed, flowers disappeared, shrubs and trees shrunk to the size of their original planting. Little by little, the vortex closed in on itself, shutting out the garden as it was today, and then, shifting and swirling, expanding it into what it had been in Jonathan's and Maddy's time.

But that wasn't the only change Sara detected. Her body began to change, her clothing redesigned itself, her hair restyled itself. Memories of Sara Wade faded to be replaced by those of Maddy Grayson. Very gradually, one last thought of Sara's passed through her mind, and then Sara Wade almost ceased to be. Maddy Grayson took shape for the very last time.

When the vortex slowed and then stopped, Maddy was sitting in the garden at Harrogate. Jonathan sat beside her smiling. "Hello, my love. Welcome home."

Maddy wrapped her arms around him and held on, happy to be home . . . finally. Then she remembered and pulled back. "Katherine? Did you tell her?"

"I didn't get a chance to. Your father came by this morning and told me that Katherine would not be marrying me after all. It seems she's fallen ill, and he's taking her to the Ursuline Convent to be cared for. They think it's yellow jack, and he doesn't want anyone else at the house to be infected. He didn't feel it would be fair to ask me to wait until she was well again."

Deep inside, Maddy doubted her father's explanation. Something wriggled at the edge of her memory. However, she couldn't bring it forward far enough to clearly make out what the memory was.

Right at this moment, she was too giddy to think on it for very long. Jonathan was hers at last. Happy that the threat of what Katherine would do no longer hung over their heads, there was one last thing she had to do.

Maddy took Jonathan's hand and led him into the house. Inside, she went upstairs to the bedroom, where a fire burned in the fireplace, despite it being mid-July. From a pocket in her dress, Maddy retrieved her diary. She walked to the hearth and dropped the diary into the dancing flames and then watched as the fire consumed it, leaving behind nothing but ashes.

Sara Wade was now completely gone forever. Maddy Grayson was back where she had always belonged—with Jonathan.

She turned to Jonathan and walked into his arms. He covered her mouth with his and drank in her spirit, making her irrevocably his forever.

It occurred to Julie that she hadn't seen Sara since she'd brought her the diary to show her the blank pages. She left her books of account on the desk and went upstairs in search of her friend. Upon entering Sara's bedroom, she found it empty. About to leave, she noticed a piece of paper propped against a candlestick on the mantel. Her name was scrawled across the front in Sara's handwriting.

Rather than lighting the oil lamp, she went to the window to use the light from the waning sun to see by. She sat in Sara's favorite chair and began to read.

My dear, dear friend, Juliana,

By the time you read this, I will be gone. Your friend, Sara Wade, will have ceased to be. Before I go, I want to thank you for your belief in me when others, including my mother, had none; your friendship when I needed it most; and your love, which sustained me through some of the darkest moments. Without you and your support, I'm not sure I could have made it through these last weeks.

I know this will be hard for you to understand. I'm not entirely sure I understand it myself. All I do know for sure is that I am going to be with Jonathan and that I will be happier than I have ever been. Please understand that this was the only way. I could not endure another lifetime without my darling Jonathan. Yes, I know I will change history, as you predicted I would, but I think the changes will all be for the good—especially one. Clarice will have her son back, and that's the most important thing for me. Both of them have suffered enough because of other people's actions.

Jonathan and I will be married, just as we were always meant to be. And, as I'd planned, we will have two children, a boy for him and girl for me. I must do this.

There are several things I want you to do for me. Tell my father I know now that he understands what I had to do and that I love him. I know it will be difficult for her to understand, but try to explain to Raina what happened. And finally, take good care of Harrogate.

Yes, we want you to have it. We know you'll love our home as if it had always been your own. Be happy and, no matter the sacrifice, find your own true love, as I have, my dear friend. Above all else, that's what really matters—love.

> Your friend,
> Sara Wade

Julie dropped the letter to her lap. Emptiness filled her. What would she do without Sara? Tears filled her eyes. She wasn't sure if they were tears of happiness for Sara or tears of sorrow because she knew she'd lost her dearest friend. She finally decided they were a mixture of both.

Though a hole now resided in her heart that previously had been filled by Sara, Julie couldn't help but be happy that Sara had found love and happiness with her Jonathan. And she couldn't remember Sara without remembering how fervently Sara had wanted to be with Jonathan. That kind of love was rare and not to be wasted. One day, perhaps she too would know what it was like to be loved with such passion.

She sat there for a long time recalling the friendship and the laughter they'd shared. Sara had been a good friend to her. She'd always been there when Julie had needed her. She'd even given her a home when she'd had nowhere else to go, and now that home belonged to her. Though Julie would miss her immensely, she could do no less than to wish Sara happiness, no matter where she was.

The shadows of evening lengthened, and still Julie remained motionless, her mind imprisoned deep in the past: the laughter she'd shared with Sara, the fussing over new gowns, the heartbreak of parting for summers at home, and the joy of reuniting at the beginning of the school year. All were treasured memories that Julie would hold close.

One in particular stood out—the day Julie found

out Sara could see ghosts. Julie had just received a letter from her father and was experiencing a rush of sadness because her mother had never lived to share her life with her daughter. By the time Sara had come to their room, a spate of self-pity had Julie in the throes of despondency. She said she'd been able to hear Julie weeping in the hall.

For a time, she'd just tried to console her friend, but then she'd hesitantly told Julie her dead mother was there, and she was very upset that Julie was so distraught. Julie laughed as she recalled how she'd thought Sara had lost her mind. Sara told her that her mother said she'd been with her all these years and was watching over her. Again, Julie had laughed. Then Sara had told her that her mother had seen her the day she'd taken off all her clothes and gone swimming in their pond.

Julie had been stunned. No one knew about that. And even if someone had seen her, the chances of Sara knowing were zero. Sara lived in New Orleans, and Julie lived in Richmond, Virginia. The only connection they'd ever had was at school. That day, Julie had become a believer in Sara's gift.

Like a *Mardi Gras* parade, the memories continued to march through her mind for hours.

Finally, when she realized the sun had long ago set and the shadows of night had darkened the room, Julie looked out the big window at the Garden of the Moon dappled in the silvery luminescence of a full moon, her heart alternately breaking and then rejoicing. The snowy white camellias, magnolias, moonflowers, and azalea blossoms glowed brightly, faces turned to the sky, and perfume saturated the darkness with their fragrance.

Her gaze wandered toward the back of the garden, where the gazebo stood silhouetted against the night sky. On the bench, two ethereal figures sat holding hands. Julie recognized them right away. Sara and Jonathan. She smiled. "Be happy, my friend, and thank you," Julie whispered. "I'll take good care of your home. I promise."

As though they heard her, the couple turned their faces toward her, then smiled and waved. They rose and walked slowly toward the edge of the garden. The woman stopped and looked back at the window.

Promise me you will find your love, came Sara's voice from inside Julie's head. *Promise me.*

Julie smiled through her gathering tears. "I promise," she told the night.

Then the image of Sara appeared to melt like hot candle wax. Just as quickly, it re-formed and in Sara's place stood a young, vibrant, and obviously happy Maddy Grayson. Maddy gave a brief nod of acknowledgment. *I'll be watching you*, she said. Then she took Jonathan's outstretched hand, and they vanished like a wisp of smoke.

"I know you will." Julie whispered, "I know you will."

Julie looked up at the portraits of Jonathan and Maddy above the mantel, where Sara had so lovingly hung them. The pictures blurred and swirled as though the painter had thrown all his paint on the canvas and stirred them with his brush. Then, slowly, they began to clear.

Moments later, Julie stared up at a single portrait of Maddy, Jonathan, and two beautiful children, a boy and a girl, both of whom looked exactly like their radiant mother. Around Maddy's neck hung a gold locket engraved with two forever-entwined roses.

Several Days Later

"Miss Julie."

Julie looked up from her embroidery. Raina stood just inside the door.

"Yes."

"Miss Clarice of Candlewick Plantation and two gentlemen has come callin'."

Surprised that her neighbor had come to Harrogate, given she had told Sara she would never set foot here again, Julie laid her needlework aside and stood.

"Show her in, please."

Raina left the room and returned a few moments later, followed by Clarice and two men. The older woman leaned heavily on the arm of a young man about Julie's age. An older version of the younger of the two men walked beside her. Although the older man was handsome in his own right, it was the younger of the two that snagged Julie's attention. His dark hair lay in heavy waves over his forehead, and his startlingly blue eyes smiled at her in a way that made her heartbeat quicken.

Embarrassed that she'd been staring, Julie dragged her gaze away from the young man. "Hello, Mrs. Degas. Welcome to Harrogate." Julie motioned to the settee. "Please have a seat."

"Raina?"

"Yes, 'um?"

"Please bring some lemonade and cookies for my guests."

"Yes, 'um." She backed out of the room.

At first, Julie had wondered why Raina never asked about Sara. Then she realized this was the first time she'd have to come face to face with the changes Sara's trip back in time had caused. Since Sara had never been born, Raina would not remember her. Julie had no idea why she'd been able to hang onto her memories, but she had, and she was glad that, at least in that way, Sara would always be with her.

Rousing herself from her thoughts, she directed her

attention back to her guests.

The young man had guided his grandmother to the settee and supported her as she sat. Mrs. Degas arranged the skirt of her navy blue gown around her legs. "It's terrible to get old. I used to be able to dance the night away, and now I need help sitting." She frowned at Julie. "Somehow it just doesn't seem fair."

"No, it doesn't. May I ask what brings you to Harrogate?"

"Nothing beyond just good manners, my dear. We heard that the heir to Harrogate had finally moved in, and since we're your closest neighbors, I just had to come meet you. I knew Alice Wade well. Lovely woman. We often shared tea together. How did you come to know Alice?"

For a moment, Julie was taken aback. Clarice thought the plantation had been left to her by Sara's grandmother. She was about to correct her; then she realized this had to be one more glitch in history that Sara's trip back in time had created.

Julie hesitated for only a moment before the words came unbidden from her mouth. "She was a very close friend." Not really a lie. Through Sara's stories of her Gran, Julie had come to know as much about the woman as a close friend would have.

Clarice laughed. A light tinkling sound imbued with pure happiness. "Now, where are my manners? It seems I've let them slip, Miss Weston."

"Please, call me Julie."

Clarice inclined her head. "Then I insist you call me Clarice. All my friends do, and I'm sure you and I are going to be fast friends." She took the younger man's hand in hers. Looking up at him with adoring eyes, she said, "Julie, this is my grandson, Etienne, and his father, my son, Phillip."

Sara would have been so very pleased that Phillip was here and not in jail. Obviously he'd gotten over Katherine and married, as attested to by the presence of his son.

"I'm pleased to meet both of you." She extended her hand.

Etienne's smile widened. He bowed over Julie's offered hand and kissed it and then, without relinquishing her hand, straightened and again flashed that enticing smile. Their gazes locked. "And I am delighted to meet you, Miss Julie Weston."

His voice flowed over Julie like warm syrup. Tingles of pure pleasure raced up her arm from where his fingers gripped hers. What on earth was happening to her?

Promise me you will find your love.

Maddy's voice echoed through her mind.

I think I may have, Julie thought, her gaze still imprisoned by Clarice's grandson's smile.

Yes, I think you have.

Julie's gaze darted to the other side of the room, where a bright light had suddenly appeared. Standing there, hand in hand, were Maddy and Jonathan. Maddy smiled, nodded, and then followed Jonathan into the light.

ELIZABETH SINCLAIR

Dora de Angelo was never supposed to be an angel. Her soul was placed with the angels instead of the mortals and, as a result, she has never fit in and has an undying wish to be a mortal. Maybe that's why she is one of the most inept angels Heaven has ever had the misfortune to employ in the Celestial Maintenance Department.

Finally, Dora is sent to Earth. For the three weeks prior to Christmas she must help a mortal family, and return to Heaven on Christmas Eve. During that time, she must help a man find his faith in family again and his ability to trust in love. Dora must also help a little girl become a child again and get past the guilt she feels for the death of her parents. Doing so, Dora finds more than just a challenge to her questionable angel skills.

Dora loses her wings. But she gains something she has always wanted with all her heart. She also finds her family . . .and discovers love. And hope for a future she's only dreamed of . . .

ISBN# 978-193383631-7
Mass Market Paperback/Paranormal Romance
US $7.95 / CDN $8.95
Available Now
www.elizabethsinclair.com

Helen A Rosburg

Lady Blue

From the independent freedom of the American cattle ranch to the stifling restraint of the prim English parlor, Harmony Simmons loses all she has ever valued after the death of her affluent parents. According to her mother's will, she must remain under the guardianship of her domineering older sister, Agatha, until she turns twenty-one, a crushing blow to her ambitious spirit. Dowdy Agatha is jealous and spiteful, resentful of her attractive sibling. A restricted existence in England promises hell compared to Harmony's former privileged life with her successful father in the heavenly expanse of the West.

When Anthony Allen meets Harmony, he plays the rogue. Kidnapping this beautiful, well-bred angel with the sapphire eyes is a risk he's willing to take to coax her into his arms forever. His Lady Blue. Never has he seen a woman like her. Never will he adore another. Later, however, he introduces himself as suave aristocrat Lord Farmington, a title she suspects is a sophisticated ruse.

Baffled by his duplicity, Harmony cannot determine whether her mysterious lover is a cavalier bandit or an honorable hero of the landed gentry. His secret ignites a fear deep inside, where her passion for him burns. What sinister shadows may lurk in his past? Does he love her as he claims . . . or is he a jewel thief and a criminal predator seeking her inheritance in an elaborate masquerade?

ISBN# 978-160542063-9
Mass Market Paperback/Historical Romance
US $7.95 / CDN $8.95
NOVEMBER 2009
www.helenrosburg.com

Jasper Mountain

Kathy Steffen

Two lost souls struggle to find their way in the unforgiving West of 1873...

Jack Buchanan, a worker at the Jasper Mining Company, is sure of his place in the outside world, but has lost his faith, hope, and heart to the tragedy of a fire.

Foreign born and raised, Milena Shabanov flees from a home she loves to the strange and barbaric America. A Romani blessed with "the sight," she is content in the company of visions and spirit oracles, but finds herself lost and alone in a brutal mining town with little use for women.

Surrounded by inhumane working conditions at the mine, senseless death, and overwhelming greed, miners begin disappearing and the officers of the mine don't care.

Tempers flare and Jack must decide where he stands: with the officers and mining president—Victor Creely—to whom Jack owes his life, or with the miners, whose lives are worth less to the company than pack animals. Milena, sensing deep despair and death in a mining town infested with restless spirits, searches for answers to the workers' disappearances. But she can't trust anyone, especially not Jack Buchanan, a man haunted by his own past.

ISBN# 978-193383658-4
Trade Paperback/Historical Fiction
US $15.95 / CDN $17.95
Available Now
www.kathysteffen.com

* 2009 BENJAMIN FRANKLIN FINALIST IN THE HISTORICAL CATEGORY*

WILD MAGIC

ANN MACELA

Irenee Sabel is a witch—a good witch, a sophisticated beauty, a member of Chicago's old money elite, and a Defender of an ancient code of ethics that prohibits the indiscriminate use of power attached to magical possessions. As a Sword, Irenee is responsible for confiscating and destroying hidden relics of the sorcery realm still employed by practitioners of the craft for self-centered reasons. Her present target: an aging warlock.

While attending a gala party at Alton Finster's Gold Coast mansion, she burglarizes his safe in search of an item of mystical mayhem. Irenee doesn't anticipate Jim Tylan interrupting her break-in. From the moment they meet, she knows this is no ordinary man.

With an undisclosed search warrant from the Department of Justice and Homeland Security, Tylan enters Finster's office to obtain covert financial records. There he finds a glowing handbag and an overpowering attraction to the benevolent sorceress holding the luminescent purse.

This mysterious encounter launches an escapade to expose pieces of the legendary Cataclysm Stone, an evil object of interest for the Defenders since the fifteenth century. In the heat of the chase, Irenee discovers that her real object of interest isn't the famed stone, but the undercover agent destined to be her lover . . . her soul mate.

ISBN# 978-193383699-7
US $7.95 / CDN $8.95
Paranormal Romance
OCTOBER 2009

TRACI E. HALL
Beauty's Curse

Galiana Montehue is beautiful, hallowed, and adored. Envied by her rivals and coveted by her suitors, this privileged lady of the manor enjoys the attention and esteem bestowed only on young women blessed with physical perfection. What more could a late-twelfth-century Welsh heroine need to shine at court?

Lord Rourke Wallis suffers a head injury at Galiana's hands, rendering him blind and dependent. He never sees the beauty she curses with vehemence. Defending her twin brothers from Rourke's drawn sword, she must live with the horrible debilitating consequences of her attack as she nurses the honorable knight. For the first time, she experiences a man's sincere affection and genuine integrity.

In his dark and depressing internal prison, Rourke discovers a depth of passion impossible to find in the superficial realm of medieval fashion and visual charms. The gentle touch of her warm, delicate hands and the arousing lavender scent of her vibrant body awaken in Rourke a fervor he cannot deny. Galiana entices him like no other, drawing him into a tactile, sensual haven.

Yet the fulfillment of his desire must wait until the completion of his mission. Stolen from King William's treasures, the magical Breath of Merlin must be recovered. This mysterious stone from antiquity contains supernatural power that royalty will fight to possess. Together they must unlock the secret to this dangerous, mystical gem, or face a future without the love they so recently discovered.

ISBN# 978-193383656-0
Mass Market Paperback/Paranormal Romance
US $7.95 / CDN $8.95
NOVEMBER 2009
www.traciehall.com

Want to know what's going on with
your favorite author or what new releases
are coming from Medallion Press?

Now you can receive breaking news,
updates, and more from Medallion Press
straight to your cell phone, e-mail, instant
messenger, or Facebook!